D0375767

A CASEY JONES MYSTERY

KATY MUNGER

AVON BOOKS NEW YORK

AVON BOOKS
A division of
The Hearst Corporation
1350 Avenue of the Americas
New York, New York 10019

Copyright © 1997 by Katy Munger
Inside cover author photo by Ricky Lee Harrell
Published by arrangement with the author
Visit our website at http://AvonBooks.com
Library of Congress Catalog Card Number: 96-95492
ISBN: 0-380-79136-6

First Avon Books Printing: July 1997

AVON TRADEMARK REG. U.S. PAT. OFF. AND IN OTHER COUNTRIES, MARCA REGISTRADA, HECHO EN U.S.A.

Printed in the U.S.A.

WCD   10   9   8   7   6   5   4   3   2   1

"THIS COULD BE A BIG ONE, CASEY," BOBBY SAID.

"We're talking very big money. Mucho dinero. Mucho publicity. Think of the glory!"

"Think of your bank account."

"Exactly." He smiled happily and bit into another doughnut. Bobby makes Henry the VIII look like Miss Manners.

Bobby D. has one good point. He pays my rent. But he also fancies himself a poor man's Nero Wolfe. They have two things in common: private investigator licenses and huge rolls of fat. The similarities end there. Brainwise, Bobby is a long way behind Nero. He pays me well to follow cheating spouses while he sits around and shovels down enough beer and sandwiches to sustain a third-world country for a week.

One day I might decide what I want to be when I grow up. For now, I work for Bobby and live in North Carolina. And that's better than being where I was.

Me and Thomas Wolfe—we can't go home again.

ONE

"This better be good or you're dead meat," I warned my midnight caller. And I meant it. I had a 26-year-old bartender parked next to my wrinkled old hide. I didn't take kindly to interruptions.

"You've stepped in it now," Bobby D. replied, his voice oozing with satisfaction. He takes great pride in pointing out my screw-ups.

"What is it?" I mumbled, tugging the sheets away from Jack. Jesus, he was a human Labrador retriever: glossy black hair, big wet tongue, sturdy chest, and a silly grin on his face when he slept.

"Your babysitting job just went sour." Bobby followed this pronouncement with a cough. I could practically feel the phlegm bubbling through the phone wires. I don't know what goes on inside Bobby's massive stomach but half the time, whatever it is, it's trying to crawl out.

"It's three o'clock in the morning," I said, fumbling for my black cat eyeglasses. "What the hell could go wrong with that woman at this time of night? She get caught breaking into the Junior League membership file or something?"

"She got arrested for murder."

"What?" I was wide awake. Mary Lee Masters arrested for murder? No way in hell. Not in the middle of the final month before the election.

Unless she had killed her husband. As a candidate's husband, Bradley Masters was a perfect specimen. As a human being's husband, he sucked.

"Don't you want to know who was killed?" Bobby asked. Our offices are only a few blocks from the Raleigh Police Department headquarters and Bobby has some clerk there paid off but good. He knows when the chief hits the can before the guy can even unzip his fly.

"Okay, I'll bite. Who was killed?"

"Don't know!" His rumbling laugh threatened to turn into a belch and I held the phone away just in case. Bobby was the kind of person you kept permanently stuffed in a closet. If you could find one big enough.

"Bobby—tell me everything straight or I'll confiscate your six-pack. I mean it." In searching for my bra, I discovered one pink bunny slipper dangling from a door knob. I tried my damnedest to remember how it had gotten there but failed. I should never have let Jack talk me into drinking Mind Erasers. And don't even ask what's in one. The recipe alone can give you a hangover.

"The call went out about an hour ago," Bobby explained. "Male body, unidentified as yet. Parked in the back seat of your client's Jeep Cherokee. Which was parked about ten feet from her front door. Stiff was covered with a tarp. State Bureau's involved. Better hurry if you want to get anything."

"Ten feet from her front door? Give me a break. She's smarter than that." Where the hell was my yellow dress? If Jack had ripped the zipper, he was dog food. I finally found it crumpled in a heap near the toilet with a suspicious brown stain over one boob like a breastplate. Forget it—I'd wear my black pants instead. Maybe even throw in my $9.98 pearls. All for the SBI.

"She's been under a lot of strain," Bobby said. "Maybe she cracked."

Mary Lee Masters crack? Not in a zillion years. Not in my lifetime. And certainly not in the middle of the night.

The woman couldn't sneeze without full makeup, nail polish, and a coordinated scarf. If she murdered, it would be a hell of a lot cleaner than this one was shaping up to be.

"Shit," I said, thinking out loud. "They aren't going to let me get near a murder. Not the SBI."

"For chrissakes, Casey. You're her bodyguard, remember? Go guard her."

For once Bobby had a good idea. I rang off in the middle of another of his gastronomic rumbles. I was sure it would still be going on when I saw him next.

No sense leaving Jack a note. I doubted his eyes could focus enough to read at this hour. Instead I piled as many prepackaged foods as I could find on the kitchen table for his breakfast. Who says the art of hostessing is dead? Not in the South, it isn't. Not in my house, anyway. At least not while preservatives live.

I stopped on the way out the door to make sure Jack was still breathing. He smelled like the floor beneath a beer keg the morning after a frat party, but he was still alive. His gentle snores purred through the silence of the night like an electric outboard motor in water. Jack was an incorrigible flirt, an overqualified bartender going nowhere fast and a smart man who preferred to play dumb. But he was also my friend—and a good friend is hard to find. I tucked the sheet carefully around his sleeping form before I left.

For once, I-40 was deserted. The invading hordes of northern commuters were all tucked in their split-level homes, sleeping quietly beneath a Carolina moon. And what a moon it was. Full and white in the October sky, like a big china plate spinning through the night. The kind of moon that used to set my grandpa howling by the edge of the swamp just to see if he could get an answer.

I felt like howling myself from the throbbing in my head but pushed onward through the pain, inching my 1965 Plymouth Valiant up to eighty miles per hour. It

began to shudder, the doors rattling like they would tear
off any minute. I knew the shimmy would stop when I hit
eighty-five. It did. I slid down the highway smooth as a
shark, wondering how the hell a dead body had ended up
in Mary Lee Masters's driveway.

Mary Lee Masters was the New Southern Woman. The
kind you don't want to mess with. The kind who comes
from generations of women used to quietly running the
family business and propping up weak front men. But
Mary Lee had gone to college in the 70's, the first female
generation to find that she didn't have to be so quiet
anymore. A hundred years of suppressed thirst for power
had exploded into one terrifyingly charming political
machine named Mary Lee Masters. She was wealthy
enough to bankroll a career in public service, well-bred
enough to crack any tier of southern society, and
pretty enough to get a good ole boy vote or two. She
knew how to bat her eyelashes, but the eyes behind them
were small and cold and blue. I admired the hell out of
her. Anyone who can wear pantyhose twenty hours a day
while taking on the fat cats—and beating them—at their
own slimy game deserved my respect.

Besides, I suspected Mary Lee Masters was the sneaki-
est creature from here to Tallahassee and I wanted her on
my side. She was from out by Charlotte way, which
meant she had started politics with a strike against her
since Charlotte wasn't really a southern city and was
considered more of a northern town wannabe. But she
fixed that problem by moving to Raleigh right out of
college and starting her climb up the state political ladder
from there. She landed a job at a local television station
reporting on consumer protection issues, then got appointed to a state commission and took on the dairy
farmers like the cows would never come home. After
marching through price-fixing schemes like a certain
nameless northern general had burned his way through

Atlanta, she moved on to arts and culture, sticking museums on every corner of the downtown area and protecting half of Raleigh from the wrecker's ball. Then she took the big leap into local politics, gobbling up the other city council candidates like a beach bum mooching off a bar full of divorcees. It took her almost twenty years, but here she was at age forty-four running for a seat in the U.S. Senate and hoping to become the first female senator in the history of North Carolina.

She didn't have a snowball's chance in hell. Everyone knew it except her. The most recent polls had her moving up all right—but it was too little, too late. I'd eat my underwear if she made it. It just wasn't the right time.

She might have had a chance in any other year, but Mary Lee Masters was running against Stoney Maloney, the favored nephew of Senator Boyd Jackson. And Senator Boyd Jackson was a man who made Strom Thurmond look a drifter just passing through.

Boyd Jackson had been senator from North Carolina for about as long as my family had been poor. He was mean. He was pig-eyed. He was a two-faced, fire-and-brimstone–breathing, handshaking, church-going hypocrite of the highest order. But he brought home more pork in the barrel for the farmers of North Carolina than could be chopped into barbecue each year. He was the subsidy king, the tobacco god, the supreme backscratcher of all time. Which meant he was invincible, unlikeable and unbeatable.

Except that he was also dying.

No one from the outside had been able to touch him for forty years, but he was rotting from the inside out. When the stomach cancer got too hot to hide and rumors started circulating in Washington, he had announced he would not run for re-election and handpicked his nephew Stoney Maloney to succeed him as his party's candidate in the upcoming election.

That left Mary Lee Masters running against the nephew of an icon at a time when the good people of North
Carolina needed icons. They were being gentrified,
northernized, and politicized into some place new—and
all the changes were frightening the hell out of half the
state. I knew Mary Lee was homegrown, but not homegrown enough. Still, I gave her credit for trying. And for
not going down without a fight.

It didn't take me long to get to her house. I knew the
way by heart. I met her there every morning at seven
o'clock to act as her bodyguard. She lived in Country
Club Hills, the first of the expensive subdivisions that
sprang up like mushrooms around Raleigh back in the
60's. By now, Country Club Hills was no longer on the
outskirts of town but pretty damn near the middle of it.
An address there was even better than the older Raleigh
neighborhoods near the universities. Country Club Hills
was "inside the Beltline," meaning you could afford to
pay a third more for your house than the rest of the
Research Triangle's newcomers. It also meant that your
era was just beginning, not ending like old Raleigh
money's—and that you had made the move down South
and the big money first, before the tidal wave of IBMers
and white-collar crowds had arrived.

Like most people on her block, Mary Lee was rolling
in the bucks. She had a ton of it from the family coffers
and a piece of just about every factory within the city
limits of Winston-Salem. Then she had married into
more of it, nabbing some walking, talking, Ken doll of an
investment banker who everyone else thought was a
dream boat but I was pretty sure was a faithless prick and
nothing more.

The faithless prick—and his car—were nowhere to be
seen when I arrived at Mary Lee's house. I wondered if
Bradley Masters was lying dead in the Jeep. He'd run
through his share of family money a few years back and
had started in on Mary Lee's. Maybe she wasn't into

share and share alike and had decided it was time for death to do them part.

I parked down the block, well back from the swirling lights. The homes and lots were big in Mary Lee's neighborhood, with yards at least an acre each. It seemed odd to be there so late at night. I usually knocked off at eight in the evening, an hour that Mary Lee had declared was too late for a stalker. I suspected she was simply too cheap to hire a night bodyguard—and not yet scared enough to open her purse strings.

A light fog leaked out of the nearby greenway, making the scene seem even more like a dream. But, if it was a dream, it was a bad one. The place was crawling with cops and agents from the State Bureau of Investigation, a sort of junior league FBI for local law enforcement overachievers.

The dark clothes had been a good idea. I inched up, unnoticed, to the edge of the driveway where I could eavesdrop on two men arguing at the curb. They stood near the trunk of a dark blue sedan. I could see someone sitting in its back seat, head down.

"I don't give a shit who you are," a short man with a bulldog face was growling. He wore a gray suit and snow-white shirt in the middle of the night, which was tantamount to wearing a sign around his neck that said "I'm an asshole." A small antennae poked out from behind one of his ears beneath a serious crew cut. He thought he looked important. I thought he looked like a Martian. "I wouldn't even bother to try, buddy," the guy added. "By morning it will be all ours."

The reply from the second man was instantaneous. "Try this on for size, Shorty: by morning it's going to be in all the newspapers that the SBI was so goddamn stupid they swarmed all over the lawn, tramping on evidence, moving the victim, and all but asking the lead suspect to dance."

I was shocked at the second man's accent. He wasn't

southern. It was the nasal twang of up by New York City way. What the hell was he doing down here?

"You're not from around here, are you?" Shorty asked. His smile was the usual power smile: flat and thin and threatening.

"Yes, I am goddamn from around here," the second man answered. "I've been from goddamn around here for three years now so don't give me any of your goddamn cowboy crap. I know the goddamn laws of this state, of this city, and of this county. This is my goddamn jurisdiction and I have a goddamn right to speak to the suspect."

Well, goddamn. The man seemed a mite irate.

"Who the fuck are you again?" Shorty asked, whipping out a notepad like he was going to write up an order for eggs and grits.

"I am goddamn William Bryant Butler, that's who I am. Allow me to make it easy for you." The tall man held out a badge and practically speared Shorty in the eye with it, reading out his number slowly. "Don't forget to put down William Bryant Butler, *arresting officer*," he said when Shorty finished penning the number in his little book of shame.

Arresting was right. Bill Butler's appearance was as impressive as his vocabulary. He stepped into the glare of a street light and I got a better look. My mind raced shamelessly for misdemeanors I might commit that would trigger a full body search.

He was tall with a slim build and solid shoulders. And he was wearing my favorite: old jeans and a black sweatshirt. He had long hands and beautifully tapered fingers. Brown eyes, longish brown hair. Long eyelashes. A long nose, long dark mustache, and a long smile. I liked the long motif and wanted to explore it further. Good heavens. And me not looking my very best.

"Excuse me," I interrupted cleverly. Both men

jumped when I stepped from the shadows. Good thing I had vetoed the puke-stained dress. "I'm Ms. Master's bodyguard and I'm concerned about her safety. Where is she?"

"Bodyguard?" Shorty asked incredulously, surveying my sturdy frame with exaggerated skepticism. "What would you do if I started to attack her like this, huh?" He came towards me, arms outstretched, ready to grab my arms and pin them behind my back.

What is it with short men? They're always trying to prove they're bigger than they are. It was time to cut this one down to size.

"For starters, I'd kick you in the balls," I said, flexing my left leg for balance as I whipped out my right, stopping an inch from his crotch with the heel of my size-nine Ferragamos ready to strike. Shorty froze.

"Nice shoes," William Bryant Butler said. It was enough. I was in love. He took his eyes off my black velvets and examined me carefully. "At ease, Sergeant," he said with a laugh. I dropped my foot, smiling sweetly at Shorty as he backed away. "Your client is in the back seat of that car," Butler explained and I noticed that he not only had brown eyes, but deep brown ones.

Oh, mamma. It felt like a million butterflies were nibbling inside my stomach. "You married?" I asked. I couldn't help it. Reflexes, you know. Besides, I pride myself on my subtlety.

Shorty stomped away toward the blue sedan, grateful for what was left of his pride, if not his balls.

"Not at the moment," the detective replied, admirably unshaken by my prying. "What about you?"

"I'm not married at the moment, either."

"A coincidence. Mind if I ask you a few questions?" He pulled out a notebook. Damn. He was a worker, not a romantic. I had a feeling I knew why he wasn't married anymore.

"Detective?" I asked.

"First class all the way." He pulled a small wallet out of his back pocket and flipped it open. I love it when they do that. The badge winked at me and he flipped it shut again. "Name's William Butler. But you can call me Bill."

"How old are you, Bill?" I asked, just to try on the name for size.

"Old enough to know better. Mind if I ask the questions and you give the answers?"

Mind? Not at all, I thought. Especially if we remove our clothes first. Oh, stop, I told myself. This is serious work. My client is sitting over there in the back seat of a car being guarded by a steroid-filled dwarf. Get your mind out of the gutter, girl.

"You know anything about local politics?" I asked Bill Butler. "You know who's sitting in the car, right?"

Bill nodded. "I know who she is. How long you been working for her?"

"About a month," I told him, flashing a quick look at the sedan. Shorty had propped his butt against the front hood. I was surprised he didn't lift his leg and pee on the bumper to mark it.

"Why?" he asked.

"Why what?" It's tough to follow a conversation when you're busy imagining the speaker naked. He had great teeth, small and even and white. It might be nice to have a boyfriend who practiced personal hygiene for a change. Everyone needs to branch out on occasion.

"Why were you working for her?" he repeated impatiently. "You on drugs or something?"

The question was like a slap. "Me? God, no. Why do you ask?"

"You're acting a little out of it."

"Well, it's four fucking o'clock in the morning," I explained. "How with it are you right now?"

"Plenty with it because I'm plenty mad. Were you lurking in the bushes long enough to hear my conversation with Runthead?" He nodded toward Shorty.

"Yeah," I admitted. "If I help you out, will you help me out?" I thought it best to get right to the point.

He had a great laugh. "I guess you aren't so out of it, after all. What makes you think I know anything?"

"All I want to know is the identity of the victim," I said. It wasn't all I wanted to know, but it was a good start.

"Who do you think it is?" he countered.

"Oh, no." I shook my head. "We need a little faith here or we won't get anywhere."

"Okay," he agreed, lowering his voice. "You answer two questions for me and I'll answer one for you."

"Deal," I said. "Then I get to talk to my client."

"Hey, I can't even talk to her," he protested.

"No problem. I can help us both out there. Shoot."

"Why were you guarding her? What's wrong with the locals?"

"She didn't trust them. Thought they were reporting back to the Maloney campaign. She might have been right. Maloney is Senator Boyd Jackson's nephew and everyone is in Boyd Jackson's pocket."

"Why did she hire you? You don't look that . . . big."

"How sweet of you to notice," I said. He had a disconcerting habit of staring intently while he waited for an answer. I was sorry I'd worn my glasses. Where were my contact lenses when I needed them?

"She wanted a woman," I explained. "Not a lot of us around."

"You licensed?" he asked.

"You've had your two questions," I pointed out. Talk about a close shave.

He shrugged. "What's your question?"

"Who's the dead man?" I stared up the steep driveway toward a Jeep Cherokee surrounded by a horde of forensic specialists in yellow windbreakers. They looked like giant hornets swarming around a dish of honey.

"Thornton Mitchell," he said. "Ring a bell?"

"Shit," I said. "You're kidding?"

"Not me," Bill Butler promised, snapping his notebook shut. "I never kid about business."

Somehow, I believed him.

Thornton Mitchell being dead made this a tough one. He could have been killed by half the state. You either loved him or you hated him. You loved him if you had sold your land to him and made a pile of money while he put up his houses and shopping malls. You hated him if you had to live down the street from one of his little development projects, enduring the endless traffic jams, noise, and loss of privacy that inevitably resulted. Thornton Mitchell had made North Carolina into his own little pie and sliced it up nicely through the years, paving and bricking his way to a fortune. He was a big contributor to political circles, but on the opposite side of Mary Lee Masters. Plus he lived in Wake Forest, a good twenty miles away. What the hell was he doing dead in her car?

A phone trilled in the sudden silence and Shorty snapped to attention. He pulled a small cellular phone from his coat pocket, unfolded it with military precision, and barked something unintelligible into the receiver. I hate portable phones. I want to rip them out of people's hands and beat them over the head with them. Pretty soon, we'll all be walking around with big cords up our asses so we can be wired every moment of our lives.

Shorty turned his back on us and whispered frantically into the receiver, nodding his head vigorously like he was on a video hookup or something. "I'm on it, sir," he said loudly and I knew he was talking to the governor, if not God himself. He began waving frantically for someone to take his place guarding the car so Bill Butler couldn't have his crack at interviewing Mary Lee. "Yes, sir. Right away, sir." He flipped the phone down to its ridiculously tiny size, stowed it in his pocket, and began to sprint up the hill.

"I wonder if Thornton Mitchell contributed to the governor's last campaign?" Bill Butler asked as he watched Shorty's stubby little legs churn up the front lawn.

"I'd have to say yes," I agreed. "Now's our chance. Follow me."

Shorty's replacement was still a quarter of an acre away when I tapped on the back seat window. It rolled down and Mary Lee's face popped into view. I was startled. I had never seen her without makeup before. She looked a thousand times better, much softer and more approachable. She had a roundish face with wide cheekbones and a thin, businesslike mouth that was usually caked with bright red lipstick. Her nose looked long on camera, but up close it had a cute buttonlike tip. She was the kind of person who had taken makeup lessons while still in high school and who spent thirty minutes each morning with a magnifying mirror making it look like she had nothing on when, in fact, she was supporting the quarterly profits for Max Factor.

"What the fuck is going on, Casey?" she asked.

Aaah, she was still the same old Mary Lee.

"Do they honestly think I'm so stupid that I would murder that scumbag and be dumb enough to leave his sorry carcass in front of my own front door?"

"Mary Lee, I'd like you to meet Bill Butler, *detective first class*." My not-so-subtle hint was received. Her public smile reappeared and her accent softened. In another five seconds, she'd be grieving for the unfortunate loss of one of North Carolina's finest citizens.

"Where's Bradley?" I asked about her husband before she could turn on the plastic charm. I had a feeling Bill Butler was not easily fooled.

"Business trip. What else?" she said. "Where is my lawyer?"

"On his way," Butler said, flashing her what I suspected was his best grin since it couldn't get any better. "I don't suppose you'd care to talk to me first? These SBI guys are giving me a hard time. I just want to ask a few questions. They're being a little overprotective, don't you think?"

"What I think is that they're giving you a hard time because you all have an extra Y chromosome," Mary Lee explained sweetly. She opened the door and motioned for me to climb inside, just as Shorty's reinforcement arrived to protest.

Mary Lee fixed him with a steely gaze, her cold eyes defiant. She was used to being obeyed. "This is my bodyguard and she *is* getting in this car. The rest of you can stay out."

I climbed inside without hesitation, knowing she'd slam the door on my leg if I was too slow. I'd barely hit the cushions before she pulled it shut with a bang.

"Men," she said, kicking her feet against the front seat. "Too bad we can't kill them all."

TWO

"I realize I'm only your bodyguard and not your lawyer, but I'd advise you not to say that again."

Mary Lee kicked the front seat again petulantly. I'd hate to have been her daddy when she was growing up. "Why would I kill that old lech?" she asked. "What I want to know is who did this to me? You're promoted."

"What?" I asked stupidly. It's hard enough to keep up with Mary Lee in the daylight. With no sleep in me, it was impossible.

"Find out who did this to me," she said, enunciating each word like I was the world's biggest idiot. "I'll pay double your bodyguard rate."

That part I understood. I nodded. "No problem. It's what I'm trained to do. Bodyguarding is just a sideline."

She knew I was full of shit and didn't care. Like the Wicked Witch of the West, she just wanted someone to do her bidding. I realized she was murmuring beneath her breath. "What did you say?" I asked.

Her indignant expression was visible in the reflected light of the street lamp. "I said that I can't believe they think I'd be dumb enough to shotgun a man to death and leave him in my own front yard."

"He was shotgunned?" I asked. "What makes you say that?"

15

She raised her eyebrows in a superior way. "The giant hole in the middle of his chest, Sherlock."

"Oh," I said. "I couldn't get near."

"Well, I got a little too near." She gave a ladylike shudder. "That shrimpboat out there who works for the SBI thought it might rattle me into talking. He made me stick my head in the car and take a peek. I about dropped my panties when I saw it was Thornton."

"A lot of women have that reaction," I offered. Thornton had been a notorious womanizer.

"When he's dead?" she asked incredulously, getting the joke but not finding it funny. That was her way. She was smart enough to figure out when you were kidding, but she didn't have a sense of humor and she didn't want one. When she wanted to be funny, she had thousand-dollar-a-day writers to make her funny.

She was staring at a tiny tear in Shrimpboat's upholstery. "I wonder who called it in?" she said. "I mean, someone had to have reported it. That would tell us who was behind it. Who would want to get me like this?"

"Get *you?*" I asked. "Isn't Thornton Mitchell the one lying dead up there?"

"Yes," she said crossly. "But aren't I the one with a crippled campaign and maybe even a murder rap hanging over my head?"

She had a point. "What have they charged you with?" I asked.

"Nothing." She looked affronted. "You think I've let them get close enough to charge me with anything? Where the hell is Hooter anyway? What do I pay him for?"

Hooter Henderson was Mary Lee's lawyer. His real name was Ambrose. But in the South, the richer you are, the dumber your nickname. Obviously, Hooter was plenty rich.

"They read you your rights?" I asked. F. Lee Bailey had nothing on me.

"Yeah, about a dozen of them. In chorus. Think they'll book me?"

A Mercedes pulled up across the street. "Ask Hooter. Here he is."

She grabbed my arm, digging her nails so deep in my flesh I could feel them through my sweater. "Listen, Casey. This isn't about Thornton. This is about *me*. Someone's trying to ruin my life. Find out who." She paused, released her grip, started to gnaw one perfect nail, then discarded the notion and twirled a strand of brown hair around a finger instead. Her forehead wrinkled. I'd seen that same look after she'd heard the results of the latest poll. "Start with Bradley. He's been acting funny. I can't divorce him but that doesn't mean I have to trust him. This feels like him, you know?"

I nodded, resolving once more never to marry again myself.

"But don't let anyone know what you're doing, okay?"

"Why do you think they call us *private* investigators?" I asked, rubbing my arm to regain some feeling in it. "I know what to do."

Her smile was thin. "I like you, Casey," she said. "You're smart. You know when to keep your mouth shut. And you don't get all hung up on rules and regulations."

"Maybe I should run for office, too?" I suggested.

She fixed me with her cold blue eyes. "Did I say you were funny? I don't think so. Tell Hooter he can come in."

Wasn't that just like her? Here she was sitting in the back seat of an SBI car suspected of murder and she was acting like she was in the parlor of some ladeedah Atlanta hotel suite, inviting in eager backers.

Hooter was shouting at the SBI man outside. "Next," I announced. He didn't waste any time arguing.

He brushed me aside and disappeared into the vehicle, leaving me to deal with the guard.

"Think it's gonna rain today?" I asked brightly. It wasn't much, but the sun was just beginning to show in a thin yellow strip at the far end of the road and I've learned to take my inspiration where I can get it.

"Who the fuck do you think you are?" the SBI man asked sourly.

"Casey Jones, private investigator," I said smartly, flipping open my I.D. It wouldn't last long in the hands of a professional in daylight but was good enough to pass the inspection of a dumb ass in the dark.

"Thanks for the info," a familiar deep voice interrupted, setting my little heart a pitter patter again. I looked up into the deep brown eyes of Bill Butler, most arresting officer.

"You still hanging around?" I asked innocently.

"Still hanging around," he confirmed.

"You two know each other?" the SBI guy demanded.

"I know everyone," I explained. "Did I mention I was also popular?"

"You don't know me," the SBI lackey retorted, pleased at his own wit.

I thumped my forehead with the palm of my hand. "Oh gosh," I said. "I can't understand how you were ever overlooked."

"Come here, Casey," Bill Butler ordered, grabbing my elbow and dragging me off toward the bushes. Regrettably, he stopped short.

"This is my card," he said, producing a small white square from one of those snug jeans pockets. I would have gotten it myself if only he'd asked. "Call me," he ordered.

"Call you?" I repeated, turning the card over to look at the back. Rats. No home phone number. No undying declaration of love.

"If you find out anything," he explained slowly. "I'm

sure you weren't in there talking politics," he added, nodding toward the sedan.

"Actually, we were," I said truthfully. "But I certainly will call you." I was about to elaborate on why when a white van turned the corner and sped our way. Its huge antenna loomed in the air like the rack of a giant moose. The local television station had finally caught on. And just in time, it seemed, to record the body being unloaded from the Jeep. I know because one of the sound men almost garroted me with a cord as he rushed past. Only the quick thinking of good ole Bill Butler saved me from strangulation.

"Does stuff like this happen to you a lot?" he asked, unlooping another cord that had wound its way around my ankle, courtesy of the cameraman.

"How did you guess?" I asked, clinging to him for support.

"You seem the type," he explained.

I wondered what *that* meant. "Gotta go," I said. I didn't like the way the conversation was heading. "Besides, I'm camera shy." Another car had pulled up to release a trio of eager reporters. They were all young. Two of them were bearded. The third had her hair bobbed for efficiency. One had a couple of cameras slung over his shoulder. All had apparently downed jumbo cups of coffee from Hardee's on the way over and were pumped with too much caffeine, too much adrenaline, and too many viewings of *All The President's Men*. For once, they had a real story and they were going to milk it for all it was worth.

Bill Butler ignored the reporters and pulled out a small black notebook though, I was sorry to see, not *that* kind of little black book. "I need your phone number." I scrawled it down. Be still my beating heart.

There was no sense in going home. Jack wasn't half so entertaining when I was sober. Besides, Bill Butler had raised my standards considerably. That's the way it is with me. That's the way it is with all women, I suspect. Go too long without getting laid and any man without a crust on him starts to look good. Get laid and you're in the mood to be picky. I was feeling extremely picky that morning.

The streets were nearly empty with only a few early commuters dotting the road. I detoured to Hardee's for a chicken biscuit, remembering to buy Bobby D. half a dozen sausage ones while I was at it. I'd need a bribe to get him to move his fat duff and I wanted my answers quickly.

Raleigh looked tired in the morning light. Maybe it was just my mood but, without people, downtown always seemed a little lost, a little too behind the times, forlorn and anxious in the postmanufacturing world it had been pitched into. I knew how it felt.

Maybe that was why I had decided that Raleigh was as far north as I wanted to go. When you're running away, it's always good to have a destination in mind. My goal had been to get far away from trouble yet stay near enough for revenge one day. I had pulled off I-95 North in Fayetteville twelve years ago and landed in the middle of what looked like a military invasion. Leaving the boys in green behind, I had hightailed it to the capitol city as fast as my poor little car could take me. And here I had stayed. It wasn't home, but it felt like home and that was more than I had expected of Raleigh. The town was big enough to get a little lost in when you had to, but small enough that people still smiled at you when you passed them on the sidewalk. I was a country girl and Raleigh, in many ways, was just a gussied-up country town.

There was plenty of parking. There always is. I pulled into a spot right in front of our plate glass window, maneuvering my little Valiant so that the bright red glare of Bobby's ''Bail Bondsman'' sign blinked a happy pink pattern on the hood. This way I could see my car from the office and run out to put in a quarter if the meter maid wandered by.

I stared through the window and watched Bobby cram Krispy Kreme doughnuts into his craw. He's too lazy to get up and adjust the blinds that line the two picture windows out front so we leave them open. This makes it easy for passersby to get a good look at whatever Bobby is eating at the moment.

He had a six-pack of Bud on ice in the trashcan next to his desk. Already celebrating the big bucks I would earn him with this case, no doubt.

"Doll!" He held up both hands in a triumphant greeting when I entered. I noticed that his Arrid had run dry and that his pants zipper had collapsed under the strain of bulging fat. His white BVDs peeked out of the gap. At least his underwear was clean. Thank god for small favors.

"Keep the volume down, huh, Bobby?" I begged. "I have a headache that could fell King Kong."

"Har. Har." When Bobby is trying to kiss my ass, he laughs at my comments. Fortunately, not too often in public. Bobby's laugh has a tendency to inspire heroic bystanders to try the Heimlich maneuver on him.

"This could be a big one, Casey," he said. "We're talking very, very big money. Mucho dinero. Mucho publicity. Think of the glory!"

"Think of your bank account."

"Exactly." He smiled happily and bit into another doughnut, chomping it down with greedy gusto. Bobby makes Henry the VIII look like Miss Manners.

"I brought you these for dessert," I told him, tossing the bag of sausage biscuits on his desk. A pile of empty fast food containers scattered and fell to the floor, joining the heap on the carpet.

"Hey, thanks," he said, genuinely grateful. Food was nothing to joke about to Bobby. "What's the occasion?"

"A favor," I replied.

"Can't do it without me, huh?" he asked, cramming another doughnut into one cheek like some grotesquely overgrown chipmunk.

I swallowed my retort. "Can you find out who called in the body?" I asked. "I need to know if it was a man or a woman, that sort of thing."

"No problem, doll," he said, adjusting his waistband as if shifting around the fat might make more room for the biscuits. "When do you need it?"

"Yesterday." I sighed and went back to my desk for the bottle of aspirin I kept in the top drawer. My box of Tampax had been moved to the other side. What a snoopy bastard he was. "You been going through my drawers again, Bobby?" I asked.

"I've been trying to go through your drawers for years!" There was that laugh again.

Why do I ever, ever ask him that question? He always answers the same damn thing.

Bobby D. has one good point. He pays my rent. But he also fancies himself a poor man's Nero Wolfe. Unfortunately, we're not just talking poor here, we're talking destitute. They have two things in common: private investigator licenses and huge rolls of fat estimated at 350 pounds plus. The similarity ends there. Brainwise, Bobby is a long way behind Nero. And Nero actually moved from his chair every now and then. Bobby is plopped on his butt when I arrive each morning and, as far as I know, stays there the rest of the day and maybe even through the night. He must go to the bathroom, but beyond that conclusion, I haven't the stomach to wonder. Fashionwise, Bobby favors stained polyester jackets. Probably because they go well with his pants. He lounges about in this sartorial splendor each day, occasionally bobbing his huge neck, which is as thick around as a tree and a startling contrast to his small, tomato-shaped head and button features. The tomato motif is enhanced by his dark brown toupee, which is styled like a 70's lounge singer, except for a large cowlick that sticks straight up like a stem. He accentuates this showstopping look with heavy gold jewelry which, frankly, I can't see Nero wearing.

Besides, Bobby D. is real. Nero, I'm sorry to say, is not.

But I leave Bobby to his illusions. He pays me well. Technically, I'm his receptionist. But only because, technically, I can be no more than that. There is the small matter of a drug smuggling conviction fourteen years ago when I was twenty pounds lighter, very much younger, and a whole lot dumber than I am now. I was carrying just enough to catapult me into the hallowed ranks of felons. Just enough to keep me from obtaining my own investigator's license. Just enough to make me quickly divorce the son-of-a-bitch who'd asked me to drive his car for him then disappeared forever. But not enough to keep me locked away for long.

Eighteen months behind bars in a Florida women's prison did a lot for me. It made me into a voracious reader and one smart cookie who can spot a phony at twenty paces. It also made me into a feminist who doesn't like women and a woman who doesn't like men but dates them with misguided optimism anyway.

My attitude serves me well when it comes to following cheating spouses or poking into the lives of the betrothed. Which is what I usually do for Bobby while he sits around and shovels down enough beer and sandwiches to sustain a third-world country for a week.

Why do I do it? I find it reassuring to watch other people screw up their lives. Participating in my own is a bummer. One day I might decide what I want to be when I grow up. For now, I work for Bobby and live in North Carolina. And that's better than being where I was.

Me and Thomas Wolfe—we can't go home again.

In fact, I won't even admit where home was. The

closest I'll come to confessing to where I'm from is to say
that, back home, we're too busy running from alligators
to stop and make pocketbooks out of them.

It doesn't matter anyway. I have a new life. I even have
a new name. It's not technically Casey Jones since the
divorce, but it's the name on my MasterCard, so why
argue? Besides, call me sentimental, but a new last name
was the one thing my ex gave me that can't be cured with
penicillin. So I kept it.

Anyway, I don't deserve to use my own name. My ex
took care of that when he convinced me to take the fall for
the smuggling charge. I was young, I was in love, I was a
sucker for a pretty face. Never again. I did the crime so I
did the time. But I never thought of how it might affect
Grandpa. He'd raised me on his own ever since my
parents had been found lying dead in a field of soybeans,
shot from behind by assailants unknown. I don't even
remember what my mother or father looked like anymore,
it happened so long ago. But I do remember the shame on
my grandfather's face when he came to visit me the
first—and last—time in prison.

One day, I will go back and prove to him that all those
years he spent feeding and caring for me weren't in vain.
And when I do, I know of at least one ex-husband who's
going to pay. And one murder investigation that will be
reopened. In the meantime, I'm learning what I can and I
call Grandpa every other week from pay phones. I never
talk long.

But enough about me. Let's talk about what Bill
Butler thought about me. I examined his card carefully.
The fact that he was carrying one at all meant he was a
little different from the rest of the jackbooted crowd a
few blocks west of McDowell Street. What was a nice
Long Island boy doing here in the wilds of North
Carolina?

More importantly, how could I weasel information out

of him while still retaining a chance to get his skinny
bones in bed when I was done?

I wasn't sure it was possible. I sighed and put the
matter on the back burner. It was time to get to work.

Five minutes later I was pulling up archived photos and
articles from the local newspaper—the *News & Observer,*
or *N&O,* as we locals call it—on my trusty Macintosh.
Bobby never moves from his chair; I never start a case
without my Mac. We all have our rituals. I learned
everything you would ever want to know about computers
in the office of that Florida prison. A nice lady from
vocational rehab taught me how to turn one on. A not-so-
nice lady, formerly of a bank in Miami, taught me how to
really make it purr. She was serving a fifteen-year
sentence for bank fraud and, like most of the inmates,
she'd only been caught because some guy she was dating
screwed up and got greedy.

NandoNet had started as the *News & Observer's*
computer network before they sold it off for a tidy profit.
It lets you surf the Internet cheaply and review reprints
from their current and past issues by pressing a few
convenient buttons here and there. I was interested in
deeper access and knew how to get it, courtesy of a young
lady who'd been caught with her hand in the ad space
money jar. She sold the code out to Bobby about a week
before the feds came to haul her away. They ought to call
it pink-collar crime. Believe me, it's the wave of the
future.

I started by reviewing the society pages. I wanted to get
a better look at Thornton Mitchell, the victim.

The South was changing, no doubt about it. The
society page was nothing like it used to be. No smiling
debutantes. No grinning daddys. No homage to the
same five last names. Instead, old money had given way
to the new elite: businessmen and political leaders.

People like the CEOs of nearby research and development firms, flanked by their thin northern wives. They were joined by the well-groomed homegrown politicos and their well-groomed but not always so thin wives. That was one thing I liked about the South. The really rich might still be really thin—especially the nouveau riche—but, face it, when you have homemade pound cake and pork barbecue and mounds of hushpuppies waiting at every fundraiser, who the hell can expect a woman to retain her girlish figure? Not the tubby male veterans of the campaign wars. In North Carolina, it was accepted practice to put on five additional pounds for each year you were in office and if your wife got a little plump too, you didn't turn her in for a new one like those northern heathens did.

I found Mary Lee all over the damn place. She was at home in society. And her weight was not an issue. She was neither thin enough to arouse envy nor plump enough to lose the babe vote. She was just right and I suspected her advisors polled the populace each week on how well-fed they liked their lady politicians to be. She had something about her, I had to admit, a shining intelligence that made everyone around her look just a little bit dull, even in photographs. Maybe it was no more real than that bright brittle cheer you find plastered all over beauty pageant contestants, but it looked real and that was what mattered. I spotted her standing next to the governor and his wife at a benefit concert, welcoming the vice president at the airport in another photograph, and opening up a new Sunday school for an acre of small black children somewhere down in eastern North Carolina. She looked at ease in every single setting.

Thornton Mitchell was a different story. For one thing, he had attended different functions. And he wasn't at the pinnacle of power like Mary Lee. He was one of those back-room guys, the kind that circles the candidates like lamprey eels searching for a soft spot. He popped up regularly in photographs of conservative fundraisers, his sleek black hair, tanned brown skin, and tailored suits making him look like a well-fed seal rising from a sea of attendees. The archivist had done a good job of bringing the *N&O* into the twenty-first century. I found shots of Mitchell in the photo library going back thirty years. I suspected he'd had a face lift or two over the years since his chins had a habit of disappearing.

One thing, however, never changed: the age of the girl hanging on his arm. In every single photograph taken during the last fifteen years, Thornton Mitchell held a drink in one hand and a very young blonde or redhead in the other. Put his repertoire together and you'd have a six-pack of Barbie dolls, all hairsprayed and squeezed into tight short dresses. I could see them now, sitting in front of the mirrors in the powder room of the governor's mansion, examining minute flaws in their mascara, adjusting their silk sheen control top pantyhose and practicing that blank stare young babes get when they don't want to say the wrong thing and are a little awed by the company. God, what were they doing with a drooling old geezer like Thornton? The thought of letting him touch me made my skin crawl.

I tried to find some sympathy for Mitchell, but failed. He was a real estate developer and, in my family's book, that made him no better than the carpetbaggers that my grandpa hated so much—a hatred passed down from his own father. Carpetbaggers had been the ones to take away our land, leading us down that rutted road to rusty trailers and broken-down trucks. How was Thornton Mitchell any different? He was destroying the South just as surely as opportunists after the big war. Just because he was raised here didn't excuse him. It only made it worse.

I noticed a funny thing about Thornton Mitchell when I pulled up all the photos side-by-side and compared them.

He was old. I figured his corpse was close to sixty-five. That gave him about forty years of behind-the-scenes maneuverings and contributions to political causes. So how come he was never in the forefront of a photo? Never standing beside a candidate? Never once taking center stage? And how come I never saw him in a single shot with the esteemed Senator Boyd Jackson, Stoney Maloney's fairy godfather uncle, the puppetmaster behind Mary Lee's opponent? It was pretty damn odd to be a conservative in this state and never shake hands with Boyd Jackson. Maybe they'd had a feud going. Or maybe something cozier.

I filed the tidbit away for further reference just as Bobby D. bellowed to me from the front office.

"I got the info you need, doll face," he hollered.

I logged off NandoNet and marched in to find out what he'd uncovered. I was smart enough not to expect him to come to me. "What's up?" I asked.

"A dame called it in," he told me. "A young woman reported the body about two a.m. last night. Said she and her boyfriend had been out parking and they'd seen a lady pull her car into the driveway then get out, acting funny. When the lady went inside the house, they looked in the car. Saw what looked like a body rolled in a tarp. Sped away and called the cops."

"How very civic-minded of them," I said dryly. "She said they were out parking in Country Club Hills?" Bullshit. The kids screwed on the fourth hole of the golf course there. They didn't drive around looking for Lover's Lane.

"That's what she said," Bobby answered, palms spread wide. "I got me some impeccable sources."

"What was her name?" I demanded.

"She didn't say." Bobby shrugged. "She called the dispatcher directly."

"Not 911?"

Bobby shook his head. "Nope. Called the dispatcher

and was all excited, blurted out her story, and gave the
address. Then she hung up.''

"What makes the night clerk think she was young?''

"She was out driving around with her boyfriend, what
else?''

"Bobby, if you were any dumber I'd make you into a
doorstop. No one is a teensy bit skeptical of a miraculous
midnight caller who conveniently knew all the facts about
the body?''

"I didn't say that," Bobby admitted. "It sounds fishy
to me, too. And to everyone else. Maybe that's why they
haven't arrested Mary Lee for murder.''

"Not that Hooter would let them.''

Bobby shrugged. "Whatever. She's been down at the
station for a couple of hours now, answering questions.
She'll probably be there all afternoon. It's driving the
reporters crazy. Happened too late to make this morning's papers and they might not even get a statement from
her in tomorrow's edition.''

"How terribly inefficient of Mary Lee," I muttered.
"She must remember to murder at a more convenient
hour next time." Then it hit me. "The station?" I asked.
Had Bill Butler won the battle of jurisdiction after all?
"Who's in charge of the investigation?" I asked.

"Joint effort," Bobby replied. "Local and state. CCBI
and the SBI. Everybody but Andy Griffith.''

"Well, surprise, surprise, surprise," I said, clomping
out to my car. I wanted to get home and sleep off my
hangover. My head was really aching. I was bone tired. I
needed to get some sleep and think it over. I ought to take
a good look at Mary Lee's husband, Bradley, but for now
I just wanted a good look at my pillow.

"Where are you going?" Bobby called after me.
"We've got work to do.''

"So do it," I told him. "If you ever want to get up,
just put your hands on the armrests and push.''

Twenty-five minutes later, I was snuggled beneath my

very own pair of cool sheets. My apartment was quiet in
the afternoon light, the silence broken only by the
occasional freight train crawling through downtown.

I had switched off the telephone ringer and muted the
volume on my answering machine. It was imperative that
I head off Mary Lee and her questions. I was too tired to
hear anyone's theories but my own.

I turned on a local radio station for the old fogies and
settled down in my bed. The sounds of Glen Miller filled
the room and I shut my eyes, thinking of Bill Butler and
how good he would have looked in a World War II
uniform. I needed music from another decade right then.
I felt transported and hoped it would last.

I finally fell asleep listening to Johnny Mathis. Helpless
as a kitten indeed.

THREE

I woke at five the next morning when the paperboy scored a bullseye on the window near my bed. It was still dark outside when I retrieved the newspaper. The cold October morning put a sting into the concrete of the stoop beneath my feet. I couldn't find my second bunny slipper. I wondered briefly if Jack had taken it, but no—a slipper fetish was too imaginative for him.

The murder took up the entire front page. Every one of those reporters had managed to score a by-line. Shrimp-boat Shorty had insinuated himself in not one, but three photographs. Bill Butler was nowhere to be seen. Rats. There was no statement from the Mary Lee Master's camp anywhere. I knew why. She never let a word out the door unless she checked it first and she'd probably been too busy downtown fending off questions to approve any official release.

Mary Lee's opponent, Stoney Maloney, had been more on the ball. The *N&O* ran his statement on page two, across from a handsome campaign photograph of him at a recent rally. Stoney had the look of a winner. He was tall with a strong build, a square jaw, clear eyes, Roman nose, and a full head of prematurely silver hair, carefully cut so that no offending strands dangled beneath his collar to provoke the church-going folks. He stood at a podium, hands spread wide, leaning toward a microphone. The camera had captured him as he was making an important point and people always look better when they're not posing. If only he could manage to be as impressive in person as he appeared in photos. He had a wooden side to him, a stiffness in public, a sort of reserve not often found in politicians. Maybe he just hated pretending to be someone he wasn't. Or maybe he had a stick up his ass.

I read his statement carefully. Depending on how you looked at it, it was either a very fair response or a carefully crafted ploy. I wanted to believe it was genuine but I knew that Stoney was taking no chances: he had surrounded himself with "paid political operatives" as the old-timers like to say, media specialists imported from New York and backed by a war chest big enough to buy television time every damn night of the autumn. One of his consultants, Adam Stoltz, was only twenty-eight years old and already rumored to be the next generation's Roger Ailes. Whether this was a compliment or not depended entirely on the speaker.

Still, the official statement had a down-home quality to it and I was willing to give Stoney the benefit of the doubt. The gist was that Stoney was aware that his opponent had been detained for questioning by the authorities and that a body had been found on the premises of her home. He wanted to let people know that the victim had been a minor contributor to his campaign—as he had contributed to virtually every pro-business campaign in the state—but that Stoney had not known him personally. Just the same, his heartfelt condolences went out to the victim's family. He did *not* mention that Thornton's family consisted of an embittered ex-wife and two alienated college-age children who had long been embarrassed by their father's immature excesses. Stoney then went on to say that he had always found Mary Lee Masters to be a woman of integrity, one who played fair and exhibited a deep moral foundation. He was positive she was innocent and felt sure that the authorities would clear up the mystery. He hoped it would be soon.

Lordy. They'd drum him right out of the party.

I didn't get the man. I truly didn't. I'd watched him at a lot of debates by now, taking on Mary Lee. He was always serious, always listening. But a little too good to be true. And, of course, related to Senator Boyd Jackson. I'd sooner vote for him if he was related to an iguana. Stoney was often flanked in photographs by his mother— older sister to Boyd Jackson—and his female sidekick of the moment, usually a quiet woman with the color and personality of putty. Any other guy would have been labeled as gay for being forty-four years old and never married, but since all of North Carolina had met Stoney Maloney's mother by now, everyone knew why the dude was still single. No one was willing to take her on as a mother-in-law.

Rumor had it that Sandra Douglas Jackson was the one who really ran the family show and had long been the force behind her brother Boyd's success as well. She was small and wiry, with a short-cropped cap of gray hair and a brittle gleam in her eyes. I'm not saying she was the type to run a concentration camp or anything, but I am saying she was the type never to hesitate. She knew what she wanted to do, and she knew what she wanted everyone else to do, and she wasn't shy about letting the world know it. I've met thousands of women like her scattered throughout the South. She could have done a damn sight better job of running things than the men but had never had the chance. Sandy Jackson was Mary Lee without the money, the attractive exterior, or the opportunity. I didn't know her and I didn't want to. I had a feeling she was the reason why old Stoney was such a stiff.

The call I had been expecting came just after I had showered, inspected my black roots in the mirror, and donned my favorite sheath dress for the day.

"Casey?" Bill Butler said, his tone businesslike, "I need you downtown this afternoon for questioning. It's official." Translation: five assholes from the SBI were at his elbows, listening in.

"No problem," I said sweetly. "What time?"

"Two o'clock?"

"I'll be there."

I called Mary Lee's house the second I hung up and got her all-around-secretary, Peggy Francis, on the line. "It's Casey," I told her. "Should I come in or not?"

"I don't think so," she told me. "The place is crawling with people. Party hacks, the whole campaign team, Hooter and his crew."

"What about Bradley?"

"Not yet," Peggy said, disapproval tight in her voice. "I tried reaching him through his office and they say he's unreachable. Mary Lee has no idea where he is."

"What a creep," I said for about the fiftieth time when it came to Mary Lee's husband. And I'd only known him for a month. Peggy did not reply. "Let me speak to Mary Lee," I demanded, hoping my forcefulness might get me through.

"She's busy." It was an automatic reflex.

"Tell her it's me," I promised confidently. "She'll come to the phone."

It about knocked me over when she did. "What did you find out?" Mary Lee asked. She didn't bother with hello. "Where's Bradley?"

"Hell if I know," I told her, a little guilty I hadn't done what she'd asked. But shoot, you'd think even the dirtiest dog would come crawling home, tail tucked under, once he found out his wife had been accused of murder.

"He has to be somewhere. What's his office say?"

"That he's unreachable." Thank you Peggy Francis. "I'm working on it. In the meantime, I've been poking into Thornton's background."

"I'm telling you, this is about me, not him."

"I think it's about *both* of you," I explained patiently. She had a bit of Louis the XIV in her.

"If Bradley had anything to do with this, I'm killing him," Mary Lee said.

"Could you come up with another expression?" I reminded her.

"Oh, yeah. Right. Listen, I have to go. We're issuing a statement this afternoon and I still haven't written it. The press is unbelievable." She did not seem entirely displeased with the situation. I wasn't surprised. What Mary Lee really craved was attention. She had it in spades now.

I promised to check in later and rang off, resolving to track down good old Bradley Masters before I went any further.

I dialed his office and wasted no time when some fresh-voiced Betty Boop soundalike answered and said, "Paradigm Investment Banking Inc." She made "Paradigm" sound like "pair of dimes" which was about all Bradley had to rub together these days in the way of capital. He was not a financial success and only family connections kept him in business.

"This is Susan Montooth from First Federal. I must speak to Mr. Masters immediately. It's urgent," I lied in my most officious voice.

"Mr. Masters is out of the office this morning. He will be back by early afternoon."

"Where is he?" I demanded, hoping to sound as if I would repossess his home at any second. "This is extremely important."

The lady kept her cool. "He is returning from a business trip abroad, Miss Montooth. May I take a message?"

I wasn't going to get anything out of her. She sounded like she'd been fielding similar calls from media representatives all morning long.

But I had an idea. If he was due in the office by early afternoon, he was coming back to town sometime late this morning. And if he'd truly been "abroad," or, at least, far enough away to miss the news about his wife, he was damn sure coming in by plane. The murder had made headlines up and down the eastern seaboard and he'd have called in if he had seen it. Chances were good that he had been out of the states. There was only one airport in the Raleigh/Durham area and only one terminal for international arrivals. I'd find the jerk first. Unless some eager beaver newscaster beat me to it, of course.

No one beat me to it. When Bradley Masters walked out through the double doors that marked the customs area at Raleigh/Durham Airport, I was the only one waiting for him. I watched him stride down the corridor and thought about what a shame it was that he was such a washout as a person, because he was truly a handsome man. If you go in for the Aryan type, that is. He was tall, his broad shoulders and flat stomach carefully sculpted through regular workouts at the most expensive gym in Raleigh. He still had plenty of blond hair, kept thick by a steady supply of Rogaine which he stored behind a stack of towels in the master bathroom. I knew. I searched the place regularly. His eyes were large and almond-shaped, tinted even bluer by the contacts he wore. And his straight nose and narrow mouth gave him a noble look he did not deserve, considering he had the personality of a weasel.

He'd apparently had nothing to declare at customs, if you didn't count the large duffel bag in one hand and the college coed in the other. She peeled off like a precision swimmer when she saw me headed toward them. I suspected she'd ducked for cover from a jealous wife many times before.

"Meet a friend on the plane?" I asked Bradley, grabbing his bag like I was being polite. I really wanted to check the weight. Maybe I could catch him with a couple kilos of cocaine and send him away for decades, saving us all a whole lot of trouble. "Been gone long?"

"What are you doing here?" he asked sourly. "God, I hope no one sees us together. What's with those roots anyway? Can't afford a bottle of Clairol? And what's with those dresses you wear? You look like a sausage. Plus that heavy eyeliner went out with my grandmother."

"You don't like the way I look?" I asked innocently.

"No one I know thinks you look normal," he answered.

"Maybe that's the point."

"What do you want?" he asked.

"Where were you?" I stared at his tan. It was deeper than his normal studio tint. "Pretty cushy business trip. She a new secretary or your new jogging partner?" I nodded toward the brunette, who had proved faster than a pro linebacker and was already halfway to the outer doors.

"Is it any of your business?" he countered.

I looked his expensive slacks over and shook my head. "Don't you know it's tacky to wear Armani in the Caribbean?"

I knew by the startled look on his face that I had him. It was more than an educated guess. He was too cheap to take a babe anywhere else.

"What do you want?" He checked his watch. "My wife send you to follow me around?"

"Your wife is a prisoner in her own home, under suspicion of murdering Thornton Mitchell."

That one stopped him. Stone cold dead. "What?" he asked, face perplexed. "What did you just say?"

His bag felt like it held a pair of swim trunks and little more. I guess he didn't need a lot of clothes for a three-day tumble in the hay. I took advantage of his shock to check the cover of a used airline ticket peeking out of a pocket on the side of the bag. He'd been in Nassau by way of Miami. "I'll tell you about it on the way in," I said. "You'd better head straight home."

"Of course I'm going to head straight home." He didn't add: "What kind of guy do you think I am?" Which was fortunate, considering the reply I kept at the ready.

"Is the press in on it?" he asked suddenly. Like I said, he was a great candidate's husband. "Do they know I've been gone?"

"Don't know," I said. "It's been pretty confusing. Mary Lee's staying out of sight. She's issuing a statement in a couple of hours." We were on the edge of the parking lot when the coed roared past in a silver Porsche. Funny, it looked just like Bradley's. I put an arm around his waist and looked up at him adoringly. She squealed the tires in rage as she turned a corner and raced away.

"Get off me!" Bradley demanded, swatting me like I was a fly. "You're a real bitch, Casey."

"Men like you sometimes think so," I confessed with satisfaction.

"For god sakes, get me home," he demanded, breaking into a sprint as we both spotted my clunker. "She can't do a press conference without me by her side. It'll look terrible in the papers."

Like I said—Mary Lee and Bradley made a hell of a pair. Like two actors playing their parts for the camera.

And that thought set me thinking: two actors, indeed.

The October day had turned into one of those spectacular Indian summer displays you only find in the Carolinas. The sky was a clear, bright blue with cartoonlike white clouds skittering around on a cool breeze.

The air smelled fresh, as if it had been replaced over a clean ocean for my lungs alone. Even the highway looked pristine, its freshly paved surface rimmed by rows of hardwood trees fluttering deep orange and yellow leaves. The ever-present Carolina pines encircled the pockets of color like the green tissue I used to stuff in boxes of grapefruit every winter after school for extra cash.

Too bad I was stuck in my car with someone I hated, instead of hiking over those peaceful-looking Piedmont hills.

"So where were you?" I asked Bradley again as we zoomed past a farm truck trundling its way down I-40 with a load of pumpkins for the yuppie supermarkets in Raleigh.

"None of your fucking business," he replied, ever the gentleman.

"Maybe not, but I can guarantee you that I won't be the last person to ask you that question."

He was silent.

"This is serious shit," I explained. "The police will want to know where you were."

"Why the hell would anyone care where I was?" he said bitterly, planting his expensive loafers on my dash simply to annoy me. It worked.

"Poor Bradley." I clucked my tongue in sympathy. "Forced to work all of what, ten, twenty hours a week? Representing wealthy business owners referred by Mary Lee. Supported in the style to which you have became accustomed by her family's money."

"Screw you," he mumbled.

"Some people might appreciate Mary Lee a little bit more," I suggested.

"Some people don't live with her like I do," he countered. "How would you like being told what to do twenty-four hours a day, your every move analyzed to see what effect it will have on the polls? Meanwhile, the whole state is laughing at me behind my back because my wife wears the pants in the family.''

Knowing Bradley, I suspected the real problem was that Mary Lee wouldn't give him a blowjob. But that would have been rude to point out, so I kept silent. Besides, if he really hated his situation, he could get out of it easily enough.

"It's your choice to stay," I pointed out.

"Spare me the marriage counseling," he replied. "I don't notice any rings on your fingers."

I decided not to show him the one in my navel.

We rode in silence after that, as I blew through quite a few red lights to get him home in time. It didn't make him any more grateful. When we pulled up to the house, it looked deserted. I had expected the place to be jammed with media cars and television trucks. "Where is everyone?" I asked.

"I doubt she'll hold the press conference three feet from where the corpse was discovered," Bradley said snidely, climbing out. "It'll be at campaign headquarters."

Peggy Francis emerged on the front stoop and glared at Bradley. "Hurry up," she called out. "We have to be downtown in fifteen minutes."

It wasn't until Bradley had disappeared inside the house that I realized what he had said. How the hell did he know where the corpse had been? I hadn't said a word about it.

I couldn't decide if I was disappointed or relieved after I showed up for my appointment downtown where only Bill Butler seemed interested in me. I guess the SBI felt I wasn't important enough. On the other hand, it gave me the perfect opportunity to pump Bill for information—and to bat my eyelashes, of course. I'd worn my contact lenses for the occasion and I considered it a real sacrifice.

"What's a rude guy like you doing in a nice town like this?" I asked as I took my seat across the conference table from where he sat, looking all spiffy in a black tee shirt and black jacket. The room had been done in early 80's Formica. Very cheerful. The muddy brown of the floor looked particularly fetching as a backdrop for the numerous coffee and grime stains peppering its surface.

"I moved down from Long Island about three years ago," he told me, sliding a cup of coffee across the table at me without asking how I liked it. It didn't matter. I wasn't planning on drinking it. I'd had the coffee before and damn near needed crowns on my teeth afterward.

"Why'd you move here?" I asked. I pretended to sip my coffee so I could look at him over the rim of my cup. In daylight he was even more attractive. His face was a little craggy. Sexy creases at the corners of his eyes. A long black mustache that made him look a little like a Mexican bandit.

"I followed someone down," he said, shuffling a stack of papers into place.

"Someone like a suspect? A girlfriend? A wife?"

"You know, Casey, I think you're a little confused. I ask the questions. You give me the answers. Got it?"

I shrugged. "Where's Shrimpboat Shorty?"

"He and his fellow agents are off playing in a sand-box," he told me.

I laughed; he didn't. "You think I'm kidding?" he said. He sighed and pulled a tablet of paper toward him. "Why did Ms. Masters hire you as a bodyguard?" he asked. "I need to know more about the specifics."

"She'd been moving up in the polls," I explained. "Against all odds, I might add. But when she started moving up, she also started getting these phone calls."

"Threatening phone calls?" he asked.

I nodded. "Seriously threatening. The caller knew where she lived, what she wore to bed, stuff like that. And he had a very specific plan for what he'd like to do to her. Weird sexual stuff, mostly. Bondage, that kind of thing. Do you want to hear the details?" I asked hopefully.

He shook his head. "Why didn't she report him to us?"

"It's hard enough being a woman and running for office in this state without having the fact that you're vulnerable in certain areas rubbed in the voter's faces."

"I get it," he said. "What else?"

"He knew a lot of personal things about her," I continued. "And he had a creepy voice. Raspy, muffled. Very scary. Mary Lee had her secretary tape a few of the calls. The guy was a real sicko."

"What's wrong with the usual state trooper guard? Or the local guys?" Butler asked. "You told me last night she didn't trust them."

He had a good memory. "A couple of times, Stoney Maloney brought up some new issues just as Mary Lee was about to release a major statement on the same issues," I explained. "It kept forcing her into reacting, rather than setting the agenda for the campaign. She trusts her staff a lot. They've been with her a long time. But there was a leak somewhere. She decided it was one of her three guards and told them all to get lost. I was the replacement."

"You replaced three guys?" he asked, his eyebrows raised.

"I could have replaced more," I confided. "But that's all that were assigned to her."

He tried to hide his smile and failed. "Did the calls stop?"

I nodded. "For a while. They've started again. I think

it's a manic depressive going through a down cycle or something. Maybe a campaign volunteer.''

"Why did she pick you?" he asked.

"I'm the only female private . . ." I stopped in time and rethought my strategy. "I'm the only female body-guard in the state. She wanted a woman."

"Why?" he asked, clearly more curious than chauvin-istic.

"Ladies' rooms figured prominently in the creep's scenarios. She was afraid to take a pee alone. My main job for the past month has been to stand outside her stall trying not to listen."

"I'm sure you're well qualified for the job," he said.

I ignored his tone. "It's no joke. Do you know how many glasses of iced tea that woman drinks a day? Hell, she hits the can more than a coke addict. And when she pees, she makes Secretariat look like a piker. I swear she has an auxiliary bladder hidden somewhere. The things I could tell you about public restrooms in North Caro-lina."

"If only I had the time to listen," he hinted and I fell silent.

"Who do you think did it?" he asked.

I felt flattered and immediately wondered if it was a trick. "Someone in Stoney Maloney's campaign springs to mind," I ventured. "Since she was moving up in the polls. Or maybe her husband did it." I hesitated. "They seem like a happy couple on the surface but that's just for the cameras. They hate each other."

"Of course they do," he agreed. "They're married."

Aha, he was divorced. It's grand being a detective. You figure out all kinds of stuff about people that way.

"What about the possibility that she really did do it?" he asked. "And tried to make it look like she was being framed?"

I considered the idea. "It's possible. Convenient, too.

All she had to do was blow the guy away and be so sloppy that everyone thought it was obvious she was being framed.''

He nodded. ''That's the idea.''

I shook my head. ''No way. What's the motive?''

''They were having an affair. She broke it off. He threatened to go public.''

I almost barfed in my coffee. ''If Mary Lee Masters had an affair it would not have been with that human hot tub. Besides, she's about thirty years and twenty pounds over the limit for Thornton Mitchell. They weren't having an affair.'' He still looked skeptical. ''Bill,'' I promised, ''trust me on this one. She wouldn't jeopardize a lifetime of public service by having an affair with someone who looked like a badly aging Engelbert Humperdinck.''

''That bad?'' he asked.

''That bad,'' I emphasized.

He sighed and drummed his fingers on the table, his eyes searching the green paint peeling off the grimy walls for clues. I waited. If you had to wait, Bill Butler was a nice diversion.

''Look, Casey,'' he finally said. ''I don't know how you fit into this, but I think you're clean.''

''You say the sweetest things,'' I told him.

''I didn't say you were perfect,'' he pointed out. ''But I asked around and, while I've noticed that no one around here has actually seen a P.I.'s license with your name on it, they all seem to think you're competent.''

''I have a license with my name on it,'' I said indignantly.

''Oh, I have no doubt of that,'' he said, his tone hard to read.

''My boss has been officially hired by Mary Lee Masters to look into the murder,'' I explained. This was only a half lie. Bobby D. had been hired, but I would be the one to do the looking. "I just help him out with the paperwork, bodyguarding stuff. Office administration. You know."

He was willing to play along but couldn't help making it obvious that he was doing so. "I've seen your boss," he said. "If he can follow anyone around without being as conspicuous as a whale in a bathtub, I'd be surprised."

"That's a pretty accurate image," I congratulated him. "What's your point?"

"You know I can't let you near this thing," he said. I shrugged in agreement. "It's a murder investigation. The SBI has gotten involved, which is rare. No way you're getting involved officially. But if you find anything of interest in your unofficial investigation, I want to know about it. I'd return the favor."

"A 'you show me yours and I'll show you mine' kind of thing?" I asked.

"Sort of," he said. "I think I have a lot more to show, of course."

"How modest of you," I pointed out. He just sat there and waited. I admired his cool. I relented finally, my dislike of Bradley Masters getting the best of me. "I picked up Bradley Masters at the airport this morning," I said. "He'd been in Nassau. At least his ticket said so. You might want to check. It should be pretty easy. If he was there, he was using his own name. He'd have to. He lives off his credit cards with the bills paid by Mary Lee's accountant. Besides, he's too stupid to cover his tracks." I didn't mention that Bradley knew where the body had been dumped. A girl's entitled to her little secrets, don't you think?

He made a note on his pad. "Thanks. We'll check. Anything else?"

I spread my hands wide. "It's your turn."

He considered it, turning the request over in his head. I

could tell he was skimming the available information, trying to strike a balance between what was really useful and what I would recognize as a throwaway diversion. I didn't care what he gave me, frankly. Anything was better than nothing.

"Well," he finally said. "The reports came back on the body. An analysis of residual silt stuck to the body indicates that the victim was probably killed somewhere along the Neuse River."

"The Neuse?" I asked. "That's a long damn river."

Butler shrugged. "It's the best I can do. Be grateful for pollution," he added. "It makes chemical analysis pretty accurate."

"What did they find?" I asked.

"Combination of sand and silt. Traces of acetic and sulfuric acids, acetaminophen, petroleum, estrogen, and a couple of carp scales. The SBI is trying to pinpoint the spot right now."

"Estrogen?" I asked. "That cinches it. It must be downstream from the sex change hospital."

He looked interested until he realized I was kidding.

"Well, thanks for the tip," I said, rising to go. I got no argument from him. "Maybe I'll spend the rest of the afternoon canoeing the banks of the Neuse in search of menopausal women."

"Whatever floats your boat," he said with a shrug.

"Aye, aye Captain," I told him and got another smile.

I didn't stay to press my luck. The Neuse was a long damn river all right, but I had a pretty good idea where estrogen was likely to land in the silt.

It was a bigger clue than he realized but I wasn't about to let on. I'd let Bill Butler check up on Bradley Masters and Nassau hotels. I had better things to do.

I was up Shit Creek but, hey, I had my paddle—and I intended to use it.

FOUR

Slim Jim Jones was being something of a jerk about lending me his canoe. For one thing, he wouldn't let go of it.

"Come on, Jim. I brought it back in one piece last time."

"It was missing the paddle."

"I wasn't the one who lost it," I explained. "That was what's-his-name."

He shook his head in disgust. Slim Jim had managed maybe one girlfriend in the past fifteen years. I'm sure he considered people who couldn't remember the names of their ex-lovers on a par with bathroom sink scum. "I didn't like all that hanky panky going on in front of my mamma's porch like that," he grumbled, holding firmly to the canoe. "You pretty near gave her a heart attack, paddling by without hardly a stitch on. You had no business bringing a stranger on my farm. You know Momma don't take kindly to trespassers."

Did I ever. I first met Slim Jim about ten years ago when his sweet old mamma got arrested for chasing a pack of teenagers off her farm with a loaded double-barrel shotgun. She'd blown a hole in the flatbed of their truck as they escaped down the driveway. No one ever thought it would get to court but, thanks to a young prosecutor who didn't know any better, it was

headed that way. That was when Slim Jim gave me a
call. He got my name from his brother, a guard down at
Central Prison who I'd run into a few times while on
the job. Slim blamed himself for not being home at the
time of the shotgun incident and explained that his
mother had a fear of burglars dating to the time her old
tom turkey had been stolen back in 1962, just a few
days before Thanksgiving. "She took that harder than
when Dad died," Slim had explained. "She was just
trying to protect her property when she chased off those
kids."

He asked me to look into the background of the
teenagers who had trespassed and, when I did, I found
a gold mine of sealed juvenile records for breaking and
entering, petty theft, assault, and—best of all—tying
up an old woman in Apex so they could steal her sole
possession of any value, a new radio. I paid the
prosecutor a visit with my information and the charges
against Momma Jones were dropped. Slim never told
her why for fear she'd go after the teenagers again, but
he paid my bill without complaint, invited me by his
farm whenever I got homesick for the smell of manure,
and, since that time, has proved to be a cantankerous
but steady friend. We share a love of cornfields and a
hatred for concrete. I steer clear of his mother, though.
They gave her back her shotgun and I saw the rear end
of the truck those kids were driving. Momma Jones
knows how to shoot a little too well for my taste.

Slim Jim interrupted my thoughts. "If your fellow had
been wearing any pants, Momma might not have got so
upset," he pointed out.

"How was I supposed to know the guy would choose
that moment to make his intentions clear?" I asked Slim,
in deference to our long friendship, not to mention the
fact that he was the only person I knew who owned a
canoe.

He scowled, his face scrunching up until it looked like an elf's perched on the end of a long stalk. "You got strange taste in boyfriends, Casey. They ought to at least be able to swim. I'm not saving any more of them for you. And next time, you give the mouth-to-mouth." He spit out a glob of tobacco juice, as if remembering.

"I don't have any taste in boyfriends at all," I pointed out. "Look, I'll muck the barn for you when I'm done if you let me use the canoe and get someone to park my car for me on the pull-off before Raleigh Beach." I knew I'd get him with that one.

He let go of the canoe and held out a brown-stained hand for my keys. "Since you're alone, I'll let you take it. But bring the paddle back this time. And no tipping."

"I had to tip it last time," I protested. "My honor was at stake."

He snorted and spat out a big wad of gooey tobacco juice. It splatted on the ground about half an inch from my hightops. He does that on purpose. "Have it back by dark," he warned me. "And just sort of duck down when you pass by the house if you happen to see Momma on the porch."

Oh, sure. I'd duck down and that nasty old buzzard would think the canoe was empty and next thing I know she'd be stroking through the Neuse with those work-hardened 74-year-old biceps of hers and I'd have to beat her off with the paddle to keep her from tipping me, ass-over-tea-kettle, into the river. Thanks, but I'd just wave and paddle faster if I saw her. Slim Jim thought his mother a delicate flower of southern womanhood but the rest of Wake County knew better. She was human ragweed: tough, unstoppable, and capable of causing people a whole lot of misery on a regular basis.

Slim and his mother owned one of the few remaining

private farms along the Neuse. I pushed off into the river and felt a pang of envy as I passed through his land. His fields stretched in flat plains up from the riverbanks in shades of tan and brown, the harvested stalks of corn drooping beneath the October sun. He'd not yet plowed under in preparation for next year. Too busy needling me, I guess. The current was slow but steady and I quickly left Slim's farm behind without a glimpse of his crusty mamma.

Soon the slow rhythm of the river seemed to rise from the bottom of the canoe and settle my hyper bones. I loved being on the water, especially sluggish rivers like the Neuse. It wasn't anywhere near as sleepy as the swamp I'd fished as a kid, but it was pretty damn drowsy. In most spots, it was no more than forty or fifty yards wide, the brown muddy current poking along between hardwood-lined banks of red clay. It was a sight to see on this sunny October day. Every tree was blazing with color, and the Indian summer still hung on so strong that the shores were teeming with basking turtles and colorful flocks of butterflies who had long since lost track of the season. Mysterious eddies formed at the water's edge where snakes slid from view at my passing.

The Neuse is a long and meandering river that reaches from just north of Lake Michie all the way to the Carolina coast. For years, it has resisted development and still remains, for long stretches, as deserted as in the days when only Indians plied its shores. But the white man was closing in on the Neuse and much of the surrounding land had been earmarked or sold for development purposes. It would not be long before the blue-gray siding of prefab vacation homes replaced the blazing hardwoods along her shores. There were people fighting the transition and organizations carefully monitoring the water quality, but they had little money compared to the developers and I feared they'd grow tired long before the fight was done.

It was precisely because of those tree-huggers, as some people called them, that I was even able to beat the flat-top boys to the punch. I knew from the report on the silt found on his body that Mitchell had to have been killed downstream from both the local pharmaceutical and textile plants that were allowed to dump their treated sewage into the Neuse. The chemicals found in the silt told me that. But the report had said nothing of human waste and I knew from a front-page article in the *N&O* that a trailer park just below Raleigh Beach had illegally disgorged a massive sewage overspill into the Neuse two days before. Water below the dam there was currently loaded with coliforms, bacteria that thrive on human waste—but the silt and water traces found on Mitchell were not. That left a three-mile stretch of river where the murder could have occurred and I'd be able to cover it pretty quickly thanks to Slim's canoe.

I was in a hurry because I knew the SBI wouldn't take long to figure it out and I wanted to get there first. They'd never let me near the spot once it had been staked off. On foot, it would have taken days. I was hoping that the rustlings I heard in the woods as I passed were SBI men hoofing it and not some mad river stalker who had done Mitchell in and was waiting for the next victim.

There was no one along the river at that time of day. It was too hot for both the fish and the fishermen. I checked first one bank of the river, then double-backed against the slow current to check the other. I was looking for a spot easily accessible to the public by car, but probably on private land or in an obscure area. Whoever had killed Thornton along the Neuse must have gotten him there willingly. He was a big man. No one would bother to kill him somewhere else, then drag him to the Neuse before carting him across the county to Mary Lee's. He must have had a meeting with someone he knew, someone who didn't want to take the remotest chance of being seen with him for personal—or political—reasons. Or both.

Some of the more popular parking spots along the Neuse were out as the murder spot, since night time was prime time for teenagers suffering from hormonal overload and no one in their right mind who wanted to be alone would expect privacy in those areas. No, it had to have been a less public pull-over spot, probably south of the U.S. 1 bridge.

I found what I was looking for two miles and almost three hours further downstream. I was sunburned and my arms were starting to ache from fighting the current on my doubling-back segments. I'm no lightweight when it comes to upper-body strength, but I'm no Arnold Schwarzenegger either. By the time I spotted a series of old campfires, deserted in the afternoon sun, I knew I was getting close. It was a remote fishing area, the charred campfire remains left behind by catfish seekers who sometimes squatted along the banks all night long, determined to haul in both breakfast and the next day's dinner by morning.

The people who fished this stretch of the Neuse weren't using fancy fly rods and they weren't doing it for the fun—they were sustenance fishermen who kept every fish, no matter how small, because they had nothing else to eat. They were often old farmers whose land had given out or been polluted beyond use by nearby industrial areas. Or, more and more these days, Mexican immigrants who had dropped off the migrant worker circuit and made Raleigh their permanent home. They'd sneak down onto private land around dusk where the pickings were good and had forged quite a few illicit paths along the river. I pulled the canoe over and beached it, so I could explore the stretch better on foot. Footprints and the usual mess humans left behind dotted the shore: flattened fast food cups, clear plastic doughnut wrappers, Styrofoam that would last until the end of time, and a million or more cigarette butts. God, but people were worse than pigs. At least pigs ate garbage instead of simply making it.

There were several trails leading from the shore's edge up into the surrounding woods, most winding over gnarled tree roots exposed by erosion, before turning into narrow lanes that criss-crossed the forest floor and fed into a wider dirt road about a quarter mile back from the shore. I was looking for a fairly big side lane, however, one wide enough to accommodate a car that had pulled off the main dirt road. Mitchell must have driven his own car and I knew he'd be the type to have a land yacht. I found one likely road, but there was no evidence of hanky panky along it.

About a hundred yards further downstream, I had more luck. The buzzing was the first sign that I was getting close. It was an odd sound, more like a sigh than thousands of insect wings beating together. I slowed and looked for the source, acutely aware that the sun was still hot and high. It would be frying any part of Thornton Mitchell that had been left behind.

At first I thought it was a dead raccoon or maybe a bloated possum getting ready to blow sky high in the heat. Flies were covering a spot about the size of a small mud puddle near the base of a tree that clung tenaciously to the steep mud bank. I stopped a good twenty feet away and cursed the lack of my glasses. Flies buzzing meant carrion and, if it wasn't an animal, it was good old Thornton. Or at least the part of him left behind. There

was no way I was going to go tramping across the crime
scene, not when Shrimpboat Shorty had gotten such a
good look at my size-nine Ferragamos.

I crept back up into the woods instead, relying on the
mat of pine needles to obscure any trace I'd been there.
Tip-toeing carefully across the tops of several large tree
roots, I made my way to the base of the tree where the
buzzing could be heard. Holding on carefully, I squatted to get a better look at the kill. A cloud of flies rose
up at my intrusion and brushed past me in an angry
swarm. I closed my eyes and fought the desire to let go
of the trunk and swat them away from my face. Taking a
deep breath, I opened my eyes and peered at what they
had so reluctantly abandoned. I was pretty certain it
was a pool of blood. The ruddy banks were stained a
deeper brown around a circle of rocks piled into an
indentation. That was what had attracted the flies.
Instead of sinking through the sand, the blood had
congealed in the hollows of some of the rocks, forming
pulsating lakes of goo. My stomach lurched but I
shrugged it off. It could have been worse. At least there
were no body parts.

I crept back to the lane leading to the spot and
examined the edges of it carefully, looking for evidence
that one or more large cars had turned around. I found
nothing until I reached the larger dirt road. There, the
recent wet weather meant that the surface was particularly muddy. It was rutted with numerous heavy tracks
criss-crossing its surface. The underbrush had been
crushed or trampled along the edges. Too much traffic,
too many tires. I'd have to leave it to the experts.

Still, now I knew where it had happened. And the
location was significant. I was at a spot on the river
almost equidistant between Raleigh and Wake Forest,
where Thornton had lived. To me, that meant his killers
had come from Raleigh and that this spot had been

chosen not only for privacy but also as a compromise: they had been jockeying for power as well. It was middle ground.

I was now convinced that Mitchell had been killed by more than one person. After all, he weighed close to 250 pounds. There wasn't a human alive who could have lifted him from this soggy bank and put him into the trunk of a car without help. There must have been two or more of them.

I got to thinking about exactly how they had managed to wrangle his body out of there and I followed the tree roots back to the blood puddle. The flies had returned so I kept my distance, searching the sand for signs of heavy dragging. I found some markings that could have been giant turtles, but I doubted it. We were hours from the coast. No, old Thornton had surely been dragged south around the tree's roots and toward a softer spot in the bank where he could more easily be pulled toward the road. What a pain in the ass for the killers. Which told me something else. The murder had been an afterthought or an accident, not premeditated. Privacy is important when it comes to killing, but so is convenient body disposal. The bank was practically quicksand. You'd have to be a masochist to want to drag a body through here.

As I knelt along the bank at a safe distance from the killing spot, contemplating the possible motives and methods of transporting the corpse, I glimpsed a flash of red moving through the trees on the opposite side of the river. I was acutely aware of how exposed I was to anyone hiding in the woods and my pulse raced involuntarily. I squinted against the sun and tuned in what Grandpa used to call my "listenin' ears." Someone was moving through the woods across the river, someone accustomed to walking silently, someone very sure of his forest footing. I could hear the faint crackle of

pine needles breaking under his weight. Sweat broke
out in my armpits and the hair on the back of my neck
rippled. I thought it a very good idea to get the hell
away from there. I quickly hiked back up the river to
my canoe and was relieved to find that both the vessel
and paddle were intact. I pulled out into the sluggish
current and headed downstream. I had no choice but to
pass directly by the killing spot. My car was waiting
half a mile downstream and I was in no shape to hike
over land with a canoe balanced on my head for that
distance.

As I neared the spot where I'd discovered the puddle
of blood, my palms grew damp and the paddle slipped
free. I lost it in the current and almost tipped the canoe
in my haste to grab it. Fortunately the river narrowed at
that spot and I was able to fish the paddle out where it
had snagged on a tree root projecting into the water.
Damn it. I had to show more guts than that. Whoever
was watching me would know I was frightened. I
paddled back to the center, forcing myself to take a
deep breath. I thought about the time I'd whacked an
alligator across the snout with a paddle when I was only
eight years old. I hadn't liked the way he was eyeing my
biscuit lunch. Or me, for that matter. My grandpa
never stopped telling the story. That was the day, he
said, that he knew I had more balls than any of the
sorry specimens our family had produced since the War
of Northern Aggression.

What did this sudden memory prove? That I could do
a little bit better than cowering in a shaky canoe just
because someone had chosen this spot for a solitary hike
in the woods. I sat up straight and paddled with dignity.
At that exact moment, I heard a whoosh like a giant
dragonfly whizzing past. An enormous arrow split the
air about six inches in front of my nose, hitting the
center of an oak on the far side of the bank right smack

dab in the middle of its trunk. I abandoned dignity and threw myself on the bottom of the canoe.

Someone started laughing in the woods and it really pissed me off. I could take a lot of indignities, especially if it was a choice between being insulted and being killed. But being laughed at was another matter. I sat back up and paddled furiously for the far side of the river.

"All right, Bozo," I called out firmly. "You've had your fun. Now come out here and talk to me."

I didn't see anyone, but a soft male voice drawled back, "What can I help you with, ma'am?"

"You can start by telling me why the hell you nearly made me into a shish kebab. This is a public river. I have a right to be on it."

"You were getting ready to set down on my land."

You must understand that "my land" is a sacrosanct term in these parts. Anyone who has managed to hang on to their corner of the earth despite progress, carpet-baggers, real estate developers, and the tax man has formed a mighty powerful attachment to property rights by now. I knew better than to challenge that particular sentiment.

"I was not getting ready to set down on your land," I said. "Why were you spying on me?"

"What were you looking at over there?" the voice asked in reply. "That's private land over there. You got no right to be on it."

"Look," I said, my voice sounding far more steady than my pulse. "I know you could have hurt me back there if you'd really wanted to. That arrow didn't hit that tree by accident. You're a good shot. I know that you were only trying to scare me. If you'd wanted to hurt me, you'd have done it by now. So cut the crap and act like a man and show yourself."

Amazing how well that works. Threaten their manhood

and the boys will come running. This one didn't run, exactly, but he did step out of the shadows surrounding a grove of birch trees and tramp through the grass to the edge of the riverbank. He was tall, with a head full of wiry auburn hair and a red billy goat goatee dangling from his chin. He was dressed in a red and white checked flannel work shirt with the sleeves cut off, a pair of well-worn jeans and sturdy hiking boots. He stood quietly, holding his crossbow and regarding me with complete calm. It was a good sign. At least one of us was calm at that moment.

"I'm Casey Jones," I told him, offering my hand. He ignored it.

"Ramsey Lee," he mumbled back. And then I understood.

"I wondered what happened to you," I said.

"Nothing happened to me," he said defiantly. "Life happened to me. You people can sit on your butts and watch television all you want. I believe in living my life and taking a stand about things that are important to me."

"How much time did you do?" I asked, curiosity getting the best of what little manners I had.

"What's it to you?" he asked back, but I noticed that he leaned his bow across a tree and was taking the time to check me out from head to toe. His scrutiny made me nervous, like he was sizing me up for a boiling pot. I was also slowly sinking in the riverbank mud. I wouldn't be able to retain my suave exterior for long.

"Hey, I admired you for what you did," I said. "I'd have helped you if you'd asked."

"How could I have asked you for help?" he replied. "I don't even know you."

"It's just a figure of speech," I explained. Jesus, where had this guy been? He acted like he'd been trapped in an

attic for ten years and just now trotted out to dry. His
social skills weren't even up to my marginal standards,
though I admit his body had its attractions. He had
unbelievable biceps and the kind of tanned, sinewy arms
that only someone who really works the land can acquire.
That kind of lean strength can't be earned in a health
club.

"I did two and a half years," he explained in a flat
voice. "I'm still on parole."

I did the math in my head. That meant he'd been out of
prison for just under a year or so. No wonder he was
people-shy.

Ramsey Lee had been arrested about four or five years
ago for destruction of property. One night, he'd visited
the construction site of a subdivision that was going up
along the Neuse just outside the Raleigh city limits.
With the help of a couple of still-unknown companions,
he had pushed a bulldozer off a cliff and ruined the
engines of at least six other pieces of heavy equipment.
A lock had been opened on several containing dams and
most of the area flooded by morning. They'd dynamited
the rest of the tract in four different spots, obliterating
all access to the site, destroying the new septic system,
and sending a good chunk of one section tumbling down
the riverbank.

Ramsey Lee had been traced by the SBI through the
purchase of the dynamite when one bundle failed to go
off. The story had dominated the news for several
months, especially since Ramsey's father was from one
of those old North Carolina families who had turned to
real estate to make money after World War II. Public
interest had died off when Ramsey quietly pleaded guilty
and plea-bargained his way to a couple of years in the
slammer. I don't think he'd ever given up the names
of his friends. The papers kept calling him an eco-

terrorist but there were a lot of old-timers in the country-side surrounding Raleigh who had openly admired what he had done, including god-fearing, church-going people that were hardly of left-wing leaning. But I was sure the SBI had a file a mile high on this guy. They'd be all over his ass once they discovered he lived across from where Mitchell had been murdered.

"That subdivision is up and thriving now," I told him. "It's practically old Raleigh these days. Ugly as hell. I don't know how people can recognize their own houses, they all look so much alike."

He nodded slowly and stroked his goatee, pressing the scraggly growth carefully between long, tan fingers. "They won't stop until the whole damn state is gone. Mark my words. One day these woods will be a parking lot."

I stared at him and his eyes locked on mine. I wasn't sure if I liked what I saw. Something stirred in me but I couldn't tell if it was fear or attraction. His eyes sparkled with the gleam of a fanatic and his voice vibrated with hatred when he spoke. But at the same time, I could feel his despair that the land he loved was being destroyed. How many of us really believe in anything? In an odd way, I was jealous of him.

"Why'd you try to scare me like that?" I asked.

"I'm getting tired of people trespassing on that land over there." He nodded toward the side of the river where I'd discovered the pool of blood. "It's getting busier and busier, especially at night. Someone ought to close off that road. It's supposed to be private. I don't like what I'm seeing and since the owner's not around, I figure I ought to protect it."

"What kind of things are you seeing?" I asked, watching his eyes for signs of evasion.

He didn't even blink. And his voice grew more relaxed. "Trespassing is all. Fishing at night. Campfires.

Noise that ruins my hunting. Smells that distract my dogs. That kind of thing.''

I didn't believe him. "You've got a problem," I said, hoping to shake him up a little. "I'm a private detective. I'm working on a high-profile case involving a man named Thornton Mitchell and a politician named Mary Lee Masters. Ever heard of them?''

"I know who they are," he said glumly.

"I think Mitchell was murdered over there a couple nights ago.''

He shrugged. "Lots of funny things happen along this river at night.''

"The cops are going to be all over you when they find out it happened across from your land. They'll want to know what you saw.''

He shrugged again, unconcerned. "That's easy. Like I said, I didn't see anything. Cops don't scare me. I'm used to them.'' He picked up his crossbow and turned his back on me abruptly. "Sorry to have scared you," he apologized over his shoulder. "But I got to be going now.''

He disappeared back into the woods, his figure blending instantly with the colors of the forest. I was pretty sure he had been lying. But about what?

I pulled away from the bank, uncomfortably aware that my ankles were now covered in bug bites. I moved quickly downstream, anxious to put room between me, the killing spot, and Ramsey Lee. Besides, I had a whole barn to muck before I could go home.

It wasn't until I was a couple of miles up U.S. 1, headed back toward Slim's farm, that I remembered something pretty damn important I'd picked up from scanning the back pages of the *N&O:* Thornton Mitchell had been one of the developers involved in the subdivision project that Ramsey Lee had been convicted of sabotaging.

He was in for an SBI rousting supreme.

FIVE

I have the kind of answering machine that blinks once for each new message. At the moment, it was strobing like a disco from my distant youth. I counted the lights and fixed myself a large Coke from one of the two-liter bottles lining the bottom of my fridge. Between paddling and shoveling, I was exhausted. It was time for a caffeine jolt.

Hmm . . . six messages in six hours. What a coincidence. That meant they were probably all from Bobby D.

What a pleasant surprise. The first message was from Mary Lee Masters. Perhaps she had even dialed the number herself. It gave me a warm glow to know how important I had become in her life.

"Goddamn it, Casey. Where were you today? You said you'd call me with an update. What's going on? Who did this to me?" There was a pause while she took a deep breath. "It is very, very important that I know who was behind this. Fast. For both professional and personal reasons. I can't afford to have this hanging over my campaign. Please, I'm begging you. And I'll give you triple your hourly rate if you get it cleaned up by early next week."

See what a tough negotiator I am? All I have to do is sit and listen and my opponent comes crawling.

"I'm begging you, Casey," she repeated. "Get these guys off my back. And hurry. I need you back. I've been getting those obscene phone calls again. Plus I hate my new bodyguard. I can't pee with the big goon standing there waiting for me to finish. It's killing me. He *listens*. I think he has a tinkle fetish.''

She hung up abruptly and I marveled at her self-centeredness. Her bladder was more important than justice. But then again, whose isn't?

The next three messages gave me more to think about.

''Casey, what did you screw up now?'' Bobby's accent was unmistakable. He sounds like a garbage truck backing up, only with a drawl. ''You're not content to have lost your own license, are you? Now you want to go and lose me mine.''

Oh, that Bobby D. He's always getting things mixed up. That's why he's a lousy detective. I never had a license. You can't lose what you don't have. Except for your virginity, of course.

''You're great for business, doll. Really great. Two of those SBI jerks came to the office today. I lost a customer when he saw them coming.''

Poor Bobby. Having to sit on his duff in an air-conditioned office telling two polite men he doesn't know a thing while his slimy bail client slips out the back. No wonder he was traumatized.

''I don't want to resort to threats, babe,'' Bobby was saying. ''But if you don't call me back in an hour, your fat ass is tossed right out the door.''

I would lose little sleep over having my fat ass tossed out his door. The next message represented a slight change in his attitude. It began with a greasy chuckle that escalated into a nervous laugh. ''Casey, babe. Jonesy, Jonesy, Jonesy. I was kidding about what I said before. Har. Har.''

Yeah. Har. Har.

''Listen, babe, I just got a call from that lady politician you've been guarding. She says she'll pay us triple if you can wrap things up by early next week. I told her it was no problem. You were a star.''

Yeah—a superstar. But I didn't get far.

"Take your time getting back to me, babe. If I don't hear from you, I'll know you're hot on the trail.'' His greasy chuckle faded as he clicked off.

I sat in the old armchair I had fished out of some garbage pile and considered my options as I scratched the four thousand bug bites on my ankles. Let's see. I could bust my ass for Mary Lee. I could tell Bobby D. to take a hike. Or, I could confess to the murder myself and seize the opportunity to throw myself on Bill Butler's mercy for an hour or two. Hmmm . . . now *that* was a concept.

But the horses weren't through running yet. The next message was from Bobby. Again. His voice was starting to give me a headache. I found an old Darvon molding on the window sill, no doubt a memento from a previous attack of mega-PMS, and popped the tranquilizer while I listened.

"Hey, babe. Just checking in to see how we're doing. We have some big bucks on the line here, know what I mean?''

We? What was he planning to do that would help? Sit on the suspect once I caught him?

Screw Bobby. I fast forwarded the message to the next one. Him again. Sorry, wrong number. Four down and two to go. Come on, Bill Butler. Pick up that phone and dial.

"Casey, babe. I've got a really great idea.''

So have I. Go stick your fat head in the can. Please. And leave my answering machine alone.

"I've got a contact at the *N&O* who would kill for an exclusive on the inside track,'' Bobby said. "In return, she could hook us up with *Hard Copy* when we're done. We could make a little more scratch and get a lot of publicity. There's no reason not to plan ahead, hey, babe?''

No reason at all. If you have no qualms about ethics. And if you have no qualms about ethics, then why aren't you running for senator yourself?

I fast-forwarded the rest of Bobby's babbling. There were more important things on my mind.

I'm not superstitious. I make my own luck. But I did cross two sets of fingers plus both my legs when the last message announced itself with a beep.

"Casey? Bill Butler here. Just called to see if you could meet me for lunch tomorrow. I'll be here late. Give me a call when you get in."

Yes. Yes. Yes. Yes. Yes. Yes.

My headache was gone.

I called Bill Butler back to confirm lunch at one o'clock in a downtown Raleigh diner that had gone upscale and had great crabcakes if you could stand the four-minute description of everything on the menu delivered by the earnest waitresses. He had a great voice on the phone. I was really starting to like the man. I wondered if he knew it and was trying to use it. I hoped not.

The next morning, I decided to get an early start on tracking down just who had lured Thornton Mitchell to the lonely banks of the Neuse and why. I was hoping to uncover a tidbit or two before lunch so Bill and I could swap something other than saliva, which regrettably was unlikely to happen.

I knew just where I would go first. I'd let others explore lofty theories and political conspiracies. I had been through a divorce myself. I know who knows where the bodies are buried. I was going to visit Thornton Mitchell's ex-wife and pump her for everything I could get.

Apparently, she had done the same to good old Thornton. Adriana Mitchell lived in Oakwood, an historical neighborhood half a mile from the governor's mansion. Real estate prices had skyrocketed there in the past decade and a lot of the old timers had taken the money and run, leaving the gentrified neighborhood to an eclectic mix of lawyers, real estate and finance professionals, professors, former hippies, and an occasional politician. I was pretty sure Stoney Maloney also had a house there somewhere and, being a detective, I suspected it might be the one with ten of his yard signs sticking out of the shrubbery like warnings. I slowed but saw no one home.

Some of the Oakwood houses were small mill homes, left over from manufacturing days. Nowadays they call them charming bungalows and charge a fortune for them but they are still dwarfed by the stately Victorian mansions, all lovingly preserved, which dotted the neighborhood. Adriana Mitchell had one of the nicest. It was big and white with green shutters and a huge porch that wrapped around three sides. The porch intimidated me. When I was growing up, big porches like that were for rich southern folk. I'd never lived in a house with a porch.

A maid answered the door, her round face scrunching in on itself when she spotted my black roots and attire. Don't people understand that recycled thrift clothes are a fashion and social statement rolled into one? Jeeze, I was going to have to start wearing a sign.

I got even. I flashed my fake I.D. badge and scared the shit out of her. Adriana Mitchell was at the door within seconds. "Yes?" she asked, stretching the single syllable into three.

"My condolences on your husband's death," I said formally. Never hurts to suck up.

"Ex-husband," she corrected me in a syrupy drawl. "And I won't pretend to be upset. We parted ways long ago. How can I help you?"

"I'm a private investigator looking into his death on behalf of the woman whose car he was . . ." Well, how *was* I going to explain it?

Apparently no explanation was necessary.

"You're working for Mary Lee Masters?" my hostess said brightly. "A lovely woman. I met her at the benefit antiques show last year. I can't imagine what Thorny was doing in her car. It must have been quite a shock to poor Mary Lee, finding a dead person in her back seat like that.''

"Who is it, Addy?" a musical voice called out from a back room. This was echoed by what sounded like a dozen more voices, all as high and flutey as dove calls.

"It's a private investigator, girls," Addy called over her shoulder. "And it's a woman."

I heard squeals and wondered what the hell I was getting into. A bevy of well-dressed middle-aged ladies emerged from a back room and pulled me into the house, escorting me to a huge screened-in back porch where you could hardly see the rattan furniture for the hanging plants. Coffee pots and mountains of those useless little sandwiches covered several card tables.

"This is my bridge club," Addy explained. "But we think cards are boring, don't we girls?"

I assumed the genteel yelping meant yes.

"A private detective is *so* much more exciting," one woman in a flowered skirt declared.

Another was more prosaic. "Tell us some good dirt," she demanded, flipping open a gold cigarette case with practiced efficiency. The cigarette dangled from between her bright red lips, bobbing up and down as she dragged on it to light it.

"I'm here to gather some good dirt myself," I cheerfully admitted. And why shouldn't I be optimistic? Hell, I'd fallen into a veritable gold mine of juicy indiscretion: a harem of women with nothing else to do but sit around and talk about other people's lives.

"Who do you want dirt on?" a plump woman with white hair asked. She looked distressed, as if scruples might enter the room at any moment. A clever distraction was in order.

"I'm famished," I announced, eyeing a plate of tea sandwiches.

The chorus of "Oh, pleases" and the rush to offer me boatloads of food did the trick. "I'm looking into Mr. Mitchell's background," I mumbled through a butter and ham sandwich square. "Trying to get a handle on who might have killed him."

"Wasn't it just awful?" one woman asked, leaning forward, her eyes glittering. "Do you know that Thornton forgot to change one of his life insurance policies? Why that thing was twenty years old and now Addy is going to get over $100,000 out of him. Is that a scream or what?"

The sighs of admiration that filled the room confirmed my suspicion that a goodly portion of the women present had been jettisoned by their husbands to make room for younger models. Addy was apparently the winner of their unofficial "milk 'em dry" award. She had managed to get a chunk out of her ex even after he was dead.

"That must have been a nice surprise for you," I murmured tactfully. It was a motive, after all.

"Oh, posh." Addy flapped a hand gracefully. "I don't need the money. My daddy left me plenty. But it tickles me. Thornton would be rolling over in his grave if he knew!"

The room exploded with tinkly laughter and I was struck by the absurdity of it: a dozen well-bred women simultaneously imagining the corpse of Thornton Mitchell rolling beneath the cold, cold ground. And finding it funny. The maid must think them all nuts. I know I did.

"Were you close to your ex-husband, Ms. Mitchell?" I asked.

"Oh, call me Addy," she insisted. "Addy Poole. My daughter saw him every now and then, but I haven't seen him or even used the name 'Mitchell' for years. Not since he took up with that one runner-up in the Miss Fuquay-Varina contest. Why, she turned out to be seventeen years old and I'd like to have died I was so embarrassed that an ex-husband of mine could act like such a fool. I went back to my maiden name. But I insist you call me Addy."

The murmurs of support that followed this statement were the cries of a curious form of sisterhood, an awakening of assertion that had taken hold of these women following their rejections. I admired them for it.

"Well, look," I said, gauging how long it would take to finish a plateful of the sandwiches vs. how long I had until I met Bill Butler. "I have another appointment later and I don't really know what I'm looking for, so maybe you could just let me know whatever you think might be useful to me in my investigation." Translation: start blabbing.

"Information about whom specifically?" someone asked, as if confirming a school assignment. "Just Thornton? Or can we talk about Mary Lee and that handsome Stoney Maloney, too?"

I held up my hands. "By all means. Include them if you like."

That was like asking a hound dog if he wanted a bite of steak. They damn near attacked me in their frenzy to snag the prize. In the space of thirty minutes, I uncovered an astonishing amount of private information that all of the individuals involved would have been mortified to know the public knew. Well, maybe not Thornton, since he was beyond embarrassment at this point. (So was I, but I didn't have to die to get there.) Those women knew that Mary Lee went to a spa twice a year for long weekends to shed weight and that her hair was tinted regularly down at Marianne's by the proprietress herself, though in a back room so no one would know. One woman declared that, at a recent catered dinner party hosted by the Masters, Mary Lee had tried to pass off the culinary creations as her own. Others knew that she went through maids like firewood, hated a distant cousin for having an affair with her husband, was exceptionally stingy with her money, and had a running feud going with her own sister.

The others fared no better. Bradley Masters was a perfidious dog who had hit upon the daughters of nearly every woman present, whose indiscretions had recently turned to college co-eds, and who was known among the husband circle as someone guaranteed to screw up your business if you were stupid enough to entrust it to him.

General consensus held that Thornton Mitchell was a horse's ass, though Addy did have *such* lovely children, and that he could have been killed by half the fathers in the state of North Carolina. There was a brief but heated debate on how his toupee had grown increasingly obvious over the years and whether his siblings would bother to bury him in it. He had recently lost his touch when it came to real estate projects, they all agreed. One woman's son worked at a bank that had called in a construction loan and another's husband had lost money investing in a shopping center deal tied to Thornton. That was interesting indeed and I tucked the information away for further examination.

But it was the dirt on Stoney Maloney that interested me the most. I inquired as to whether he lived in the neighborhood and numerous voices assured me that he did.

"Right next to Elaine," one woman offered.

Elaine smiled, pleased with the attention. "He does indeed. He has a lovely yard. Of course, it's a gardener's work since he's so busy."

"Are you voting for him?" I asked out of curiosity.

"Oh, no," most of the women said, explaining they preferred to see a woman take the seat. Besides, their ex-husbands were all conservative and they were tired of being told how to—

"I'm voting for him," Elaine interrupted playfully. Her ploy worked. All eyes once again turned on her as she giggled.

"Why, Elaine. You're a Yellow Dog Democrat. How can you say—"

"Because he's so handsome," she admitted. "All that silver hair."

"Oh, Elaine," one woman said in disgust and I was impressed. Until she continued. "That handsomeness doesn't do any of us any good. He's *that way*." She dropped her voice and managed to give the impression, without actually saying so, that Stoney Maloney spent his evenings dressed in tight muscle tee shirts dancing the night away with hordes of gay men on the rooftops of local discos.

"No, he's *not*," Elaine assured them, laughing with the superior air of one who has inside knowledge.

"Tell! Tell!" a dozen voices chorused at once.

"I think he has a lady friend and not one of those mousy-mousy types, either. His mama would split a gut if she knew."

The room leaned forward as one, all eyes riveted on Elaine. I took the opportunity to snag a deviled egg.

"Every Wednesday night for the past month, he's gone out of his house very, very late at night."

"How do you know?" someone asked.

"Because I was *watching*," she explained, mystified that there could be any other answer.

"Does he leave the house alone?"

"Of course he leaves it alone," Elaine said crossly.

"Then how do you know he's meeting a woman?" Addy asked.

Elaine had the good grace to color slightly. "I happened quite by accident to overhear a message on his answering machine when I was weeding my marigolds a week ago."

"Weeding marigolds in October?" one of the women cried. "Shame on you, Elaine! You were *skulking*."

The laughter that met this statement quickly gave rise to what sounded like a football cheer for details.

"It was definitely a woman's voice and she was saying that she couldn't wait to see her 'Rockman' later that night."

"Rockman?" a white-haired woman asked. "What does that mean?"

"Helen!" someone exclaimed. "You're not *that* old."

The pragmatic guest with the gold cigarette case translated with admirable brevity. "It means he's hard as a rock in bed, darling."

"Heavens," Helen said and fell silent. I wondered if Stoney had just scored another vote.

"Is this helping?" Addy asked me politely.

"Oh, yes," I said, nodding vigorously and chancing one more eensy-weensy bite of a chicken salad sandwich before I left. "Heaps!" And it was the truth. After all, Thornton Mitchell had been killed on a Wednesday night and Stoney Maloney had not been home at the time. Bill Butler would be impressed with what I had to offer.

However, an hour later, Bill Butler proved quite unimpressed with my morning's haul. It rather pissed me off, despite the way his green polo shirt accented his big brown eyes.

"We know Mitchell's business dealings were going sour and we also know where Stoney was that night," he explained when I was done relating what I'd learned. "We interviewed him yesterday."

"So tell me where Stoney was that night," I demanded.

"Casey, it's none of your business. And it's not important to the case."

"None of my business?" I asked incredulously. "The whole world is my business."

"Apparently you think so," he said. He had ordered the crab cakes at my urging and, thanks to my fortification with several pounds worth of tea sandwiches, I had thus far managed not to wander over onto his plate with my fork in order to compare seasonings. "Look," he said, as if peeved that I hadn't done better, "I asked you to lunch to see if you had learned anything useful that might help me out."

"Sure you did," I said ominously and flashed him a sunny smile. If you can't seduce them, confuse them. That's my motto.

"What's that supposed to mean?" he asked suspiciously.

"It means it's time for you tell me something," I said. "I already told you what I know. It's not my fault you're overlooking the importance of my information to the case." I smiled again. He was still confused.

"Look," I spelled it out for him. "Did you check the husband's alibi *thoroughly?* I mean, double-check it?"

"We're working on it," he said impatiently. "But I got a feeling he's clean."

"Can't you tell me anything about the case?" I complained, hoping for his ex-wife's sake that he wasn't as stingy with his alimony payments.

"I can't comment on the case right now. It's at a critical stage."

"Really? How critical?" I innocently popped a hush puppy in my mouth and chewed while he fidgeted. I swallowed and decided to surprise him. "In other words, Mary Lee Masters is no longer a suspect. You've arrested someone else and now you're questioning him."

"Maybe." He looked uncomfortable.

"And Ramsey Lee won't say a thing."

This time he looked astonished. "How did you know that?" he demanded. "Is there a leak in my department?"

"No leak," I promised. "I'm a detective, remember? I'm great at putting puzzle pieces together."

"That's too big a piece to pull out of the air." I was a little put off by the suspicion in his eyes. I'd hate to get on his bad side.

But it didn't stop me from persisting. "Really? How's this for a puzzle piece? The SBI has determined that Thornton Mitchell was shot along the banks of the Neuse where his head hit a pile of rocks, then dragged through the sand and dumped in the trunk of his own car before being driven to Mary Lee's house. Because the spot where he is killed is across from land belonging to Ramsey Lee—and because the SBI has a boner the size of Cleveland for said Ramsey Lee—he's been arrested. They've wanted to nail him bad ever since he got off light for blowing up that development project and this is their big chance.''

"You *are* going to tell me how you know that," Bill warned. He glared at me but it was exciting rather than intimidating. I knew I had it right. And I knew something else as well.

"They're wrong, Bill," I assured him. "I won't tell you how I know where he was killed or who the SBI arrested. But I will tell you that you're wrong."

"What makes you so sure?"

"Ramsey Lee wouldn't blow a man away with a shotgun. He'd use a rifle or a crossbow and it would be clean, right through the heart. He wouldn't even have had to leave his own land to do it. He'd have been able to stand across the river and fire away. And he damn sure wouldn't have dragged him through the sand like that and parked the corpse in Mary Lee's driveway. Why would he? What does he have against her? And why drag the body off that piece of land at all?''

"Because it's across from his own land. The fact that the body was moved is essential."

"It certainly is," I agreed. "But not to Ramsey. Because he didn't do it. But someone did and I'd like to know why it was so important to get the body off that land."

"Ramsey's a good collar," Bill insisted. "He has a connection with Mitchell. He has a record as thick as this table."

"He has a *surveillance* folder as thick as this table," I corrected him. "He has a criminal record about as thick as Shorty's dingaling. Which is to say, maybe one teeny weeny centimeter wide.''

He ignored me and continued. "Well, explain this then: they found Mitchell's car on his land.''

"What?'' I asked. "They found Mitchell's car on Ramsey Lee's land?''

"Yeah, Sherlock. Does that convince you?''

"Yes,'' I said, nodding my head. "That I'm right.'' He rolled his eyes and I continued. "They find his car across the river from where he was killed? How did it get there? By ferry? Someone drove that car and dumped it on Ramsey's land on purpose. It's not exactly a convenient dumping spot. In fact, it is the single least convenient spot of all. They'd have to drive about fifteen miles out of the way and cross a bridge and double back. What kind of crap is that? And why would Ramsey leave the car on his own land? He's being set up and so are you. You guys are acting like idiots.''

I sounded sure because I was sure—and Bill finally got the message.

"What are you on to?'' he asked, his tone changing from anger to curiosity. We were getting somewhere at last. "Come on,'' he asked as nicely as he could. "Give.''

"I gave it all to you already,'' I said with a shrug. "And you can either work with me or work against me. But if you don't want to end up looking like a fool with those SBI guys, I'd stick with me, kid. I'm going to find out who did this.''

SIX

We ended the lunch crabbier than the cakes, leaving my hopes for romance in ruins and me even more determined to embarrass the whole lot of those overtestosteroned jerks. I was the most intrigued by Bill's comment that he knew where Stoney had been the night Thornton Mitchell was killed. Why wouldn't he tell me? Identifying the cavegirl to Stoney's Rockman was going to be a wee bit difficult on my own, but I felt up to the challenge.

I returned to the office in mid-afternoon to check Stoney's schedule for the week. The *N&O* printed a weekly political calendar each day and I had been following it carefully. Wednesday nights seemed to be strategy nights. Traditionally, all the candidates returned to their headquarters to recoup in midweek and plan out the next week's events. This week had been no different, putting both Mary Lee and Stoney in Raleigh when Thornton Mitchell was killed. But the days still ahead showed them scattered throughout the state. My best shot for catching Stoney in action was that night, before he left for an appearance in Asheville. He was scheduled to speak at a fundraising dance sponsored by the political clubs of several local colleges. Maybe I could spot his lady love lurking nearby in the crowd.

There was a photo of Stoney on page one that showed him issuing his statement in defense of Mary Lee. I studied it carefully. No wonder his eavesdropping neighbor Elaine was voting for him. He was one of those lucky guys who get better looking as they age. Who was the woman he met on Wednesday nights, I wondered. And what was the big secret? Was she a campaign aide? Someone's wife? Who knew. Maybe I could find out tonight. Maybe I never would. In the meantime, I had work to do.

"Bobby!" I shouted, kicking my door open so he could hear me over his own gastronomic ruminations.

He replied with a rumbling belch. If I'd had a herring, I would have tossed it to him.

"Sorry, babe," he explained. "There's a new Mexican restaurant opened down the block. They deliver."

They'd prosper, too, with him as a client. The most amazing thing about Bobby was that he had a love life. Yes, there were women in Raleigh, North Carolina willing to date a 360-pound man who dressed in polyester clothing, wore heavy gold chains, sported a bad toupee, and groped them with fingers that resembled greasy sausage links.

"Know anyone down at the county registry of deeds?" I asked.

"Sure," he rasped. "Girl named Nancy. Long-legged blonde with a nice pair of credentials and great legs. Bad marriage."

"Tell her I'm on the way, okay? Ask her to pull the file on the plot of land along the Neuse belonging to Ramsey Lee. Pull the deed for the plot directly across the river from it, too. I don't know who owns it or any of the plot numbers. Can she find them for me anyway?"

"Sure, babe. Nancy could find anything. Especially in the dark."

I didn't want to know. I grabbed my pocketbook and made a beeline for the door. Someone had suggested that Thornton Mitchell meet him in the middle of the night in the middle of nowhere. I wanted to find out who. The owner of the land was a logical start. Not that I necessarily believed in logic.

The nice "girl" named Nancy was no spring chicken. Fried was more like it. She had bleached blonde hair—but who was I to throw stones?—a dubiously perky bustline, and the kind of leathery face you seldom find north of Boca Raton in these skin-cancer–enlightened times. But she did have great legs, I'd give Bobby that. They scissored toward me, expertly balanced on four-inch heels. "You Casey?" she asked, snapping her gum as if the pop were a question mark at the end of her sentence.

"That's me."

"How's Big Daddy doing?" she asked, sliding two folders my way.

Big Daddy? *Please*. Not even Tennessee Williams would have found Bobby D. captivating.

"He's fine," I admitted. "Large and in charge, as they say."

"I'll say." She leaned over the counter, giving me a good look at the tops of her breasts. They were the color of coconuts and looked just as hard. They were not, I am grateful to say, as hairy. "That man can make my motor run, know what I mean?" As if to prove it, her nasal voice softened to a purr. I did not ask for details. "I need this back in twenty minutes," she said, raising an eyebrow at the two folders. "My boss is mad at me on account of I told him he was sexually harassing me. So he's not taking kindly to any personal favors I may hand out these days, know what I mean?" The gum cracked again, on cue.

I nodded wisely, woman-to-woman, as if Bobby spent his afternoons chasing me around the desk and I could really relate. In truth, the last guy to sexually harass me—without permission, of course—wound up with hot coffee in the crotch.

I stuffed the folders in my bag and went outside to read them, choosing a nice spot on a brick wall nearby. There was the usual new construction project clogging traffic on the outskirts of the Fayetteville Street Mall. Probably another hopeful office building going up in this no-man's land of urban dreams.

Nancy knew her stuff. She'd pulled the deeds and deed histories on both Ramsey Lee's land and the plot across the river. Ramsey had been left the property by a grandfather fifteen years ago and had held on to every inch of it since. The other deed was even more interesting. The land across the river had belonged to a former councilwoman for the city of Raleigh. She'd donated it to the city about a year and half before for future use as a public park. Apparently there had been some sort of holdup, because there sure as hell was no park on the plot. The file's checkout history on the outside of the folder showed that it had been a hot item over the past six months. Everyone from a city planning committee representative to a parks and recreation commissioner to several lawyers whose names I recognized had been taking a peek. Plus, guess who? Yep—Thornton Mitchell. Something was going on with the land all right. If Nancy didn't know, I'd search NandoNet for news on it.

"Yeah, a lot of action on that folder," Nancy admitted when I returned it. "Don't follow that stuff myself." I had slipped her a twenty and it disappeared faster than you could ask for change. "Why, thanks. That's right nice of you. Can I get you some photostats?" I nodded and handed her the other file.

She took the folders without comment and disappeared into a back room. She was back in less than two minutes with full copies neatly stapled in one corner. She handed them to me with a sunny smile and I realized that Bobby D. was right: she did have a lot of girl in her. "Here ya go, honey," she said with a wink. The crack of her gum had grown merrier with her twenty-dollar windfall and she sounded like microwave popcorn heating.

"Thank you," I said. "Clairol Ash Blonde?"

"L'Oreal," she replied. "Because I'm worth it."

I made it back to the office in time to do a little cyber surfing and put Bobby on the case of the park that was not yet a park. He was still in the same position, what a surprise, and eager to do what he could to earn that triple fee.

"There's something going on with the piece of land where Mitchell was killed," I explained. "The file on it's been checked out a lot over the past few months. I'm going to comb the press clippings. What can you do?"

"Leave it to me, doll face," he promised, reaching for the phone.

I logged on to NandoNet and launched a search using the name of the property's former owner. I got several hits right away. The land had been in her family for generations, but she had deeded it to the city on the stipulation that it be used as a public park for the education of local school children on the importance of natural resource management. After flexing her liberal muscles, she had packed her bags and left with her husband for new digs in Colorado, leaving the land behind for local politicians and developers to squabble over like coyotes fighting over a dead sheep.

Over the last four months, several related proposals concerning the land had been introduced and then tabled during city council meetings, all outlining what construction should take place in order to bring the dream of a Neuse River Park to life. The version I suspected Thornton Mitchell was connected to called for the development of a wide recreational beach along that strip of the Neuse, complete with an artificial pool for swimming alongside its banks, water slides, a huge snack hut, and an intricate network of roads that led north and south into the woods. I had no idea what purpose these roads served, but thought I could guess: he was hoping to use the park as the centerpiece for a new residential subdivision. A surrounding park was a great magnet for home buyers. It guaranteed that, while you might be spoiling the land and view for others, no one could return the favor.

I peered at the color photograph of an elaborate architect's model that accompanied the article. It was complete with miniature trees, Lilliputian gravel walkways, a shining strip of pseudo-Neuse, and a scaled-down eating complex. There was even a tiny Ferris wheel near the beach. It was painted bright red and yellow. Hordes of miniature people streamed toward the Ferris wheel, as if the entire city of Raleigh had been waiting for generations just to get the chance to eat cotton candy along the banks of the Neuse. No wonder the proposal had been shelved. In Raleigh's current climate—which was moving toward development backlash—a project like this was a guaranteed political disaster. I wondered how much Mitchell had had to do with it.

I'd have to wonder a little bit longer. It was time to face the hordes at Stoney Maloney's fundraiser and see if I could track down Madam X. I printed out a copy of the article and left it with Bobby as I dashed out the door. "I need to know who the potential investors in that piece of nonsense were," I told him over my shoulder. "That architectural model must have cost them plenty. Who paid?"

He held the copy of the photo up to the light and squinted. "Man, I love cotton candy," he said.

My wardrobe for the evening was hopeless. Everything was either too low cut, too tight, too short, or too transparent for a conservative college boy shindig. I'd be fighting off drunken frat boys like a dog in heat intent on preserving her honor from the neighborhood studs. I finally settled on a sleeveless white dress with a low scoop neckline that almost, but not quite, hit my belly button. It was a little tight on top and I made a mental note that I needed to cut down on the upper body weight machines because I was starting to look like a fire hydrant. But I thought I might be able to salvage the look if I used my ingenuity.

I had a remnant of red satin I'd been considering for

curtains and wound it around each breast and over my
shoulders like Miss Liberty. It concealed my cleavage and
lent a patriotic air to the ensemble. I then tracked down a
bright blue negligee that some misguided soul had given
me. I wound it into a belt, tying it off with a perky bow
that perched on top of my butt as if my rear end was a gift
for the entire party. All I had to do was unearth my red
pumps, wear pink lipstick, and slap one of those goofy
straw campaign hats on my head to hide my roots in order
to blend in. Of course, I looked like a float in an election
day parade, but we must all suffer for our art.

It cost me twenty bucks to get in at the door and, to
cover the cost of what I intended to spend on cocktails, I
reminded myself to tell Mary Lee it had been fifty. The
fundraiser was being held in the smaller of two basketball
gyms at North Carolina State University. The cramped
coliseum was not exactly the swankiest of milieus. I'd
seen the women's team play there a couple of times, but
tonight they'd shoved the bleachers back to one side in
order to make room for a raised platform at each end of
the court. Long tables lined the remaining side of a large
dance floor and served as a cash bar. In a burst of
originality, the ceiling and walls had been decorated with
red, white, and blue bunting as well as matching bal-
loons. All I had to do was grab onto a rope and hoist
myself up into the air if I needed to blend into the crowd.

One of the platforms held a podium and a row of empty
chairs. The other held an aging beach music band that
was cranking out ancient dance tunes. The crowd was 100
percent white. The band was 100 percent black, a
veritable six-pack of Shaft lookalikes left over from the
seventies, decked out in knit suits and iridescent open-
necked flowered shirts. They were long and lanky, and
looked monumentally bored as they moved in time to the
familiar sounds of a North Carolina college crowd. It was
a time warp. The dance floor was filled with young men

and women dressed in madras shorts and light blue or pink work shirts—sleeves rolled up—all wearing sandals or worn topsiders on their sockless feet. They looked exactly like their parents had, as had their parents before them. It was a strange and rigid species. Gold add-a-bead necklaces winked at the throats of the girls, while the boys were distinguished by their common glassy-eyed concentration. The kegs of beer lining the walls behind the makeshift bars explained the stares. These folks were about as politically aware as slugs. They just wanted to get drunk and dance. And what the hell, they were young—and half right.

I approached the closest bar and asked the middle-aged man behind it for a margarita, straight up, no salt.

"You gotta be kidding, lady," he said. Hmm . . . a northern import, no doubt. "I can give you frozen from the vat." He flipped a thumb over his shoulder at a large commercial freezer drum, the kind that used to churn frozen custard at Dairy Queens everywhere. Now you most often found them at yuppie bars, spitting out endless ropes of frozen green goo like some kooky apparatus from a Doctor Seuss book. I groaned. Frozen margaritas could really slow you down and I needed a drink to cope with this crowd. Oh well, what's a girl to do but risk brain freeze and make the best of it? I accepted a huge plastic glass of the mixture and noted that, as compensation, the concoction was loaded with enough tequila to put down a moose. I hoped the party organizers had remembered to line the dance floor with puke barrels.

I wandered through the frantic crowd, bumping into sweating college bodies, shrugging off overeager paws and sympathizing with the occasional adult who stood huddled in solitary misery like a disapproving school-marm. Working my way across the floor was a bruising experience because the place was jammed, but I'm an expert at negotiating crowded bars and I was able to elbow my way to a corner near the empty platform without spilling a drop of the margarita down my well-draped bosom.

"Nice outfit," a kid inexplicably dressed in a satin smoking jacket told me. He held a pipe and I wanted to tell him that the days of Hugh Hefner were over. But at least he wasn't smoking a cigar. He admired my dress again. "Kind of retro," he added.

I smiled vaguely. What the hell did that mean? I refrained from telling him that he looked like Jerry Lewis in *The Nutty Professor*.

"Like the band?" he asked, blowing pipe smoke in my face. "I think beach music is sort of passé, but the hordes seem to find it amusing."

I thought pretentious little whippersnappers who tried to pick up older women were even more passé, but I kept my opinions to myself. "They're perfect for the occasion," I said instead. I had noticed mass movement of bodies toward the empty platform over on the far side of the gym and was pretty sure that Stoney Maloney and his crew were heading for the podium.

As if on cue, the band broke into a sloppy version of "Bony Maronie," originally a Cajun tune that had been bastardized into a rock-n-roll hit in the early 60's and was now being further bastardized into Stoney Maloney's theme song. I clung to my margarita, listening incredulously, as hundreds of young white conservatives raised their voices in anthem, screaming Stoney's name to the music and throwing themselves on the floor to alligator on their bellies across the now-slimy wood like refugees from a remake of *Animal House*. I downed about half of my drink in a single gulp, brain freeze be damned, while I reflected on how silly white people looked when they danced. Just as Stoney and his aides took the stage, the singing escalated to a roar. Two hefty young men took up positions on either side of an enormous piece of blue bunting that dominated the wall behind the podium. Grasping ropes, they tugged on the curtain and it fel[1]

the floor, revealing a huge banner that read STONEY
MALONEY—THE ROCK OF CAROLINA. A roar went up
from the crowd and I almost dropped my drink. For a
moment I thought it said THE ROCKMAN OF CAROLINA.
The idea opened up endless possibilities. Why, he could
go from door to door seeking out female constituents
and . . .

My dirty thoughts were interrupted when the ambitious
young organizer of the fundraiser began to introduce Stoney.
The crowd grew even wilder, hooting and thrusting fists in
the air as the kid made one bad joke after another. Of
course, this group was so well-lubricated they'd have sent up
a cheer if the guy simply stood there and wet his pants. I
wondered if the band could hear him and if they appreciated
the humor, but when I looked over they were nowhere to be
found. Probably smoking pot in a back hallway. Anyone
who still wore their hair in an Afro these days had to have
been smoking pot for a long, long time.

Stoney finally stepped up to the podium and began his
speech. I have no idea what he said as I could not hear a
word above the cheers. But the crowd loved him. They
roared whenever he looked up from his notes, waving
their plastic cups of draft beer in homage and squealing
approval through drunken lips. I kept my eyes glued on
the podium, searching for a female who did not belong.
Several were scattered among the official party but no one
looked particularly smitten by the words of the Rockman.
And, frankly speaking, none of them looked attractive
enough to be worth risking a political career over.

Stoney Maloney was nobody's fool. He kept the
speech short and ended it by exhorting them all to drink
and dance their way to victory. As he raised his hands to
a final deafening roar of approval, the band wandered
back on stage and obligingly broke into "Tighten Up" by
Archie Bell and the Drells. The crowd packed together,
dancing itself into a drunken frenzy duly sanctioned by

the ability to vote. I fought my way to one side where I
could finish my margarita in peace.

Stoney was lingering on the platform, reaching down to
shake hands in the crowd. He worked the huddled masses
expertly, smiling, joking, and ignoring the drunken
weaving of his fans. The coeds loved him and you could
practically smell the hormonal overdrive in the air. But
the Rockman kept his distance and lingered with no one
too long. He was all business, with nary a personal smile
to break the monotony of his plastic grin. And he stayed
that way all night long. For the next hour, I dogged
Stoney determinedly throughout the coliseum, surveying
his entourage, gauging his reactions, keeping my eyes
peeled for a particularly favored damsel. It got me
nowhere. I finally called it a night after some pie-eyed
pudge face stole my makeshift blue bow and ran through
the crowd with my negligee on his head. I would have to
find out the identity of Stoney's lady love some other
intrepid way. Political appearances were just too jammed.
I finagled another margarita from the bartender for the
drive back home, reminding myself that tomorrow was
another day.

I slept like a college drunk that night, dead to the world
and all its ambiguities. When I woke the next day, I
reminded myself of how good it felt to be clear-headed
instead of hung over, not to mention unencumbered by a
snoring young man who would hoover up my pantry's
contents within the hour. But I doubted this lesson in
sober self-reliance would last. I knew myself too well.

I-40 was remarkably deserted, the empty lanes stretching out invitingly in the morning breeze. I could have
driven forever, but duty called. I made it to downtown
Raleigh in under thirty minutes.

"Looking good, Casey," Bobby D. whistled through a
mouthful of the ubiquitous cheese and peanut butter

snack known in the South as "nabs." Garishly orange crumbs peppered his chin and masked the twinkling of his single gold tooth when he smiled. "You get a makeover down at Thalheimer's or something?"

"Yep," I replied. "And I'm scheduled for a personality transplant at noon." His little dig did not bother me a bit. I did look good—and for good reason. I was considering storming the gates of the Citadel that day, or at least trying to see the great white hope himself. If Stoney Maloney was in the mood. So I was dressed accordingly in white linen pants and a short matching jacket over an ivory tee shirt. I felt like a giant vanilla ice cream cone, but I looked respectable and that's what counted.

It's hard to look respectable when you're built for trouble. I am a big girl and, since I have no choice in the matter, I try to make the most of what I've got. My grandpa explained it to me when I was twelve years old and brokenhearted over my treatment at the hands of the enlightened local youth during a disastrous school dance. Now, these young men were fated to grow up and possess an average of six teeth apiece, while I was fated to grow up to be strong enough to relieve them of those teeth. But at the time, I didn't know it. I just knew that I had stood against the wall of the school gym without having a single boy speak to me for a solid three hours, except to call me Refrigerator Butt. When I got home and confessed all to my grandpa, he sat me down and set me straight.

"Casey," he said. "You're gonna be a big girl like your grandma was. No doubt about it. So you can either be one of those big girls that eats like a bird and looks like a corpse or you can work those muscles until you're strong enough to whip the tar out of anyone who takes offense to the good body that God has seen fit to give you. If you're willing to stop whining, I'm willing to show you how to get strong and stay strong. We can start tomorrow morning. Ain't nobody gonna be messing with you if you're strong."

I chose door number two and Grandpa turned out to be right. By a year later, there wasn't anyone in the entire county that dared call me or my butt a name I hadn't chosen for myself. And I grew to like the feeling of being able to take care of myself. Today, I look chubby at first glance and stocky at second. Or strong as hell to those in the know. My shoulders are wide and my rib cage is a barrel. But I don't have to take any crap from anyone but the strongest of men and I feel it's a fair trade-off over all.

I took off my jacket and hung it on the back of the door, where Bobby's greasy fingers were unlikely to wander. "Any messages?" I called out as I inspected my drawers for signs of snooping.

"Hell, yeah I got messages," Bobby bellowed back. "Whole stack of 'em."

"Why the hell didn't you tell me when I walked in the door?" I was once again struck dumb by his cheerful stupidity.

"Well, babe, I was busy complimenting your personage," he said. He sighed and leaned back, folding his hands over his big belly. That meant he had some real news for me and could afford to make me beg. I smiled at him. He smiled back.

"Give it," I demanded.

"Half the triple fee," he countered.

"Done." I was in no mood to bargain. "But it better be good."

He consulted the tattered yellow legal pad he keeps by his phone. That pad ought to be designated as an historical marker. I don't believe he's ever used a fresh one since I've known him. "First of all, the SBI has dropped any action against your client. They announced that forensic tests prove that the Mary Lee Masters vehicle was not driven in the vicinity of the murder spot." He pronounced vehicle "vee-hick-el," like it was something I could suck on.

"What a revelation," I remarked. "Damn, those guys are good."

Bobby ignored me. "Instead, they are focusing on Ramsey Lee, the eco-terrorist fellow on account of he owns the land across the river from where this guy was shot."

"Another big surprise," I said.

Bobby regarded me coolly as he took a swig of Budweiser. "He also was involved in blocking that Neuse River Park project you asked me about. But I guess since you know all this, there's no need for me to run down the list of investors in it. I apologize if I have bored you this morning."

"Give it, Bobby, or you die."

He smiled in triumph and consulted his notes. "Just who you'd expect. Mitchell was the biggest investor, which is unusual because he likes to be the general partner and avoid putting his own cash on the line. A dozen or so smaller individual investors, the usual suspects from the ranks of local real estate hustlers. No one mentioned yet in connection with the murder, but there are two companies listed as investors. I've got someone down at the secretary of state's office looking into the ownership of them now. I think we're gonna find out what we need to right there. Follow the money, I told you. Always follow the money."

"What was that about Ramsey Lee helping to block the project?"

"I know a gal works at the city council meetings," Bobby explained. "She takes down notes, helps the T.V. crews tape the meetings, kisses the mayor's ass. She's the one who placed the microphone that caught that damn fool mayor calling the rest of the council a bunch of fuckin' idiots last week. Only thing he ever said I could agree with. Anyway, she says that there's some smart group of environmentalist types who are using the threat of court action to force developers to back down on projects around these here parts. They think Ramsey's part of it and that his family money is bankrolling their efforts."

"That's not very specific," I pointed out.

He wiggled his eyebrows suggestively. "I think a dinner or two will get me the details you crave. Rome was not built in a day."

"Only because they failed to pay off the right senator," I assured him. "Anything else?"

Bobby shook his head. "Nothing important. Guy named Adam Schmaltz called. Northern fellow. Kind of pushy. Talks through his nose. Works for that candidate guy."

I stared at him incredulously. "Adam Stoltz?" I asked.

He shrugged. "Sounds right." He rummaged in his upper desk drawer and drew out another pack of nabs, snapping open the cellophane wrapping with an expert twist of his teeth.

"Bobby," I explained calmly, though my hand was itching to boink him over the head with his empty beer can. "Adam Stoltz is Stoney Maloney's media advisor. What time did he call?"

"Well, hell, baby. Wasn't that long ago. I was still on my doughnuts."

That meant Stoltz had called at least an hour ago. The doughnuts didn't last more than ten minutes after Bobby arrived. I wondered what the guy wanted. I also wondered if it was too late to weasel my way into a meeting before Stoney took off on another campaign tour.

As it turned out during the course of my brief phone call with Stoltz, I didn't have to beg for an audience. Stoney Maloney wanted to see me. As soon as possible. I told the northern fellow who talked through his nose that I'd be over there before you could skin a squirrel.

I got the feeling he had no concept of time because he hung up like I'd just belched in his ear.

SEVEN

Maloney headquarters befitted the Rock of Carolina. It was a square brick building in the middle of an asphalt parking lot about half a mile down Hillsborough Street from the capitol building. The lower floor was lined with plate glass windows plastered with MALONEY FOR SENATE signs. The joint had been a fast food franchise, one of those retro-fifties drive-in places with great milkshakes and nothing else you could stomach. It had folded about six months ago, just in time for the campaign. You could still see traces of the neon decor around the door and window frames, and the floor was a screaming yellow and blue check. I was tempted to keep my sunglasses on, but reminded myself that respectability was key. I wanted to get some answers and being a smart ass was not the best way to go about it.

The air conditioning blasted me with full force. It was like getting slapped in the face with an icy wet towel. "Can I help you?" a perky young girl in a blue mini-dress asked before the door had shut behind me. She was perched at a huge reception desk stacked with bumper-stickers and signs. A small break in the stacks accommodated her tiny frame. Her smile was stretched so wide it looked like a rubber band about to break. Maybe it was frozen in place.

"I have an appointment with Stoney Maloney and

Adam Stoltz," I told her in the undertaker tone of voice I reserve for perky people.

She regarded me coolly. It was those black roots again. I was at least two months behind her in the Clairol. "You have an appointment with *Mr.* Maloney?" she repeated with disapproval. Her face pinched in on itself like she had just taken a bite of green apple.

I checked my watch. "Yeah. And he needs to make it quick. I have to be somewhere in an hour." I fixed her in my high beam smile and she scurried into the back of the cavernous main room, her plastic grin long gone.

I never saw her again, but a lanky kid of no more than twenty-eight came hurrying out of the back rooms, his hands in his pockets as he jangled loose change nervously. He was over six feet tall and weighed just enough to keep his pants up. His skin had a perpetually flushed look, like he was having trouble making friends with the humid Carolina climate. His buzzed haircut confirmed that we were in conservative headquarters but he had been too busy for his weekly trim and a few loose curls wound hopefully toward the neon ceiling lights like he was starting to sprout. He had an angelic face, a lot prettier than my own: large brown eyes, a graceful narrow nose, and perfectly formed lips that stretched half an inch wider than normal as he tried on a professional smile and failed miserably. The grin slid off his face like melting ice cream. That was when I noticed that his suit was slightly rumpled and the collar of his white shirt was grimy.

"I'm Adam Stoltz," he said, lanky arm outstretched. His voice was startlingly deep for such a childish face. It sounded like it was coming from a speaker embedded in his chest.

I introduced myself and made a point to wring his hand dry during the handshake. I like people to know I could flip them over my back as soon as shake their hand. It helps to keep them in line.

"This way." He gestured behind a stack of cardboard boxes and led me around tables full of campaign workers manning telephones and stuffing envelopes. Everyone looked like they had just popped out of the showers at a Mormon church retreat. Lord, what a well-fed and well-scrubbed bunch they were. Young, too. I was feeling like Methuselah by the time we reached the private offices in back. Old and gray and tired.

Stoltz paused before a shut door that was marked PRIVATE. "I may as well be upfront," he whispered. "I think this is a bad idea. I don't know why Stoney wants to get involved with this mess at all. I told him to make a statement and leave it alone. But he won't listen to me. So if you can't help, say so and get out."

"Nice to have your support," I told him, pushing past to open the door myself. And there he was: the Rock of Carolina. Stoney Maloney was sitting behind an enormous oak desk. He was framed by a wall-to-wall window that was carefully shuttered against the blazing Carolina sun. His head was bent low over a stack of papers and he was murmuring to a small older woman ensconced in an armchair by his elbow. Both looked up as I entered. The woman's eyes lingered on my hair and its black roots. The candidate's lingered on my bustline.

"Ms. Jones, it's a pleasure to meet you. Call me Stoney," he said, rising to his feet with the kind of elegant grace you only find in men who really appreciate women.

His hand was firm and smooth. I decided against the death grip, but let the handshake linger. A small electrical current ran through his fingers right to the center of my heart before proceeding in a southerly direction. No wonder he was raking in the female vote. I had seen him on many occasions, but I had always been busy scanning the crowd in my role as Mary Lee's bodyguard. I hadn't had the opportunity to appreciate him up close until now. He was taller than I remem-

bered. And he was built solid, without an ounce of extra
fat. His shoulders were wide beneath his tailored white
shirt and his tie had been loosened half an inch. It hung
down slightly as if inviting me to tighten it for him. He
removed a pair of small gold-rimmed glasses and stowed
them away in a breast pocket of his shirt, giving me a
chance to check out his blue eyes. I'm usually a brown-
eyed girl, but his were enough to make me change my
mind. They were wide and clear, a deep blue, not those
pale-eyed versions that make you think of serial killers
and selfish hearts. His chin and cheekbones were slightly
wide for his long face and his nose fit the picture
perfectly. His silver hair gleamed in the sunlight filtering
through the blinds and was set off perfectly by his deeply
tanned complexion. I got a little lost examining his
candidate smile up close, but a sharp voice brought me
back to reality.

"I don't believe we have met, young lady. I am Sandra
Douglas Jackson, Stonewall's mother." A determined
hand poked me in the side.

I retrieved my professional pride and tore my eyes off
Stoney. His mother was a poor substitute. She was one
of those tiny, inescapable women who hardly eat a thing
but keep on ticking until well past midnight when the
rest of the world is exhausted and just wants to go to
sleep. Her nervous energy invaded the room, setting my
teeth on edge. She was no more than five feet tall and
wore an expensive designer pantsuit that could have fit a
munchkin. The pantsuit didn't intimidate me. Hey,
mine was Anne Klein. And I'd gotten it for twenty
bucks at the PTA thrift shop while hers had probably set
her back a grand. That made which one of us smarter?
Her white hair was cut about thirty years too young for
her age, which I put at sixty-five or so. She was a little
young to be a senator's mother, that was for sure. Must
of plopped out Stoney a long time ago, before she
soured. Her head was too big for her fashionably

emaciated body, making her look like a marionette when she moved too quickly. I guess they still haven't invented a weight machine that can reduce that pesky skull circumference.

Her delicate features clashed with her disapproving expression as she scoured my face for signs of gullibility, cowardice, or any other exploitable weakness she might find. I wouldn't have called subtlety her strong suit. She was an operator, all right, and I believed all those stories naming her as the force behind her brother's decades of success and, now, her son's.

I dredged up what I knew about her from my mental store of trivial knowledge. I didn't know much. I knew that she loved to play the southern steel magnolia in Washington, acting as hostess for her widowed brother. I knew that her own husband never seemed to be mentioned; he was either dead or long gone. I'd heard a rumor that he had died in the Korean War but, looking at her in person, I began to wonder if the battle hadn't been a little closer to home. Underneath all the expensive clothes, I suspected she was really just a tough old bird from a farm in Eastern Carolina. When I first moved here, I remember that she won the female division of the turkey shoot at the North Carolina State fair three years in a row. Which didn't intimidate me. I could shoot the eyes out of a snake at a hundred paces. And had. So I didn't mind bringing her down to size—and letting her know it.

I touched her brittle hand as quickly as I could. "You're not Mrs. Maloney then?" I said.

Her eyes narrowed. The gauntlet was thrown. "Stoney insists on using his father's name," she said a shade too politely.

"Can't blame him," I admitted. "Stonewall Jackson seems a little heavy-handed, don't you think?"

"Good point," the candidate said as he pulled a chair out and swept an arm over the back of it, indicating that I should sit if my pretty little feet were just too fatigued to continue standing. "I must think of all those northern transplant votes."

I liked his style, especially when he turned to reclaim his seat behind the desk and let his hand brush slowly all the way across my wide shoulders, as delicately as butterfly wings fluttering past.

"Can we make this quick?" a deep voice asked from the door. Adam Stoltz still stood there, determined to remind me that he was a lot more important than I was, at least in this room.

Stoney smiled an apology. "You've met Adam?" he asked. "Adam is my media advisor, a necessary evil in these technologically advanced times." He shrugged. "I know when I'm out of my element and so I frequently take his advice on how best to communicate the issues I believe in."

"Not frequently enough," Stoltz interrupted.

Stoney turned his clear blue eyes on his advisor and Stoltz backed away slightly, as if some force were driving him into submission. "Adam is rather adamant that seeing you is a bad idea," Stoney said.

"So am I," his mother snapped in her tightly wound southern drawl. "There is no need to go wading into the mud just because everyone else is."

Stoney held up both hands. His mom looked away and Stoltz slid into a chair obediently. "We've gone over this enough," Stoney warned them. "Now that Ms. Jones is here, I think we can move forward as a team." He smiled at me and it was a curious sensation: I do believe he meant it. It was as if little old me being there in front of him in his office made him happier than a herd of pigs storming an outhouse.

"Why did you call me?" I asked him, meeting his gaze. I can bat my baby greens with the best of them and my eyelashes were working overtime.

to

Stoltz grunted like it pained him to hear Stoney's reasons again while Mrs. Jackson abruptly crossed, then recrossed her legs. Jeeze, the two of them could have used a couple weeks worth of Prozac. It wasn't like I was from the campaign reform committee or something.

"I understand you are working for Mary Lee Masters in the capacity of private investigator," Stoney said. His voice was much more mellow when he wasn't giving a speech. An undertone lingered in the room when he fell silent, as if he longed to say more to me in private but that such things would just have to wait until a better time. Wee doggies, but that was an effective technique that I didn't think he had learned in Speech 101. The boy had been born with charm that the squirming old biddy beside him lacked.

"How did you find that out?" I asked.

He shrugged. "People call me and tell me what they think I need to know."

Mary Lee had been right, I decided. Someone in her camp was reporting to the Maloney campaign.

"No point in hiding it," I said. "She's asked me to look into the Thornton Mitchell murder. She's anxious to clear her name and she doesn't trust either the SBI or the locals to find the solution."

"Not trust the authorities?" Stoney asked. "Why, if we can't trust them . . ." His voice trailed off regrettably and I couldn't decide if he was kidding or not. I decided he wasn't. Especially when I noticed his mother crossing her legs again and whipping out a cigarette to calm her nerves. Yeah, someone in Mary Lee's entourage was singing all right and I suspected Momma was the choir master.

"So why did you want to see me?" I asked again, figuring he was unlikely to rip my clothes off and take me on the desk with his mother present, so I might as well get the ball rolling.

"To offer my cooperation," he said. "I am anxious to put this matter to rest so that the campaign can continue to focus on the real issues."

Stoltz groaned and I felt sorry for the guy. He was having trouble controlling his protégé.

"Is this a joke?" I asked, scanning all three of their faces. "I know. You want me to run out and let the press know that you're cooperating, is that it?"

"No, no, no," Stoney assured me, his hands lifting off the desk in emphasis. "I assure you I am not offering my services for publicity's sake. I am entirely serious. Mary Lee and I are old friends, you know, we go all the way back to our college days. I went to Duke and she went to the University of North Carolina but we often met at parties. Duke is a tradition in my family, my mother went there as well." He smiled at her and she relaxed a little. "She was homecoming queen one year, I believe."

Well, whoopee doo. That made me like her a whole hell of a lot better.

"Adam here, of course, is one of our northern brothers." Stoney smiled apologetically and, being a sucker, I felt a flash of sympathy for Stoltz. He had been a stranger in a strange land for many months now. "He graduated from Harvard, but we won't hold that against him, now will we?" Stoney smiled at his advisor. I did not join in. I had decided to hold everything against Adam Stoltz, if possible.

"How can you help me?" I asked him. "Are you aware of the nature of my investigation?" I knew damn well that he was not, since I hadn't updated anyone. I was getting the feeling that maybe that was the purpose of this visit. Did he want to pump me for information on my leads? Was there something personal in this for him?

"Am I aware of your investigation?" he repeated. "Well, in answer to your real question, I am not trying to trick you into divulging anything confidential, I assure you."

Well, ouch. The guy was so upfront it was ridiculous. What was I going to do now? "So you're just offering to answer any questions I may have for you that might possibly help in my investigation?" I said. I thought his advisor and mother would pass out when I phrased it that way.

Stoney nodded. "If they are pertinent to your investigation, yes. Like I say, I would like this to be over."

"He means he will answer any questions relating to his relationship with Thornton Mitchell," Adam Stoltz clarified. "But only on the proviso that his answers remain confidential and that they are not leaked to the press in an attempt to help the Masters campaign."

On the proviso? Geeze, is that how they talked in the North? "I am not a paid political operative," I assured him. "I've never even stayed at the Watergate."

He didn't even get the joke. Good god. How old was I anyway?

"Stonewall, this is too much," Mrs. Jackson interrupted, distress lending an owl-like screech to her voice. "We must call Uncle Boyd and ask his advice before we go any further. Can't you see this woman does not have your best interests at heart?" She pointed at me like I had just caused three young ladies to drop to the ground and writhe in agony under my spell.

"Mother," Stoney said, his composure cracking for the first time since I'd met him. "I am a big boy. I do not need to ask Uncle Boyd's advice. I did not offer him advice during his campaigns. I let him run his office in the manner he saw fit. I expect the same courtesy for myself. Give it up. I am not going to call Uncle Boyd with trivial matters. Let him die in peace."

"Don't repeat that!" Sandy Jackson cried at me. "You did not hear that!"

"Hear what?" I asked innocently. So, Senator Boyd Jackson was closer to death's doorstep than I—or anyone else—realized.

"You must *not* repeat that," Mrs. Jackson insisted again. "It invades our privacy."

"I'm not a political reporter, either," I assured her. "Calm down."

"I am perfectly calm," she snapped back, tugging her jacket down and settling back in her chair like a petulant child. Jesus, and I thought my own mother had been a drag. At least mine had been upfront about torturing me.

"I should not have said that," Stoney conceded. "And I would consider it a personal favor if you keep the true nature of my uncle's ill health confidential." I shrugged and he took it as a yes. "To get back to the matter at hand, if it helps, I can fill you in on some of the information you may need. I did not know Mr. Mitchell personally. Indeed, I have never met him that I can remember and he is a virtual stranger to my family. But he did contribute to my campaign, I will concede that. How much was it?" he asked Stoltz.

"The maximum," Stoltz grumbled. "Four grand."

"Does that include his PAC contributions?" I asked brightly, knowing that Mitchell probably single-handedly supported the mother of all political action committees in this state. PACs are a nifty way to circumvent the legal limits on individual contributions.

A long silence greeted my remark.

"His company did make additional contributions through a PAC," Stoltz admitted glumly.

"But the pertinent thing is that we did not know him," Stoney pointed out like the lawyer he was. "He has attended several fundraisers for both myself and my uncle. Most of them, in fact. But that was the extent of my family's relationship with him. I am sorry I cannot provide you with more useful information on Mr. Mitchell. Perhaps you have some questions for me? I would be glad to answer them if you do. In return for our cooperation, I hope you will let me know in advance what the outcome of your investigation is.''

That was when I finally figured out his angle.

"After checking with Ms. Masters, of course," Stoney added. "She is a gracious woman and I am sure she would want to let me know before the press gets ahold of any information you may uncover."

Lord, he would make a good senator. He had charm and nerve in spades. He wanted me to let him know in advance so he could prepare his reaction and come out looking calm, cool, and collected.

"If Mary Lee agrees, it's a deal," I said. I knew she wouldn't.

"Good. Then I'm glad we had this talk." He stood and beamed his hundred-watt smile at me. "Is there anything else I can do for you?" he asked.

"Sure," I admitted. "You can tell me where you were the night Thornton Mitchell was murdered. Since you weren't at home."

His smile switched off. His advisor groaned. His mother shifted abruptly and let one leg fall to the floor with a thump.

The candidate sat back down in his chair. "Who told you that?" he asked calmly.

"It doesn't matter," I answered. "You offered to cooperate. Now's your chance."

"I warned you!" Stoltz interrupted in his deep voice, but his control had slipped and it boomed out like a foghorn cutting through the mist. Everyone jumped and he looked embarrassed. "I warned you," he repeated in a lower voice. "Not everyone is going to act like a gentleman, Stoney. You can't follow some code of honor that no one else is following. You're trying to play some sort of honor game but you're the only one following the rules. You can't win that way."

Huh? I always get lost during macho sports metaphors. I suspect I'm supposed to.

"Mother, could you leave us alone?" Stoney asked politely. His voice was soft but the look he turned on his mother was not. She rose without a word and left the room, slamming the door behind her.

The silence that followed was broken by Stoney's polished voice. He was calm, I gave him that. Very calm. "Ms. Jones," he said evenly. "It is true that I was not at home the night of Mitchell's murder. The police are aware of this fact, as well as the circumstances of my whereabouts that night. They have confirmed my alibi, if you wish to call it that, and are satisfied. While I understand your desire to know the details, I cannot satisfy your curiosity. There are certain things a gentleman does not tell. I'm sorry."

That weird thing happened again. I believed him. I sat there staring at his determined but apologetic face and could not tear myself away from his clear gaze. He had been with someone and he wasn't going to tell because he cared about her. Lucky lady.

"I'm sorry to hear that," I admitted. "It would make my job easier."

"Sorry to inconvenience you," he apologized again.

A knock at the door interrupted us and the receptionist in the blue minidress stuck her head into the room. "Mr. Maloney," she squeaked in excitement. "There's a man here from one of those tabloid shows. They're doing a segment on the murder and they want a statement."

Stoney exchanged a glance with his advisor and I knew at once that they had discussed this eventuality days ago. He was prepared. "I'll be right out," he told the girl.

"Okay," Stoltz commanded, my presence forgotten as he assumed an air of authority. "Let's get out there quick so this looks off-the-cuff. But remember, stick to the statement you gave earlier. You're above it all. You can make it casual, if you want. This is television and any stiffness will work against you. In fact, let's do it in short sleeves." He actually scurried over and unbuttoned Stoney's shirt sleeves, pushing them up his arms so the cloth bunched around his elbows like he'd been toiling over hot legislation for days. "Repeat at least twice that you and Mary Lee are on good terms and you're sure she's not involved. The middle-of-the-road vote is important and polls show we're attracting center voters that your uncle would never have reached. And don't laugh, whatever you do, a man has been killed after all. Be courteous, but remember that the whole experience is just a little too sleazy for you."

"The whole experience *is* just a little too sleazy for me," Stoney replied, heading for the door. Stoltz scurried after.

That left me as part of the furniture. I contemplated putting on my sunglasses and furtively slipping behind Stoney, pinching his ass on camera as I breezed past to leave all of America wondering who the bleached blonde with black roots could possibly be. But more practical matters beckoned. Instead I searched Stoney's desk drawers for evidence of a romantic liaison. If he didn't want to give the woman's name, chances were good she was married. That meant hotel or motel time, someplace where no one would be watching. And that meant credit card slips. But the drawers yielded nothing more exciting than a three-pack of red, white, and blue American flag condoms. The box was unopened so it was possible it was a gag gift and not a megalomaniacal fetish on his part. The pockets of his suit jacket were equally barren, though I did find three notes with girl's names scrawled on them, along with their phone numbers. All three were written in different handwritings. I guess women threw these scraps at him all day. They were slightly less obvious than tossing brassieres. I considered tucking my card in with the stack, but refrained. I never did like being part of a crowd.

I had just finished replacing his jacket on the back of the chair when I heard noises in the corridor. I dashed back to my chair and was innocently smoothing the legs of my pantsuit by the time Stoney and a small crowd of minions returned.

"Perfect," Stoltz was saying in satisfaction. "Your mother is a good touch. Having her in the background answering phones makes it clear you're independent, but her recognizability factor is so high they can't ignore her and have to ask how she is. So we get the family vote. Perfect."

Stoney didn't look as if it had been perfect. He looked like he was getting an ulcer. His shoulders slumped as if he were weary of the entire game and wouldn't mind warming the bench for awhile. "Leave me alone with Ms. Jones for a moment," he commanded. Stoltz and the three volunteers behind him hesitated halfway out the door. "Just a few minutes, Adam. Then we'll leave for Asheville." The advisor and his lackeys took their leave reluctantly.

"I hate that stuff," Stoney confessed when we were alone. He did not return to his seat behind the desk but instead pulled up an armchair until it was only a foot or so from mine. He plopped down in it wearily and ran his fingers through his hair. It was thick and springy, like teddy bear hair. I wouldn't have minded running my fingers through it myself. And maybe patting him on the back and rubbing the kinks out of his shoulders while I was at it. The Rockman looked exhausted.

He sighed and exhaled a good five seconds of air. "Listen, this really does suck," he said. "Mary Lee doesn't deserve this kind of crap hanging over her head and all anyone is asking me about is the murder. I'm tired of it. I was running a good campaign, a clean campaign, until this. I want it cleared up and cleared up fast."

"But not enough to tell me where you were on Wednesday night?"

"Look, Casey," he confided, leaning toward me until I could smell his aftershave. Yum. "I had to tell the police, I know that. And I had to use some family pull to get them to keep it quiet. I didn't like that, but it had to be done. But I won't tell you and I won't tell anyone else. The woman in question is married and any disclosure would cause her and her family a great deal of pain. I can't do that to her."

"Does your mother know?" I asked, partly out of curiosity and partly because I was pissed that he wouldn't tell me.

He flinched. "No. She knows something is going on. She doesn't know with whom. That's a battle I'll have to fight on my own."

"How long do you expect it to go on?" I asked. "Are you planning to sneak her into your D.C. pad or what?"

He sighed. "Look, I don't expect it to last. There are too many problems. But I'm not giving her up until I have to."

"I'm sorry," I said. The words surprised both of us. "Really, I am. You haven't got a private life and I know it's difficult. I can tell just by looking at your mother."

He nodded. "The trouble with my mother is that she's usually right. She knows North Carolina politics better than anyone in the state. But I could not walk away from this . . . woman. And I won't until I have to. I hope you understand."

"I hope you get to keep your secret," I said.

He smiled thinly. "Want to have a drink with me when this is all over?"

"What?" I almost dropped my drawers.

He looked up at me, his face a little sad. "No, I mean it. I like you. You're smart and you don't hide it. You're strong and you let people know it. I know who you are. How many people can you really say that about?" His blue eyes bore into mine like he really expected an answer. He didn't get one.

"Well, maybe I'll ask you again sometime," he finally said.

"You do that," I answered, standing to go.

The corridor was crowded with volunteers and paid workers, including Stoltz and Stoney's mother. They watched silently as I walked down the long hallway, my thoughts filled with more questions than I'd had when I arrived.

I couldn't figure Stoney Maloney out. He was not what I had expected at all. He seemed genuine about wanting to help. Yet it was a dangerous offer for him to make. He had nothing to gain except a little advance notice of anything I unexpectedly uncovered. And he had a lot to lose if my path led to him or his campaign. I struggled to separate the real man from his image. I was starting to believe that he was the rarest of people, someone whose heart led the way. Yet I felt downright naked without my cynicism.

EIGHT

Let me explain what happened next. I appreciate a man with principles (when I can find one) but that doesn't mean I go so far as to trust a guy just because he makes my cooter twitch. After leaving Maloney headquarters, I circled back to Hillsborough Street and parked behind the dumpster of the nightclub across the street. I had my eye on a little red Mazda Miata waiting near the back door of campaign headquarters. I knew it was Stoney's and I knew I was going to search it. Then I would trust him. Maybe.

Half an hour and two lukewarm Diet Pepsis later, a black stretch limo pulled into the parking lot of Maloney headquarters and slid to a halt near the rear entrance. The building door opened and an entourage emerged, blinking into the sun. Adam Stoltz looked around nervously as if he knew I were watching, but Stoney was too busy consoling his mother to be suspicious. He had his arm draped over her shoulders and was bent low, talking intently as she scowled. Several volunteers brought up the rear, their arms piled high with promotional giveaways. The driver of the limo hopped out of the front seat and went around to the trunk to help the campaign workers dump their loads of buttons and bumperstickers inside. Stoney wasn't big on ceremony. He opened the limo door himself and climbed inside, leaving Mom on the outside looking in. Adam Stoltz and the volunteers joined Stoney and the car pulled away in a cloud of exhaust. Sandra Douglas Jackson stared after the tail lights. She watched the car for as long as she could, then marched back inside Maloney headquarters as if she were in need of a few good people to kick around.

Leaving my Valiant nosed in between two dumpsters, I dashed across Hillsborough Street and slipped behind a large hedge that sheltered Maloney headquarters from the dental offices next door. I emerged from the boxwoods ready for action, my trusty Slim Jim in hand. It's a nifty curved piece of metal that can jimmy the lock on just about any car door, especially Mazda's—which are as easy to open as a can of tuna. The back door of Maloney headquarters was firmly closed and the only noise was the steady hum of the air conditioner. I slipped the Slim Jim down between the inner and outer hulls of the driver seat door, sliding and pulling it until I hooked the right assembly and the lock indicator popped up. I was in the front seat within seconds, sprawled across the soft leather so that I was invisible to anyone walking by. At least I hoped I was. Chances were good my refrigerator butt was poking up a few inches. But I'd just have to risk it.

Stoney was something of a pig when it came to his car and I felt a certain kinship between us. The floor was covered with political pamphlets, fast food wrappers, one black sock, and two empty Mountain Dew cans. I decided not to hold his beverage of choice against him. There were no empty beer cans, open liquor bottles, or patriotic condoms to be found. The console between the two front seats held a supply of quarters and I wondered why. There were no toll roads near Raleigh. Phone calls perhaps? To his secret love bunny? I saved the glove compartment for last, preferring to draw out the suspense. Hey, I take my kicks where I can get them. When I finally opened it, a Niagara Falls of registration and insurance papers, crumpled napkins, aspirin bottles, sunglasses, plastic fast food sauce packets, and badly refolded road-maps tumbled to the floor. It was awkward lying sideways across the seat with oozing ketchup packs plastered to my forehead, but fortunately I'm used to suffering.

I heard a door slam and froze, contracting my muscles in a attempt to shrink to a size I could never hope to attain. Voices approached, two women arguing about some man named Artie and whether it was okay to have an affair with a married man if his wife knew and didn't care. The one who was all for hopping in the sack and damn the torpedoes was on the verge of convincing the other of her viewpoint when they passed by, high heels clicking on the asphalt just inches from my twitching ear. A cramp shot up my right calf and I winced, shifting slightly to ease the pain. The gear shift poked into my bladder and I felt an intense urge to take a pee. It's easy when you're a guy and can whip it out and whizz into a can. Us females on stakeout have it harder. I silently willed the two intruders to get the hell on with their lives. Obligingly, their voices faded and I began scrambling through the pile of documents before the rest of the world passed by.

Among the fascinating facts I discovered about Stoney Maloney was a propensity to speed, a disregard for local parking laws and a habit of failing to have his car inspected on time. I wondered if he bothered to pay for all the tickets or if they just sort of disappeared into that never-never land of good old boy favors.

I found the motel receipts stashed inside a AAA towing assistance wallet, gummed together with bits of ketchup from another burst packet. The imprint was blurred on most, the carbon bleeding from exposure to the ravages of vinegar and tomato paste. He wasn't using his real name, or rather, he was using a variation on it. It looked like his alter ego was S. Pickett Jackson Maloney. I examined the

crumpled slip marked for the Wednesday night Mitchell
died and realized I was holding Pickett's charge in my
hand. Talk about brushing up against history. What in the
hell had possessed his mother to name him Stonewall
Pickett Jackson Maloney? Did she think he never intended to travel above the Mason Dixon line? But worst of
all, the name of the hotel was about as legible as grammar
school graffiti. I turned each slip sideways, upside down
and even held it up to the light above me but about all I
could decipher was the word "Inn." The jerk at the front
desk had been sloppy with his charge slips; every one of
them was imprinted way to the left so that the name of the
establishment trailed off one side. I'd lodge a formal
complaint with the management to fire his ass on the
spot. But first I had to find the spot.

I rammed the mess back into the glove compartment,
arranging the layers as best I could to replicate his unique
storage system, grabbed a couple of campaign flyers for
their pictures of Stoney, and got the hell out of there. I'd
barely dashed to safety behind the hedge when Stoney's
mother stomped out the back door of the building with
several volunteers following. They climbed into a cream-
colored Lincoln Continental and pulled away, Sandy
Jackson sitting in the front passenger seat with some poor
browbeaten-looking fellow at the wheel. The driver cow-
ered nervously as he passed by my hiding spot, then
proceeded to jerk and sputter his way down the avenue.
Talk about stop and start driving. They'd have whiplash
by the time they reached McDowell Street.

It took me five phone booths to find an intact phone
book but at least the directory was only a year out of date.
I found six motels with the word "Inn" in their name,
ripped the pertinent pages from the book—hey, none of
us is perfect—and spent the rest of the afternoon checking out the decor and friendliness of smooching spots
across town.

I was on my third motel when I spotted the tail. I would have noticed it sooner, but I wasn't expecting one. I thought Bill Butler and the Raleigh Police Department had blown me off as a crackpot. I had just pulled out of the circular driveway of the Plantation Inn north of Raleigh when I spotted a blue sedan lurking behind the dumpster of the convenience store next door. Now, come on, people—I had just gotten through lurking behind a dumpster myself. The driver could have been a little more original.

Pulling out into traffic behind me, he stayed about five cars back. He was relatively subtle, which was why I had missed him until now. Plus the little bugger was persistent. I couldn't see his face because he was wearing these discreet black sunglasses that wrapped around his temples and were about as subtle as a sign on his ass saying "I'm a cop." But I could see enough to know he'd barely met the minimum height requirements of the force and that he wouldn't need to worry about RPD haircut guidelines for much longer if his balding forehead was any indication. I tried shaking him at a couple of stoplights, but there was a pair of retirees in the car in front of me who were managing to piss me off every three feet with some new boneheaded driving maneuver. They were an insurance company's nightmare the way they wandered back and forth across the lanes and stopped at every yellow light. God, when I grow old I'm going to move up North and spend my days driving really slowly up and down their superhighways.

I finally said the hell with it, let him follow me, and headed toward the airport to try the Courtyard Inn. There, the lovely girl at the counter refused to answer any questions, but she didn't have to. There was a pile of charge slips next to her elbow that matched the ones in Stoney's car. Plus, she would never make it on Broadway. Her painted eyebrows almost kissed her bangs when I showed her Stoney's pamphlet and asked if she recognized him. I returned to my car in triumph, though I did admit I didn't know all that much. I knew where Stoney took her and that Stoney took her, but I didn't know who "her" was. I had five days until next Wednesday night and, if he chose to chance their regular spot, I could spend the evening in the parking lot and catch them that way. What it would accomplish, I wasn't sure. But at least I had confirmed that his liaison was no figment of his imagination. The Rockman lived.

I wasn't through with my tail. I'd done my job and now it was time to play. I visited six more motels at random. It was easy since the airport area offered plenty. I popped into each lobby, used the restroom, or had a Diet Pepsi in the air conditioning, and once stopped for a vodka gimlet straight up because the bartender was cute and I was getting tired. I stretched my game out for a good two hours, determined to make the guy tailing me earn his overtime. On a whim, I led him out to Garner, a small country town next door to Raleigh, and pulled into the gravel parking lot of the Babydoll Lounge, a joint I recognized from Bobby D.'s topless bar wanderings. I parked my butt at the end of the bar, ignoring the horny construction workers and tired old geezers who were trying to decide whether I was more likely to put out than the professionals grinding away on the pathetic stage behind the bar.

When I saw my tail walk in and take a booth near the front door, I struck up a conversation with the dusty redneck next to me. He had three teeth total, all on the right side of his mouth, but I needed him for distraction purposes, not for marriage. I bought him a beer and told him the sad, sad tale of my ex-husband, a former cop turned bad, who couldn't seem to let me go. After years of beating me, I confided, I'd finally broken away but he just couldn't stand to let me live my own life. The guy's biceps bulged further with each new atrocity I invented and his eyes gleamed more dangerously with each beer we shared. I finally left him, saying I'd be right back, I just had to shake the dew off my lily. I stayed in the ladies room long enough to make my tail nervous and, sure enough, when the cop left his front booth and followed me into the back of the lounge, my barside companion followed him. I could hear them arguing on the other side of the bathroom door.

"Hey man, it's history between the two of you," my toothless paramour was sputtering. "Give it a rest, man. She's a lady."

"Who the fuck are you?" I heard my tail answer.

I didn't wait for the rest. I hopped up on the toilet and opened the single window in the bathroom, shimmying out onto the gravel parking lot. It cost me a few snags on my now grimy Anne Klein pantsuit, but it couldn't be helped. I was gone in sixty seconds flat. I was sure the guys would work it all out. Testosterone and alcohol is such an interesting combination.

"What the hell happened to you?" Bobby D. demanded. "You look like shit." It was nearly nine o'clock and he was still hard at work, munching on a pizza.

"Wild goose chase," I explained. "I was the goose."

He grunted but didn't ask any questions. When he's eating, Bobby likes to concentrate.

"I'll take one of those," I said, grabbing the largest slice I could find.

"Hey!" he barked. "Go easy. I need to keep my blood sugar up."

I almost choked on my pizza I was laughing so hard, but Bobby D. managed to stop me in mid-guffaw.

"There's a guy waiting for you in your office," he mumbled through a mouthful of pepperoni and cheese.

"What?"

"There's a guy wants to talk to you. He's waiting in your office."

"Why the hell did you put him in there?" I whispered.

"He didn't want to stay out here and I thought it might be important."

I knew why the guy didn't want to stick around and watch Bobby eat. I didn't know why Bobby thought it might be important.

"Bobby, that's my goddamn office," I hissed. "I have confidential information in there."

"Like what? Box of Playtex Supers in the bottom drawer?"

"How about an Astra Constable in the top right-hand drawer?"

"You keep that one locked," he retorted. "It's a pussy gun anyway."

"How about I go unlock it and let you get a real close look?" I said. "We'll see how pussy you think a .380 semiautomatic pistol looks up close."

"Take it easy," he said, swallowing a wad of mozzarella. "I recognized the guy. He ain't going to hurt you."

"Who is it?" I demanded.

"I can't remember his name. I've seen him on television."

Oh great. Probably on "America's Most Wanted." I left Bobby to his gluttony and carefully inched down the hall. I wasn't in the mood for surprises. I got one anyway. My visitor was sprawled backwards in my plastic client chair, his long legs stretched out in front of him as he snored. I decided against waking him until I could figure out who the hell he was. I tiptoed up and scrutinized his face. He was thin and his brown hair was even thinner. He had a sad-looking face, like a disappointed hound, and a pair of wire rim glasses that were slipping off his nose. His eyebrows were bushy and pulled into each other, like two caterpillars crawling toward true love. His eyelids twitched as he dreamed and one leg kicked out; he was in the middle of some heavy-duty rem sleep. He did look familiar, but I couldn't think of the name. He was a television reporter, I thought, for a local station.

"Hey!" I kicked the bottom of one of his shoes and he jumped like he'd just been bitten by a copperhead.

"What?!" he cried and it was my turn to jump. He had one of those baritone media voices and it filled the room. Then he began to wheeze violently.

"Take it easy," I said, afraid he'd choke to death in front of my eyes. "You came to see me. Remember?"

He looked completely baffled. "Who are you?" he demanded as his wheezing subsided to a strangled whistle.

"Who am I?" I snapped my fingers in front of his face. "Wake up, buddy, you're the one who came to me."

He stared at me for a moment then swiped a weary hand through what was left of his hair. His eyes cleared and he focused on the office around him. His breath returned to normal. "Oh, yeah," he mumbled. "Sorry. It's been a hell of a week."

"I guess so." The guy looked pretty harmless. Confused but harmless. I pulled out my chair and sat in it gratefully, parking my feet on the desk. I don't wear high heels, I'm not that dumb, but you do need a little height to pull off Anne Klein and my doggies were barking from a hot day pounding the pavement in two-inch dress shoes.

The guy was gulping in air and slowly waking, going through all the little motions people invent to reclaim their dignity. He straightened his tie, evened out the cuffs of his pants, ruffled his thinning hair back in place and rebalanced his glasses on his nose. "Listen, you don't know me but I know you," he said when he had pulled himself together.

"Yeah?" I asked helpfully.

"Well, you helped a friend of mine get out of a lousy marriage without losing his shirt. And I've seen you a lot during the campaign. Working for Masters."

"I don't remember seeing you," I said, not caring who his friend was. I knew I'd never remember the name—*all* my clients want to get out of lousy marriages.

"I'm usually off to the side filming my commentary. Don't you ever watch the public television station?"

"I don't watch television at all," I told him.

He looked at me like I was downright un-American. "Not watch television?" he repeated.

"Why don't you just tell me who you are and why you're here?" I suggested. "You do look familiar," I added, hoping to loosen him up.

"My name's Frank Waters," he said. "I do statewide political commentary for WUNC. Didn't you see my series on environmental law last month?"

"No," I confessed.

"Oh." He recovered quickly from this blow to his ego. "Let me just cut to the chase."

"Please do."

"I was in the middle of preparing an exposé on Thornton Mitchell when he was killed."

Now he had my attention.

"He's been popping up around the edges of a lot of local stories for a couple of years now," Waters explained. "But he was really smart about it. Forget about all the young girls and the public image. He acted stupid about some things but, take it from me, he was sharp when it came to business."

"What do you want from me?" I interrupted. "In exchange for this information?" I like to know what I'm going to owe before I buy.

His breath started coming faster, like another asthma attack was on the way. "I need your help. I thought you knew that."

"Help in what?"

"There are some missing pieces in his story and I can't get anywhere without them. I'm convinced it crosses over into your investigation. I need your help filling in the holes. I think we can help each other."

"Maybe," I said doubtfully.

"Not maybe. Definitely. Just hear me out before you decide. If you don't feel you can help, fine."

A television reporter giving away information for nothing? Something wasn't right. "What's going on?" I persisted. "Tell me the truth."

He hesitated. "I am telling you the truth, but there is something else bothering me. Maybe you can help me with it." He took a deep breath and his Adam's apple bobbed in his scrawny neck. His breath grew more rapid until he sounded like a little locomotive chugging away. His hands shook as he spoke and I couldn't decide if he was the nervous type or had the DT's. "I think maybe I'm in danger here. Someone might be watching or following me. I was getting these phone calls right before Mitchell died. Someone was calling me and hanging up. It's happened before when I was working on a story, but no one ever got murdered in the middle of an assignment. What if I've uncovered something I shouldn't have?" His face grew even paler and I was afraid he might pass out right at my feet.

"Take a deep breath," I told him. "And hold your head between your knees." I helped him assume the position and waited patiently. Why me, Lord? Why me?

After a moment of deep breathing, he continued. "Every time I think about Thornton Mitchell with a big shotgun blast in the middle of his chest, I wonder if I'm next. I need help finding out what's going on. The cops aren't an option. We're on different sides. You already know Mitchell's story, maybe even more that I do. You've got to help me. I'm after the truth but I don't want to be killed for it. I'm so nervous already that I've started having panic attacks. That hasn't happened since I was a kid. They could wreck my career. I can't go on the air with asthma. And I'm not sure this story is worth my life."

"Someone might think so," I pointed out.

He gulped again. "I know. That's why I need you."

"Okay." I nodded. "I'm listening. Relax and tell me what you know."

"I've been following state politics for over ten years," he explained. "It's my beat and I'm good at it. I know everyone involved, including the guys you never hear about who operate behind the scenes. I spend most of my time watching the legislature work. I'm there physically and I see who's waiting out in the halls, who hides behind closed doors and who picks up the check for dinner. I grew up around here. I know how to blend in. No one ever notices me. It's amazing the things I see."

Looking at him, I could believe it. He was that putty color you see on office desks and computers. The guy was so bland he would blend in with the hallway paint.

"There's been a lot of controversy about development in the Triangle over the past few years," he continued, referring to the area of North Carolina formed by the three cities of Raleigh, Durham, and Chapel Hill. "Ever since that stupid magazine article came out naming this area as the number-one place to live in America, we've been invaded."

"I know," I agreed. "Time marches on. What can you do?"

"Well, some of us do different things," he explained. "And some of us forget about anything but making as much money as fast as we can off the situation."

"I thought reporters were neutral," I said.

"Our coverage is supposed to be. Our souls don't have to be. I've been following environmental issues in particular, especially the relationship between overdevelopment and local legislation. All this, of course, has a lot to do with my political beat. It doesn't take a genius to figure out that one side favors real estate development over the other. And that the men who are making money off the development are funneling a big chunk of it back to the politicians making it possible."

"That's the way it's been done for two hundred years," I said.

He nodded. "Yeah, but the stakes are getting higher every day. There's more competition for the development, the opportunities are shrinking as people decide they've had enough but because of demand the potential to make big, big money is getting bigger. You see the paradox?"

I nodded. I know big words. I wondered what he was getting at.

"I began to follow the links between real estate development in this area with contributions to local political campaigns," he explained. "In the past, people weren't too sophisticated about it. It was a pretty straight path from your local construction company owner to the mayor's campaign or whatever. But the more you move up the political ladder now, the less straightforward the path becomes. In part, because state and federal laws kick in, limiting the amount you can give. I started looking into state legislature and gubernatorial campaigns, tracking down the contributor and PAC lists, charting instances where the money came back to real estate developers or companies with business before the state."

"And Thornton Mitchell's name started popping up?" I guessed.

He nodded. "He was quiet about it. He hardly ever gave money directly and sometimes I had to go back two or three holding companies to finally put my finger on him. He was making a whole hell of a lot of money, especially in Eastern North Carolina. He made a fortune off vacation home communities along the Carolina coast a few years ago."

"So he's the one who ruined the Outer Banks?" I said.

Waters nodded. "Him and his cronies."

"His cronies being?" I asked.

"That's what I can't figure out." His voice dropped to

a whisper. "I couldn't see a pattern when it came to Mitchell. His representatives would go up against this zoning committee or that state commission and just when you thought he was going to be refused, he'd propose some sort of minimal compromise that allowed him to squeak through. He seemed to have a friend in every pocket of the state. I couldn't pinpoint anyone specific."

"The whole state?" I asked. "How hard is that to figure out?"

Waters nodded. "I know. It had to be someone big. And the biggest guy is Senator Boyd Jackson."

"Stoney Maloney told me that no one in his family knew Thornton Mitchell personally," I said. "And I got the distinct impression he meant his uncle as well."

"It could be true," Waters admitted. "I can't find a single photograph or mention of Thornton Mitchell meeting with Boyd Jackson or Maloney. But that alone makes me suspicious. I think they've been hiding the relationship for years—and there has to be a reason why. I know there's a connection between them."

"Because of the special treatment Mitchell received?" I asked.

"Because over the past twelve months, Mitchell started getting turned down for the first time. He'd submit proposals and get nowhere with them. He lost his magic touch. His rezoning requests started getting denied. Investors started losing money as soon as his cash flow took a big dive. He always funded cash distributions for past projects by dipping into seed money for new ones. It was a legal pyramid scheme. But the house of cards started collapsing as soon as his new projects started stalling. And I started thinking about the timing . . ." His voice trailed off.

"That was when you realized that Thornton Mitchell's fall from grace coincided with Boyd Jackson's dying from stomach cancer?" I asked.

Waters nodded. "The family's been trying to keep it

quiet, but everyone in government knows that Jackson is going down fast. He's been missing tons of committee meetings in Washington, pops up for votes but skips all the debates, and has all but disappeared after hours. His aides keep up the press releases and public appearances, but if you look closely you'll see how gaunt he is when he does appear in public. They save his strength for the most visible occasions and I think he's probably bedridden in between."

I could have told him more, but the semi-promise to Stoney weighed on what little shred of conscience I had. I kept it quiet for now. "The family's been waiting it out until after the election," I said.

Waters nodded again. "If Jackson had pulled out a year ago when he was diagnosed, the governor would have been able to appoint his replacement. And the governor is not aligned with Jackson at all. In fact, they hate each other. Stoney Maloney would not have been the appointee."

"Meaning someone else would have inherited an incumbent spot and been sitting pretty for this election?"

"I think so," Waters agreed. "Anyway, the point is that I think there's an arrangement between Thornton Mitchell and Boyd Jackson, whether Stoney Maloney knows it or not. First, Boyd Jackson goes down for the count, then Thornton Mitchell follows. That's not a coincidence. But I think the connection has to go way, way back because I've looked into forty years of Mitchell's dealings and forty years of North Carolina politics and I can't find where their paths cross yet."

"So go back even further," I suggested.

"Look," he said and I noticed a fine sheen of sweat on his brow. "I won't kid you or pretend to be brave. I'm scared shitless. This is getting pretty hot for me. Like I say, I've been getting these phone calls." His voice trailed off as he regrouped his resolve and tried to regain his breath. The guy was starting to make me nervous and

I'm pretty unflappable. "I'm not running away, but I am taking a breather," he said. "I'm heading out for a week or two, some place quiet and far away."

"And you want me to do your dirty work for you while you're gone?" I suggested.

"You can look at it that way," he said. "Or you can look at it as me giving you a lead you'd never think of otherwise."

"A lead or a theory?" I countered.

"A lead," he said emphatically. "I think the whole key to this mess lies in unofficial connections, like family ties. Family is family in North Carolina. You know how it is. Those are not ties to be taken lightly. You have the resources to track them down as well as me. Isn't it your job to find missing people and investigate birth records and stuff like that?"

"Mostly I spy on unhappy marriage partners," I pointed out.

"Perfect," he said.

"And you want me to give you the information for your story when you come back?"

He shrugged. "Maybe. But I don't even know about that. Mitchell is dead. And I'm not sure I'm comfortable being the one who picks at his corpse. But there is a story in this and it's whoever killed Mitchell. Someone murdered him and even if I didn't agree with his politics, that's crossing the line. I think they ought to be caught. And that could be a bigger story than the one I was working on."

He had a point that had gotten lost over the last few days. Maybe there weren't a whole hell of a lot of people mourning Mitchell's death, but someone had crossed the line big time. And that line protects us all. Whatever he'd done, Mitchell deserved justice as much as the rest of us. Whoever had appointed themselves his judge and jury ought to be brought down. Before they did it again.

"Okay," I agreed. "Thanks for the tip. I'll start looking into family ties tomorrow."

His smile transformed his face from mournful to boyishly handsome. The intellectual look wasn't so bad after all, I decided.

"That's great," Waters said, leaping to his feet and pumping my arm like he was trying to bring up water. "I'll call you in a couple of days to see if I can help with whatever you find."

"I could call you," I offered hopefully, tricky as ever.

He shook his head. "No thanks. I don't want anyone knowing where I am. No offense."

He was out the door before I could argue. I watched him hurry nervously down the deserted sidewalk, looking over his shoulders as he dashed past the forlorn concrete buildings of downtown Raleigh at night. I wondered just how much real danger he was facing. The guy wasn't a goof. He might have a point. That meant I could be in real danger, too.

I unlocked my top drawer and took out my .380. It had been awhile since I had even held it and it lay heavy in my hand.

I don't like guns. Too many morons wave them around. Especially since the wise leaders of North Carolina voted to let any yahoo with a permit carry one concealed on their person (not on state property, of course, the legislators aren't stupid enough to allow guns near their place of work). But I don't like walking into trouble unarmed, either. I slid the clip from the grip and removed the first bullet, just to be safe. Then I reloaded and dropped the gun into my pocket for the trip home. It almost tore the thin knit cloth. It didn't matter. The pantsuit was history. I could burn it while I made myself a nice tall gin and tonic. Maybe I would even wrangle another piece of pizza from Bobby on the way out. After all, now I was armed.

NINE

Bill Butler was the strong-and-not-very-silent type. The next morning, he left a message on my answering machine that would have curdled the milk in my coffee had I not been the black, no sugar type. I was smart enough not to pick up the phone.

"Damn it, Casey, that little trick of yours last night was not funny," he said. "Randy was one of my best undercovers. He damn near dislocated his shoulder. It cost me three hours sorting out what the hell happened and voiding the arrest of the poor drunken bozo who thought he was protecting your dubious honor. The guy started blubbering, for chrissakes. His mother had to come pick him up from the station. It was pathetic. I hope you're happy."

I was happy. Just the sound of Bill Butler's voice made my toes tingle. I listened to another few minutes of his lecturing while I dressed once again for maximum respectability.

Bill's harangue was followed by an equally hostile phone call from Mary Lee Masters. I decided not to pick up on that one either. "Casey? Remember me? I'm the person paying you triple your usual fee. It might be nice to hear from you once in awhile." There was an ominous silence before she continued. "These press idiots are driving me crazy and Maloney is up three points in the polls. Plus, I got another one of those obscene phone calls today. Could I have a little help here? Call me or you're dead meat.''

Maybe she had a point. She *was* paying my fee. I would fill her in on the highlights but keep some of the tidbits to myself.

"About time," she barked when I called her back. "I knew you were standing there listening. Make it quick. I have some stupid appearance at a peanut factory in thirty minutes."

"Nuts!" I said.

"Just give it."

I gave it. She didn't like it when I got to the part about investigating Thornton Mitchell's past, starting when he went to the University of North Carolina.

"What the hell good is going through old school records?" she demanded. "Half the state went to UNC. Big deal."

"True," I conceded. "You did, too, as I recall."

"What the hell is that supposed to mean?" It was a challenge and I wondered what was eating her.

"Look, Casey," she continued. "That's a complete waste of time. I don't like my money going for a wild goose chase."

And I didn't like my clients telling me what to do. What was the big deal about me spending the morning in Chapel Hill? What the hell was she trying to hide? Ooops, there goes my lack of trust again.

I changed the subject. "Bradley is in the clear. He was in the Bahamas."

"I should have known," she said bitterly. "How old was she?"

Oops. I changed the subject again. "They have a suspect in custody," I said. "His name is Ramsey Lee."

There was a short silence. "He didn't do it," she said flatly.

"I know," I agreed, silently wondering how she could be as sure as I was. Did Mary Lee know him?

"So, if he didn't do it, find out who did!" She hung up before I could ask her any questions. Talk about PMS.

There are some things you simply cannot do on a computer. I could cruise school records and hack into transcripts, but without names to search for, it would do me little good. What I needed to know would take some old-fashioned legwork and that meant paging through dusty school yearbooks. There was no way around it. Carolina here I come.

Chapel Hill used to be a quaint college town. Now it's overcrowded with rich white retirees and urban professionals who have highly inflated ideas about property values. Housing developments and shopping centers have replaced the sleepy farmlands that used to welcome you into town. My grandpa would have puked at it all.

Fortunately, the University of North Carolina had resisted the changes around it. Huge oaks and massive stone buildings surrounded grassy central lawns where hundreds of students dawdled between classes, basking in the sun and smiling at each other, free from any worry greater than their next term paper. Enjoy it, I thought as I passed a group of retro-hippies lounging on the lawn. It ain't gonna last long.

The student library was dark and cool. I was tempted to curl up in a corner and take a nap. Instead, I trundled my butt up to the third floor and pulled out several years worth of what was now called the *Yackety Yack,* the dopey annual put out each year for the graduating class. It was frightening how little life on campus had changed over the years. Or maybe I was envious. I don't think I've ever been isolated from reality in my life. I knew when Thornton Mitchell had graduated, so I started a few years earlier and worked my way up. As I suspected, he had pledged a fraternity by the end of his freshman year, was active in intramural sports and a member of various business-oriented campus clubs. I noted that even back then he had preferred to work behind the scenes: I spotted him in several photos, lurking in the background, always just a little too soft-looking, a little too overweight, but with an amiable grin on his face that never faded.

After I found Mitchell, I concentrated on identifying his old buddies. Thanks to the deeply ingrained fraternal system still thriving in the South, it wasn't hard. He had been inducted into the Order Of The Golden Fleece, ostensibly an academic organization. But a quick glance at their page in the annual told me that, even back then, parties had been their real priority. Those Golden Fleecers looked permanently disheveled, slightly shame-faced, and most definitely hungover in nearly every shot. The girls hanging onto their arms in the casual photos looked like female versions of the same: smart and spirited party girls brought in from nearby women's colleges for conversation—and cocktails—with Carolina's intellectually inebriated. The girls were all a little too plump and not quite blonde enough to have made it within a more traditional sorority system. On the other hand, they didn't look like a bunch of tight asses.

I photocopied several years worth of group shots for names of people that might have known Thornton Mitchell way back then, before he'd turned Golden Fleecing into his lifetime's work. I'd zip back to Raleigh and get on the phone, trying to track down former classmates. I knew that in the South, college was the time-honored place for sowing the seeds of your future good old boy network.

Just for the hell of it, I looked up Mary Lee Masters in her senior yearbook. I was curious as to why she had made such a stink about it and I wanted to know more about her possible connection to Ramsey Lee. I knew from the newspaper accounts of his original sabotage arrest that he had briefly attended UNC around the same time as Mary Lee.

I didn't know Mary Lee's maiden name, so I scanned

the entire graduating class of 1974. When I found her, I was in for a big surprise: Lee *was* her maiden name. All this time, I had thought she was simply afflicted with the Lee syndrome, a southern tradition that dictates the use of the name Lee after virtually any first name in the world: Ricky Lee, Bobby Lee, Jordan Lee, Linda Lee, Jerry Lee. You get the picture. But damn if Lee wasn't her last name, her full maiden name being Mary Watson Lee. I knew she was a member of the moneyed Watson clan, but I hadn't realized that Lee was an offshoot of that hallowed crew. I stared at her face carefully, looking for signs of her future in it. She was ridiculously perky-looking and her fifties housewife flip stood out as particularly dorky in a sea of 70's shag haircuts.

Then it hit me: I had been incredibly stupid. Mary Lee was related to Ramsey Lee or I'd eat my Hanes Her Way underwear. Why hadn't she told me? Half the South was named Lee, of course, but none of them had any money except for *those* Lees. Ramsey had money, plenty of it. And so did Mary Lee Masters. They had to be from the same gene pool. No wonder she'd been so sure that Ramsey hadn't been the one to set her up.

I couldn't find Ramsey Lee in the annual but I paged forward to see if Mary Lee's husband, the vapid and vain Bradley Masters, had also attended her fair alma mater. He was there, all right, looking like a cross between Dudley Do-Right and one of the Beach Boys. How could anyone have teeth like that for real? I wondered if he and Mary Lee had been engaged by their senior year. Or did people like that schedule engagement and marriage for the summer after graduation?

I considered Xeroxing their embarassing photos, perhaps for blackmail purposes, but decided I'd get started tracking down former classmates of Thornton Mitchell instead. After one more small errand, that is.

I knew Thornton Mitchell had a daughter who attended

Carolina. Maybe she would know something about her father's death or, at the very least, be able to steer me toward some of his friends. I looked up Andrea Mitchell's address in the student directory then set out for the center of campus where her dorm was located. I felt as old as the hills by the time I got there, not to mention overweight and out-of-style. Silly me, I should have worn my shredded blue jeans.

The girl who answered the door could not possibly have been Andrea: she was tall and slender with a dancer's grace. She was also the color of light brown leather and had a headful of dreadlocks bound back by strips of brightly colored cloth.

"I'm looking for Andrea Mitchell," I told her.

"Go away." The girl tried to slam the door on me but I was used to this kind of treatment. Big feet are good for something. She barely got it closed another inch.

"I'm not with the press," I explained.

"Then who are you?" the girl demanded. Geeze, UNC must have imported her from the Bronx.

"I'm a private investigator looking into her father's death," I explained. I flashed my badge but she didn't look impressed. Where was my .380 when I needed it?

"Do you want to talk to her, Andi?" the girl called back over her shoulder. Her arms were crossed resolutely, as if it would take a battering ram to get by her.

A slender blonde emerged from the back of the large sunny room, dressed in a pink terrycloth bathrobe. She was drying her hair with a towel. She paused in her scalp scrubbing to stare at me, her face an immovable mask of suspicion. "I don't believe you," she finally said.

"Look, I'm not with a newspaper. I'm not with a television station. I work for myself. I've been hired to look into your father's murder by someone who was originally suspected of it but has since been cleared. Don't you want to find out who did it?"

"The police will find out," she said calmly, rubbing the towel over the back of her head. I could smell peroxide in the air. Ah, another sister in subterfuge.

"You believe that?" I asked. "Do you really think the cops are on the right track? Have you even been reading the newspapers?"

Her gaze was defiant. "I have faith in the police. And no, I haven't had time to read the papers. I've been a little upset, know what I mean?"

"You seem real broken up," I said dryly.

"You don't know how she feels," her roommate interrupted angrily. "She's been crying herself to sleep for days. Now go away and leave us alone." She was mad, and fury lent her strength. This time she succeeded in slamming the door shut and nearly took off my big toe in the process.

"I'll just slip my card under the door," I hollered calmly through the heavy wooden panel, acutely aware that other doors were opening up and down the hall so the residents could get a better peek. Didn't anyone ever go to class around here? I slipped my card under the crack of the door and a shadow passed over the sliver of light as someone reached to pluck it from the rug.

"Can't you at least give me the names of some of his friends?" I asked her. Silence.

"Call me if you want to talk to me," I said. I was greeted with more silence and left.

Bobby was on the phone when I returned to the office and ignored me completely. Even more unusual, he was ignoring the double cheeseburger sitting on the corner of his desk. Perhaps he was on to something big. That made one of us.

I started off with a phone call to Mary Lee's secretary, demanding a call back from Her Majesty as soon as possible. We had to straighten a few matters out.

Next I booted up my customized snoop computer program and searched all the local North Carolina

telephone directories for the names of everyone who had
been in the Order Of The Golden Fleece with Thornton
Mitchell. I got three hits in the Raleigh area and ten more
statewide. Three hours later, I had spoken by telephone
with the spouses of most of the out-of-towners, contacted
several at work, been hung up on twice, and unearthed
exactly zippo that might help. I was saving the locals for
last. Of the three in the Raleigh area, one did not answer,
one claimed to be the wrong Hubert Pupkins, and the last
was a woman who answered the phone in a high,
trembling voice. I recognized the tone immediately. The
dear lady had been drinking all afternoon, probably with
no one but a faithful dog for company. All of the spouses
I had reached had sounded a little lost and a whole lot
lonely. This one sounded lonelier than most.

"Hello?" she quavered. "Mrs. Alice Hampton Mackie
speaking."

I explained who I was and why I was calling. Older
people often got nervous when they heard I was a private
dick. It makes them feel less than respectable. This one
just wanted someone to talk to.

"Oh, yes," she said in a slurred Southern drawl. "Harry
and I have been talking about poor old Thorny all week. It's
just terrible to die that way and to be stuffed in some
stranger's car. I was so depressed just thinking about it."

"Did you know Thorny in college?" I asked. Hey, I
knew him as well as anyone by now.

"Oh, yes." she said. "Quite well. He and my husband
Harry were both in the Order Of The Golden Fleece. My
daughters attended UNC as well. We don't have any sons."
She admitted this sadly, as if she had failed poor Harry in
not producing a future generation of Golden Fleecers.

"Are you busy this afternoon?" I asked. "Could I talk
to you in person, Mrs. Mackie?" My theory is that you
can't be too respectful of your elders when you are
sucking up to them for badly needed information.

"Of couse. I'm not busy at all," she said eagerly. "Do

come right over." I felt a little ashamed that she sounded instantly cheered at the prospect of company. I reminded myself that I was not exactly hustling a lonely old lady for secrets. I was just doing my job. I wrote down the directions to her house and hung up. The phone rang almost immediately and I grabbed at it, anxious to be on my way.

"Yeah?" I grumbled, hoping it wasn't Bill Butler and a new lecture.

"It's me," Mary Lee announced. "What do you want? What's so important? I suppose you spent the day prying through my life at UNC?" Her voice was strained. I guessed the campaign was not going well.

"I went there to pry into Thornton Mitchell's life, not yours," I reminded her. Had she always been this megalomaniac or was she getting worse?

"What did you find out?" she asked in a tight voice.

"I found out that Lee is your maiden name," I said. "Why didn't you tell me that in the beginning? You're related to Ramsey Lee, aren't you?"

There was a short silence. "Is that all you're calling about?" she asked and laughed. "He's my first cousin. So what? I have about five hundred first cousins. I thought you knew. Some detective you are."

I let out a deep breath. "I want to talk to him again. Set it up."

"What makes you think I can get him to agree to see you?" she asked.

"Gee," I said. "Maybe it's because you make Hitler look wishy washy."

Good god if her laugh didn't sound pleased at the comparison. "I'll see what I can do." She hung up. I couldn't wait to return the favor one day. I flew out the door, anxious to interview Mrs. Alice Hampton Mackie before she sobered up.

I needn't have rushed. Mrs. Alice Hampton Mackie would not be sobering up for some time. She sat in a white wicker armchair surrounded by framed family photographs, steadily downing a pitcher of gin and tonics while we talked. I had declined the offer of a drink. Something about her dignified tipsiness made me want to stay sober.

"Thorny was a dear boy," she said after she had warmed up by probing my family origins and quickly switching to a more tactful fifteen-minute monologue about her garden. "He was one of those boys who preferred to stay behind the scenes and let someone else take the spotlight. He knew everyone on campus who counted, though. And he always had lots and lots of money to spend. He enjoyed flashing it around, you know. It was sort of sweet. He had no idea he was being gauche."

"His family had money?" I asked.

"Oh, no. Thorny's family was as poor as church mice. He was just good at making money in different ways. I never understood any of it. I was just a silly girl back then. All I cared about was the football brunches or whether my daddy would buy me the car I wanted. That sort of thing. It was a lovely time." She sighed. "My husband Harry was so handsome back then. He still had his hair."

"How about Thorny?" I asked. "Was he a ladies man? He seems to have been rather, um, popular as he got older."

A disapproving frown crossed her face. "That was just foolishness brought on by middle-age. My own Harry went through the same thing but I told him I would stand by him and never divorce him. He grew out of it. I think maybe poor old Thorny was just making up for the past," she continued dreamily. "He was always shy with the girls back then. Tried to use his money to impress us, but he wasn't very good at it. He was never terribly good-looking and always a little overweight. Looks really count in college, you know. When Addy Poole agreed to marry him, we were all surprised. I didn't say so, naturally, but I thought Addy could have done better."

So did I. "Was Addy his girlfriend all through college?" I asked.

"Oh, no." She shook her head and the ice cubes rattled forlornly in her empty glass. "Thorny didn't start going out with Addy until his senior year."

"Did he have a girlfriend before that?"

"Not exactly," she explained carefully. "He was just crazy about Sandy Jackson, but she was from money and went to Duke and wouldn't have a thing to do with him." She paused for a moment. "At least, not after a few dates she wouldn't. But they became good friends and when that unfortunate business happened, Thorny was very helpful to her."

It was what I had been waiting for and it made the entire afternoon of wasted phone calls worth it. "Sandra Douglas Jackson?" I asked. "Senator Boyd Jackson's sister?"

The old lady nodded brightly. "Yes, that's the one. She didn't go to school with us. They wouldn't let women attend UNC until their junior year back then, you know, unless they were pharmacy students. She was a Duke girl. But they all came over to Chapel Hill looking for beaus. Those Duke boys could be so serious. They just weren't any fun. Her and her brother Boyd both went to Duke. How their daddy paid for it, I can't imagine. I believe he was a well-to-do peanut farmer, but still. Duke is so expensive."

"What was that about an unfortunate situation?" I asked her.

Mrs. Mackie's face flushed a deep pink. "Unfortunate only in the sense that Sandy didn't finish her senior year. She moved to South Carolina for awhile. Got married and didn't come back for quite some time."

If I knew my 50's euphemisms, that meant that Sandy Jackson had gotten knocked up her senior year, had a shotgun wedding, and been packed away to distant relatives until the baby was born.

"You're talking about Stoney Maloney's mother?" I confirmed. "She left school to marry Stoney's father?"

"Oh, yes," Mrs. Mackie said, nodding her head vigorously and looking with longing at the by now empty pitcher. "She was definitely married when Stoney was born. Everyone knows that. But she gave up school. That's why she pushed her brother so hard. She was a brilliant student, but left with just a year to go. She is making up for lost opportunity, you see, that's why she may seem a little bit pushy about her son's career."

"Who did she run away with?" I asked. "What was his name?"

"Why, Albert Maloney," Mrs. Mackie said. "Everyone knows that. He was someone the rest of us hardly knew. I believe he was in my zoology class, or maybe it was biology. But I can't think how Sandy even met him. We were all quite surprised when the two of them turned up missing. None of us ever saw Albert again after that since he wasn't really in our circle. And we didn't hear about Sandy again for another ten or so years, not until her brother began running for office and we all noticed that she was being quite a help to him. That didn't surprise us. She is the brains in that family."

"Is Albert Maloney still alive?" I asked. "I heard he was killed in a war or something."

"Killed in a war?" Mrs. Mackie laughed, transforming her face into one of lost beauty. "Albert would never have been in a war. He wouldn't hurt a fly. He was a quiet boy, more quiet than Thorny. No, he is still quite alive. I believe my husband Harry told me that he lives somewhere on the Outer Banks. He has a charter boat business. He's a very lonely man, Albert is. Always was.

He likes to be alone. I can't imagine why." She said it
with the conviction of someone who knows. "I don't
think he even sees his son and everyone knows he's going
to be the next senator from North Carolina."

"I don't understand how everyone could know this
family's history and me not have read a word about it in
the press," I complained.

"My dear," Mrs. Mackie said, patting my hand
soothingly. "Of course you haven't read about it. This is
not Washington, D.C., you know. We have better things
to do than point the finger at others. The Jacksons are a
fine North Carolina family and Stoney is a good boy.
None of us can afford to throw stones and none of us
wants to get started. Anyone who has ever lived in North
Carolina knows that there are things that you can discuss
in private but would never mention in public. It's just not
done."

Had I been from North Carolina originally, her voice
implied, or from a little more money, or maybe a slightly
better family, I would surely have understood. But she
didn't mean it unkindly and I didn't take it as such.
Instead, I thanked her for the information and stood up.

"Oh," she said. "You're not going to stay for dinner?
My husband Harry called and won't be able to make it.
I've made a ham and fresh biscuits. I was hoping that you
might join me."

I had plenty to do. And I could have used an evening at
the bar. But Mrs. Alice Hampton Mackie was a nice
woman and the house was so quiet you could hear the
grandfather clock tick. Besides, I've always loved fresh
baked ham. What the hell. It wouldn't kill me to stay and
eat. It was the least I could do. She had helped me. Why
not return the favor?

TEN

It rained hard that night. I know because I sat up late and watched the downpour knock the red and yellow leaves from the trees in my side yard. By morning, they would be bare and part of autumn would be gone. The thought depressed me. So did thinking about Mrs. Alice Hampton Mackie. So did everything about the case, come to think of it, not to mention the fact that I was alone and sober enough to hate it.

What was really bothering me was the fact that Stoney Maloney could very well be a big fat liar. I wanted to believe he was real. But someone, somewhere wasn't telling the truth. There was definitely a connection between Thornton Mitchell and Stoney's family— perhaps the most important link of all. Why would Thornton Mitchell and Sandy Jackson be close friends in college and then spend the rest of their lives avoiding one another? And why would Albert Maloney abandon a highly successful son to spend his days ferrying drunken fishermen around the Atlantic? The only thing I could figure out was that Albert Maloney wasn't Stoney's father at all. Which left Thornton Mitchell as the leading candidate.

This was truly a repulsive thought. Had Mitchell threatened to blackmail Stoney by revealing his status unless Stoney agreed to grant him special favors once he was in office? Would it have made any difference to the voters if they had known who Stoney's father really was? It was a possibility. Stoney's strongest support was among the moral right. They didn't like anything that smacked of someone else having had more fun than they had. But I didn't like the theory. There is such a thing as genetics, as numerous pitiful specimens of my own dying family tree could attest. If ever two people looked different, it was Stoney Maloney and Thornton Mitchell.

On the other hand, it made sense. Sandy Jackson gets pregnant. It's the fifties and she's in danger of disgrace. Mitchell won't marry her. So she finds a man who will— Albert Maloney—and they lie low for a couple of years before they part. The experience makes Sandy Jackson and Thornton Mitchell lifelong enemies, each kept from revealing the truth for their own selfish reasons. Inevitably, the reasons eventually conflict.

If Stoney knew all this, then he was the big fat liar I feared he might be. Or worse, a possible murderer of downright biblical proportions.

I wanted a drink, but knew it would only depress me more. Besides, the more it rained, the more my apartment seemed to shrink in size. There was only one way to deal with the situation. What I needed was a road trip. I'd find Albert Maloney and ask him myself. If anyone knew the truth, it would be him, but the phone wouldn't do the trick. I'd be harder to ignore if I was standing in front of him and I could also read his face if he tried to lie. I checked my watch. The Outer Banks were about four or five hours away, depending on how fast I could push my Valiant on the deserted highway. If I left immediately, I'd be there before sunrise. If Albert Maloney ran a charter fishing boat business like Alice Mackie seemed to think he did, I might be able to question him before he headed out for the day.

I was pretty sure he'd be around. October is a good

month for fishing off the Atlantic Coast. But I didn't want to waste time unless I had to. I called directory assistance in all of the towns along the Outer Banks, starting at the Virginia Border. I found him listed in Nags Head. I phoned the number and a male voice answered on the third ring.

"Hello?" the man mumbled, his voice heavy with sleep. "Who is this? What time is it?"

"Albert Maloney?" I asked.

"Yes?"

I hung up the phone and reached for my car keys.

The rain stopped just outside of Lake Gaston. I rolled down the car windows, letting the cool night air fill the car and sweep away my bad mood. The never ending strip of black highway calmed me and I began to relax. By the time the sun was inching up over the horizon, I could smell the tang of salt water in the air and my head cleared.

I stopped for coffee and hot biscuits just outside of Nags Head at an empty diner that probably thrived in the summer but was barely kept alive in off-season by the occasional truckers passing through. The woman behind the register was napping with her head down on the steel countertop when I arrived. But the coffee was strong and, better yet, she knew just where the charter boats left the docks.

I followed her instructions and arrived before the sun did, snagging a parking spot near a long row of cabin cruisers bobbing gently in the quiet waters of the bay. Most of the boats were empty but a few twinkled with lights that winked in the early dawn. Isolated crew members climbed here and there, checking hatches, coiling ropes, and preparing for the morning run. The air was cold and sharp with the smells of tar, brine, and drying fish. Overhead, gulls wheeled in the mist, their sharp cries spoiling the morning quiet like momentary quarrels.

I knew Albert Maloney the minute I saw him walking toward the dock. And I also knew that my trip had been in vain. He was a tall man, trim with huge shoulders and a shock of white hair above a handsome, weather-worn face. Stoney looked just like him. His firm jaw was locked in thought and he did not look up as he passed by me. I waited until he had boarded a large boat near the end of the row before I approached. He was already busy at work on the captain's deck, a small upper platform high above the water where he could spot schools of fish. I was halfway up the ladder before he noticed me.

"Not going out today, miss," he said, dismissing me with a disinterested glance. His voice was clogged, as if he seldom spoke. He returned to calibrating a dial that was blinking neon green numbers. "You better try one of the other fellows down the dock."

He didn't stop me when I joined him on the captain's deck. "Are you Albert Maloney?" I asked.

"Yep," he said suspiciously, unsettling me with his dispassionate gaze. He didn't care what I looked like, I realized, he just wanted to make sure he could take me if I started to cause trouble.

"I'm Casey Jones. I'm a private detective investigating the murder of Thornton Mitchell."

"I read about it. Why do you want to talk to me?" As he buried his hands in his coat pockets, I realized I was cold. The mist was clinging to the backs of my legs like a washcloth. I shivered, wishing I had worn my jeans and a heavier jacket.

"I don't know," I admitted. "I just didn't know where else to turn."

He laughed, a short barking sound that drifted over the water and alarmed a flock of sea gulls perched on a nearby pylon. "Then I guess you made your trip for nothing, because I sure don't know how I can help."

"I know your son," I told him. "He's a nice man."

He turned his face away and stared to the east, where the sun had risen only to be obscured by a heavy gray cloud that merged with the flat pewter of the ocean. "I suppose he is," was all he said.

"He is your son, isn't he?" I asked. "Stoney Maloney?"

"Who wants to know?" he replied. "What difference does it make?"

"Look," I admitted. "You don't have to talk to me and if you haven't seen your son in a while, maybe what I'm asking is painful for you to answer. But there's a man in jail right now charged with Mitchell's murder, and I don't think he did it. My client wants me to find out who did. Maybe you're part of the puzzle and don't even know it."

Albert Maloney shook his head. "Thorny never did know when to quit," he said. "I'm not surprised it came to this."

"So you knew him?" I asked.

"Sure, a long time ago." He leaned back against the outer railing, scanning the clouds for a clue to the day's weather. "I knew him back in college. He was one of those men who don't want you to see them coming. He was always trying to make a buck here or there off his friends. I didn't like him much. But I never liked anyone much, so that's not surprising."

"Did you like Sandy Jackson?" I asked.

He stared at me. "Course I liked her. I married her, didn't I?"

I was embarrassed. "I thought maybe . . . you weren't Stoney's father after all. That maybe . . ." My idea seemed ridiculous in the daylight.

His laugh cut me off abruptly. "I know what you're getting at. But you're barking up the wrong tree. Sandy would never have let Thorny get near her. She was saving herself for someone better, believe you me."

"That being you?" I asked cautiously.

He cleared his mouth and spit over the side of the boat, creating a small silver arc that glinted in a sudden ray of sunlight and disappeared. "She thought so for awhile. Guess we were both wrong."

"But how did you . . ." I stopped. "I guess it doesn't matter anyway."

"Look, miss," he said, not unkindly. "Let me put you out of your misery. Yes, Stoney Maloney is my son. And, no, his name was not my idea. And, yes, I haven't seen him in a very long time. And, no, that wasn't my idea either. I embarrass his mother. I don't fit into her image of the kind of life she wants to lead. If you knew Sandy, you'd understand. Sandy doesn't like making mistakes. She doesn't like messy situations. She likes things one way—her way. And I was her one big mistake." He spit again, as if ridding himself of the memory. "Yes sir, I am the one mistake that Sandy Jackson made in her carefully planned life. But we were young and, well, we were young. When we realized that she was going to have a baby, I did the right thing. I married her. But I moved out a month after my son was born. Because she wanted me to and because her father offered me $20,000 to leave and never come back. And you know what? I took it and I bought my first boat with that money. I guess that makes me worse than any of them. But believe you me, I earned that money. Besides, she didn't love me anyway, not after she figured out I'd never be what she wanted me to be. Thought I'd be a brilliant scientist." He shook his head. "She should have asked me first. I could have told her." He stared at a group of fishermen bumbling their way along the dock, noisy and boisterous with the anticipation of a full day ahead and the full cooler they dragged behind them. "I never did like people much, you know?"

"I know how you feel," I agreed.

He examined my face. "I believe you might. I guess you see what people can do to each other in your job."

"That I do."

"We're a mean species," he declared. "We don't deserve the earth we've been given." His hair gleamed silver in the sun that had finally ascended above the clouds and was flooding the still waters of the bay with long fingers of light. He pointed over the water. "Have you ever seen anything more beautiful than that?" he asked.

"No," I admitted. "I don't believe I have."

He ran a hand over the white stubble that peppered his chin and focused his eyes back on the horizon.

"Have you seen your son since he was born?" I asked, unwilling to go so soon after such a long drive.

"Have I seen him?" He looked at me, then away again. "I've seen him. He hasn't seen me. Folks around here don't know about him. I'm not planning to tell them."

"Don't you want to know him?" I asked. "He's your son."

"It's not as simple as that," he replied. "You don't know Sandy like I know Sandy. She'd keep me from seeing him, count on it."

"Have you seen your ex-wife since you left?" I asked.

He shook his head. "Nope. Don't plan to, either."

"What about Thornton Mitchell?"

He shook his head again. "He'd never have bothered with someone like me. What good could I ever have done that man? Him and Sandy, they were alike in that way. They only wanted to know people they could use." He smiled bitterly. "She should have lost her head with him instead of me."

"Maybe," I said, not knowing what else to say.

"Shoot." He looked overhead at the sky above him. "It all happened a long time ago. None of it can be undone. No sense poking it all up now."

"You never married again?" I persisted.

"Nope." A brief twinkle flared in his eyes. "Why, you looking?"

I had to laugh. "I'm prone to seasickness," I said.

"Then you better keep looking." His laugh was short but genuine.

"I guess I ought to be going now," I said. "Thank you for your time."

"No problem, miss." He returned to his dial and squinted at the reading, my presence already forgotten. But when I glanced back at him from the far end of the pier, I found him staring after me. Even at that distance, I could read the regret in his face.

I returned to my car, breathing in deep gulps of fresh sea air. I was no closer to finding Thornton Mitchell's killer than I had been the night before. But somehow, I felt better.

I skipped changing clothes and headed straight to Raleigh. I was back at my office by noon. "Geeze, babe," Bobby D. said when I walked in. "You look like you've been up all night."

"You should see the other guy," I said, searching through my drawers for a bottle of aspirin. I'd gone without sleep plenty of times, but seldom so sober. I felt a little lightheaded from the hours on the road. I stripped off my clothes and changed into fresh underwear. I lock it in my gun drawer to keep Bobby's paws off it. I slid into the dress I kept hanging on the back of my door for emergencies and was dismayed to find it a bit snug. I had to cut back on the biscuits. Starting tomorrow.

"I'm hungry," I yelled to Bobby when I was presentable again. "Got anything to eat?" This was like asking the pope if he went to church.

"I got me an extra ham and swiss I could spare." His mumble told me where the other one had gone.

I snagged the sandwich before he changed his mind and parked my butt on his desk where I could reach the jumbo bag of barbecue potato chips he was busy demolishing.

"Messages?" I asked through a delicious wad of meat and cheese. Bobby knew his sandwiches.

"That dame you're working for is getting on my nerves," he answered. "Called about three times this morning asking how you're doing."

"*Three* times?" I pulled his copy of the *N&O* toward me to check the political calendar. "What's the big deal all of a sudden? I don't hear from her in days and now she's all hot to find out my every move?"

Bobby reached for a beer out of the trashcan filled with ice at his feet. "Maybe she's on the rag?" he suggested.

"I find your psychological insights penetrating," I told him, but my sarcasm was wasted. All he'd heard was the word "penetrating," one of his favorites. I flipped through the newspaper, scanning each column. "Okay, listen to this. Mary Lee Masters has got three appearances scheduled for this morning alone: at a rest home, church, and Kiwanis Club, all near Charlotte. A pretty busy schedule, if you ask me. So why does she keep calling me? And why did mankind ever invent the car phone?" I checked the rest of the schedule. "Stoney's heading back from the mountains for a debate with Mary Lee tonight in Charlotte, sponsored by the League of Women Voters there. Meanwhile, Stoney's mother is busy berating the poor saps in Greensboro to vote for her beloved son. She's opening a tractor exhibit there. No mention of Bradley Masters. I guess he's scheduled to boff a couple co-eds by nightfall."

"Sounds like everyone is getting somewhere except you," Bobby said.

I stole his new beer before he wrapped his fat lips around it and glared. "Thanks for your support."

"Well, babe. Let's face it. Your working style seems to piss people off. You got a couple calls from that Butler guy today, too. Do me a favor. Keep on his good side. I don't need trouble downtown."

"I know," I said. "I'll call him back." Making

friends with Bill Butler again was for the common good. I
might need him the next case out, more personal ulterior
motives aside. Time to swallow my pride.

I figured I'd get a lackey or something, which was why
he surprised me with my mouth full of potato chips when
he answered on the first ring.

"Mmmrphf," I mumbled. "Sorry. We have a bad
connection. There's potato chips on the line."

"So, the great Miss Casey Jones surfaces and deigns to
give the authorities a call," he said.

"That's Ms. Jones to you." I couldn't help it. I rebel
in the face of authority.

He sighed. "Is it safe to assume you've been receiving
my messages?" he asked.

"Yes. I'm sorry about your man. But you should have
told me. That was a rotten thing to do, putting him on me
in the first place. I'm absolutely shocked at your lack of
trust. You don't have to put a tail on me. I haven't lied to
you. Yet." I decided that omitting details didn't quite
qualify for fabrication status. "You don't think it's
Ramsey Lee either, do you? Or you wouldn't be bothering to keep tabs on me."

He ignored me. "Find out anything that might interest
me?" he asked.

I spared him the details and went for the summary.
"No."

"Keep me posted," he asked, his voice losing its hard
edge.

"I will," I promised. "What about you? Find out
anything that might help me?"

"Bradley Masters checks out. He was in Nassau all
right. That guy's a weirdo, if you ask me. He's down
there with some coed but he spends most of his time
calling home."

"What?" I asked.

"We checked the hotel's switchboard records. He
made at least six calls home over the span of three days."

"Checking his answering machine?" I suggested.

"Maybe," Bill replied. "If so, he gets a lot of messages. Some of his calls have lasted ten minutes or more. But he sure wasn't around to kill Mitchell."

I was silent for a moment, puzzling it out. If he had been calling home, why had Mary Lee acted as if she didn't know where he was?

"Look," I finally said. "What if I told you that Bradley Masters knew where Mitchell's body had been dumped. Without anyone telling him?"

"I'd tell you that a local station here in Raleigh is the CBS affiliate in the Bahamas. The prick heard all the details on the evening news. He just wanted his wife to suffer alone."

"What else?" I asked, disappointed. "Learn anything else you can give me?"

There was a long silence.

"Come on, Bill. You can't expect me to—"

"Okay," he interrupted. "I *don't* think it's Ramsey Lee. The forensic tests aren't panning out and he's being too upfront about how much he hates the victim and is glad he's dead. I think the guy is clean. But I also think he knows something that he's not telling us."

"And the SBI?" I asked. "What do they think?"

"They're still trying to make it fit," he said. "But I smell mutiny in the ranks."

"Thanks," I said and meant it. "I owe you one."

"I know," he answered and hung up.

But he'd be the one owing me, I thought, if I saved his ass from embarrassment and handed him the answer on a silver platter. Right now, though, the chances of that were looking pretty tarnished. I told myself I just needed to meditate on the possibilities awhile but, before I knew it, I was asleep. Bobby woke me an hour later with a bellow from the other room.

"Weirdo on line two for you," he shouted. "Says you've been waiting for him to call."

That could be just about any man who'd appeared in my life so far. But I suspected it was probably Frank Waters, the terrified television reporter.

"Casey Jones," I said, stifling a yawn.

"He'll see you," a male voice whispered, as if he feared being overheard. "But it has to be this afternoon. They're moving him."

"Who is this?" I asked. "Who'll see me?"

"Ramsey Lee will see you," the voice said. "My name doesn't matter." He hung up, leaving me staring at a silent phone. Where had I heard that voice before?

And what was it about people and secrecy these days? Did everyone think they were starring in a made-for-television movie?

Bobby was busy cooing into the phone and dipping into a vat of french fries. He was the only man in Raleigh, North Carolina who could convince McDonald's to deliver.

"Where are they holding Ramsey Lee?" I interrupted.

He covered the mouthpiece and glared. "I'm trying to work here."

"I'll bet."

"He's at Central but the feds are trying to move him."

"They're succeeding," I said. "Found out about those shell companies?"

He looked affronted. "I'm working on it right now." He returned to whispering into the receiver and I steeled myself for a trip to Central Prison. I wasn't looking forward to it at all. I'd been a visitor there before and you had to check your soul at the door. No matter how much you reminded yourself that you could walk out of there at any time, no matter how much you felt the men imprisoned there deserved it, it was still a place without hope or humanity. I prayed the ordeal would be worth it.

I had some time to kill before visiting hours began so I spent it wisely: I visited the local Gap store and bought a

black cardigan. There was no way I was entering the stone
cold walls of Central Prison with my breasts showcased in
the tight orange dress I was wearing. Between the dress
and the sweater, I looked like someone about to introduce
a Halloween pageant. But it was better than imagining a
hundred guys ripping off in their cells while they thought
of me.

The man at the visitor's desk was so gray he looked
like he'd had the life boiled out of him. He was also so
distressed at my request to see Ramsey Lee that he
squeaked something about checking with his supervisor
and scurried away. The supervisor turned out to be a tall
black woman who had a drop dead gorgeous figure clad
in a well-fitted blue suit. She must have caused a riot
each time she walked through the population areas. On
the other hand, the look she gave me was enough to
freeze my kidneys and I made a fast decision not to mess
with her.

"This way, Ms. Jones," she said curtly. "You appear
on the inmate's list, which is a complete surprise to me,
so I can't deny the visit. But you will have to limit your
time to twenty minutes. He's scheduled to be interviewed
at four o'clock by the authorities."

Probably by J. Edgar himself, I figured. Hoover might
be dead, but he still had more on the ball than half the
bozos working this case.

We walked through the cold stone hallways in silence,
her frosty look communicating that I was either a
prostitute or Ramsey Lee's white trash girlfriend. Oh
well, I'd been accused of far worse. I could sense life
stirring behind walls and huddled in doorways, like rats
in the sewer who preferred the shadows. Where was a
rosary when you needed one?

"No physical contact," she warned me as we neared
one of the visiting areas, "or the visit will be termi-
nated." She led me into a well-lit room furnished with
puke-colored linoleum tiles, soft-drink machines, and

half a dozen scarred plastic tables. There were few
visitors in the middle of the week. The womenfolk were
no doubt busy slaving away at a host of underpaid
occupations, trying to make up for the wages lost when
their losers were sent away to the slammer. I sat at one
end of a bench at a middle table, as far away as possible
from an overweight blonde woman whose roots were
worse than mine. She was sobbing into a dirty handker-
chief while her loved one, a skinny man as pale as a slug's
underbelly and with about as many teeth, patted her fat
pink fingers helplessly.

Ramsey entered the room a few minutes later, his
hands and feet bound by shackles. Overkill, I thought,
since no one else in the room was attired in such a
fashion. Unless you counted the teenager in black leather
and chains who was tongue kissing her biker boyfriend at
the next table.

"Hello, Ramsey," I said quietly when he sank down
on the bench opposite the table from me. He leaned
forward so that his head nearly touched mine, anxious
that no one overhear. The guard behind the glass tore his
eyes off the smoochers to glare at us. I guess jamming
tongues down each other's throats didn't count as physical contact for some people. I doubted they'd extend the
same courtesy to Ramsey Lee.

Ramsey was so close I could feel his warm breath on
my cheek. I expected a state secret, at least, but I guess he
was just being cautious. "You're my first visitor," was all
he said.

"Really," I whispered back. "I'm surprised, what
with all those cousins of yours. How is good old Mary
Lee anyway?"

"Awwhh," he said, trying on that phony ah shucks
facial expression that country boys pull when they're
about to get the best of you. "You're just pissed I didn't
tell you we were related."

"I'm pissed *she* didn't tell me," I explained.

"You can't hardly blame her. It's bad enough it looks like she killed someone. Now her cousin gets arrested for it instead. Have you seen anything about it in the papers?"

I shook my head. "Not yet. I'm kind of surprised I haven't."

"It makes me nervous that it's being kept quiet," he confessed. "No one knows I'm here except for you and a few other people and the cops. If I vanish, it's going to be up to you to let folks know what happened to me."

I stared at him skeptically. After all, this was North Carolina, not Argentina. Still, he seemed genuinely concerned and I hastened to assure him that I'd raise bloody hell if he disappeared.

"Thanks for seeing me," I said once I had calmed him down. "What made you change your mind about talking to me?"

"Mary Lee sent me a message. If I'd known you were working for her, I would have talked right away. Why didn't you say she was your client?"

"It's hard to concentrate when someone is trying to turn you into a shish kebab," I told him.

He laughed and the guard leaned foward, pressing his face against the glass. Maybe laughing was forbidden, too. "I am a good shot, aren't I?" he asked.

"You are," I agreed. I was becoming uncomfortably aware that, up close, Ramsey Lee was a very handsome man. If you defurred him, that is, stripped away his ruddy goatee and mustache then trimmed back his hair, you'd have a man with high angular cheekbones, deep-set eyes, and a wide, thin mouth that curled up a bit at the corners, as if laughter might erupt at any moment. I realized I was wasting valuable visiting time and coughed. "Sorry," I said. "I was just admiring your beard."

He laughed even more softly and if he was laughing at

me, I didn't feel insulted. I smiled at him—then unleashed my ammo. "What aren't you telling me, Ramsey?" I asked.

"I didn't do this thing," he answered. "I only kill what I intend to eat."

"Is that why you tried to kill me?" I teased him and was rewarded with an unexpected blush. Hmm . . . perhaps the thought had crossed his mind.

"I know you didn't kill Thornton Mitchell," I assured him. "Besides, you wouldn't have botched it."

"That's true," he said, pleased at the thought. "But I don't think these SBI fellows are going to accept that defense."

Beneath his good old country boy drawl, he was a well-educated and articulate man. A dangerous combination, I thought to myself. Smart on the inside, and seemingly innocent on the outside. "How well do you know Mary Lee these days?" I asked.

"Not like I used to," he admitted. "When we were kids, we spent whole summers together, down at my parents' farm near Gastonia. But then we grew up to be real different. She's not as bad as she seems, though," he added earnestly. "Really. I know what she looks like to you, but she has a big heart beneath all those designer clothes and the makeup."

"I'll admit she has a heart," I said. "I draw the line at saying it's big."

His laugh rumbled softly against my ear. "She wasn't always like that. College changed her. That creep she married changed her, too."

"So why does she stay married to him?" I asked. "Dump the bastard."

"You know why," he said. "It'd be the end of her career."

"Why'd she marry him in the first place?" I asked.

He hesitated before he spoke. I wondered why. "Maybe there's things we don't know," he said. "Or maybe she's like most of the people in this world and got scared there was no one for her. She just married the first good-looking guy that came along.''

"You're not one of those people, are you?" I asked. "The kind who are always looking for someone?"

"Wouldn't do me any good," he admitted, his arm inching closer to mine. I could feel the hair on his forearms brushing against my hand. "I like being alone too much. No woman would put up with it."

"Maybe a woman who likes being left alone a lot?" I suggested.

His smile made it clear that he was pretty sure no such creature existed on the face of this planet. "Why are you helping Mary Lee?" he asked.

"She's paying me," I said. "Why are you? Even if she is your cousin, you aren't particularly close anymore."

Ramsey shrugged. "I think it would be good for the land if she got elected. She wouldn't sell out to the developers like that other guy. I want to see her win. You've got to clear me before all this gets out and hurts her chances even more."

Maybe the guy was even more innocent than I thought. Because I doubted Mary Lee would hold out for ten minutes in the face of big-buck contributions if she thought she could get away with it and still keep the left-wing vote. "Give me something to help clear you," I told him. "Were you along the river that night?"

He leaned even closer, so that his lips nearly brushed the edge of my right ear and his beard tickled the base of my neck. I hadn't enjoyed so much foreplay since high school. "I heard people along the riverbank that night," he whispered.

"Thornton Mitchell and his killer?"

"Someone else, too," he explained softly. "I heard voices arguing. More than two people. Maybe three or even more."

"What kind of voices?" I asked. "Male or female?"

"I don't know. I was pretty far back from the riverbank. I was up at my house, sitting on the porch, admiring the full moon. Sound carries pretty good. I know there were at least two male voices but I can't be sure of the others. It could have been a girl."

"A woman," I corrected him.

"A woman," he repeated obediently, his eyes dropping to my chest. How do you like that? The man was into more than wildlife after all.

"I remember the moon that night," I said. "It was pretty bright. Did you see anything?"

He shook his head and a lock of his hair brushed against my cheek. The guard stuck his head in the door and called across the room, "You've got five more minutes, folks," he said.

Ramsey waited until the guard was behind the glass again before he spoke. "No, not what you want anyway. I heard the shot and that was when I started out through the woods to see if maybe someone was poaching on my land. But three of my dogs were out and tried to follow me. I didn't want them getting in the way, especially if someone had a gun out there. Damn fool city men get full of liquor and decide they want to go out hunting. They'll shoot anything that moves, including my dogs. So I stopped to put them in the pen."

"How long did that take?" I asked.

"Held me up about fifteen minutes because one of the dogs kept running away from me. If he hadn't been a champion, I wouldn't have bothered. But I couldn't afford to lose Big Red. By the time I got there, the riverbank was empty. I could hear people arguing in the woods over near the road and a couple of car engines after awhile. I figured it was just someone screwing around and I went back home."

"Oh." I was disappointed. It wouldn't help me much.

"There's something else," he whispered, his warm breath seeming to snake down my ear canal and right to my heart, setting it thumping more quickly. "I saw a campfire on the bank, about a hundred yards or so downstream from where you were the other day."

"So?" I asked cautiously.

"So someone else was out there," he explained. "A fisherman, maybe. I don't bother them if they're peaceful about it. He might have seen or heard something. Maybe more than me."

"Who was the fisherman?" I asked him.

He shugged. "Hell, Casey, I don't know. You're the one who's a private detective. I'm just a country boy."

"That's the biggest crock of shit I've heard all week," I told him. "Don't try to put one over on this country girl. Speaking of which, who called me this afternoon to let me know you would see me?"

He hesitated. "One of my associates," he said.

"Well, your associates are a little paranoid, aren't they?" I asked. "He wouldn't even tell me his name. What does he think? He'll be thrown in jail for opposing real estate development?"

"Well, I'm here, aren't I?" he asked.

He had a point. "I'll get you out," I promised. "I heard the forensics tests didn't match, anyway. They can't keep you forever."

"My dogs," he said.

"What?"

"My dogs. They're still in the pen. Someone's got to check on them. I tried calling a friend but couldn't get through. They've got enough food to last a week, but I need someone to go check on their water. Sometimes the pipe to the trough clogs up."

"I can do that for you," I promised. "Don't worry about them. You'll be home soon anyway, I promise."

"Thanks. I'm sorry I didn't trust you before."

Then damn if the guy didn't kiss me. He brushed his lips right across my ear and over my cheek and planted one right on my mouth. I kissed him back, of course. And let me tell you—shooting arrows wasn't the only thing that boy was good at.

"Time's up," the guard interrupted. "Let's go."

Oops, we had violated the no touching rule. Gosh, I bet we lost a whole thirty seconds for it.

It had been well worth it.

ELEVEN

I decided to call Bobby from Sadlack's, a sandwich bar on Hillsborough Street, to see if he had tracked down the owners of the companies investing in the failed Neuse River Park project. I also silently kicked myself for failing to ask Ramsey Lee about his involvement in stopping the project. Had distracting me been his intent all along?

Sadlack's is famous for its tolerance of rabble-rousing liberals, destitute students, and scruffy losers just this side of the law who have scraped together enough bucks for a night of beer. It was the perfect place to unwind after my trip to Central Prison since an appreciation of personal freedom was the one trait that every patron there shared. The bartender had sideburns like Elvis and an attitude like Genghis Khan, but he let me use the house phone when the pay phone turned out to be broken.

"Get in here now," Bobby said the second he heard my voice.

"You've got the names?" I asked eagerly.

"Soon," he promised. "Just get your ass in here now. I can't deal with your latest visitor."

That meant it was either a child or a crying woman. Turns out it was someone in between. When I arrived at the office, I was greeted by the sight of Bobby stuffing cold pizza into his mouth while Thornton Mitchell's daughter Andrea looked on in horror. A rope of cheese trailed out of his mouth like an albino mouse tail. It dangled and twitched when he chomped, a sight so appalling that the girl had momentarily forgotten her tears. She was sitting as far away from Bobby as possible, staring at him the way you'd view a sexually aroused gorilla at the zoo.

"It's the guy's kid," Bobby mumbled, nodding toward our guest.

"I know," I said. "Thanks for your sensitivity."

"I want you to help me," Andrea pleaded, rising to her feet before collapsing in a fresh round of sobs and sinking back into her chair.

"Get her out of here, will ya?" Bobby demanded.

He was all heart. I led her into my office and shut the door, waiting patiently until her sobs turned to hiccoughs. Her eyes were red and mascara rivulets ran down cheeks now smeared unevenly with blush.

"Want some water?" I asked, when her hiccoughs continued.

"No, I'm fine," she gasped, then proceeded to hold her breath until her face turned nearly Carolina blue. After a minute of silence, she expelled a whoosh of breath, dabbed beneath her eyes, settled back and stared forlornly at me. "I remembered what you said about looking into my father's death," she whispered.

"What makes you want my help now?" I asked.

"No one else is doing anything," she said. "Now I understand what you meant about the newspapers and television. I'm the only one in the world who seems to care at all that he's dead." Her voice broke.

I offered a short and silent prayer that she not start crying again.

"Everyone made fun of Dad," she explained. "Mom made jokes about his girlfriends, my brother hated him, the papers only printed photos that make him look like some dirty old man. But he wasn't that bad, honest."

"What do you want me to do about it?" I asked.

"I want you to make people stop treating his murder like a big joke. I want you to find out who killed him and why. My Dad had changed a lot over the last year. He was becoming a better person. He should have had his chance to do that, but someone killed him first."

"How was he becoming a better person?" I asked skeptically. This was certainly a new tune she was playing.

"He said that the last year had made him realize life wasn't just about money," she said, sounding as if she agreed with the sentiment. Maybe the kid wasn't so bad after all—if you could ignore the fact that she was wearing a pink buttoned-down shirtdress in October.

"How had your father changed over the past year?" I asked.

"He was around a lot more," she answered slowly. "I'd hardly seen him for years. But he started visiting me at school after his heart attack a year ago. He was going to a clinic at Carolina for follow-up treatment. That's why he was in town so often. I didn't tell my mother, but he would pick me up and we'd go driving around and have lunch together. He felt bad that he couldn't give me more money for school, but I told him not to worry. Mom had plenty. I just wanted to spend some time with him. We never had before, he was always too busy working."

"Why was he losing so much money over the past year?" I asked. "What happened to his business?"

She shrugged. "He said that everything just seemed to go wrong at once. First his health and then his business sense. He said that his edge was gone but that if he could just hold on for a few more months, his luck would change. He had a secret weapon, he said. An ace in the hole."

"A secret weapon?" I asked. "What was it?"

"I don't know. It's just the way Dad talked."

"When did you last see him?" I asked.

"The day before he died. He picked me up from my dorm and we went out to eat at a barbecue place in Cary. He's not supposed to eat pork but he loves barbecue so much . . ." Her voice trailed off. "He used to love it," she corrected herself.

"Did he say anything to you that might help me find out who killed him?" I asked.

A few fresh tears trickled from each eye. "He only said that things were going to be different from now on. That he had learned his lesson, that family was the most important thing in the world. That he'd be able to help me out more and I shouldn't worry. He said, 'I helped one of theirs and now they can help one of mine.'" She paused. "I was the only one in the whole family who would talk to him, you know. The only one."

This confession triggered a new round of tears and I was still waiting it out when Bobby bellowed in from the other room.

"Another weirdo for you on line one."

"You're a wonderful secretary," I yelled back.

It was no weirdo. Well, maybe it was. It was Frank Waters, ace television reporter and world-class chicken. And he was quaking in his Jockeys, if his panicked voice was any indication.

"Casey," he squeaked. "Don't ask where I am."

"I wasn't about to," I said, eyeing Mitchell's daughter carefully. She seemed too absorbed in her misery to eavesdrop, but paranoia is one of my more healthy personality traits.

"I'm somewhere you wouldn't expect," he confided, his voice trembling. "I lied to you. I'm not on vacation. I'm still on the story. And I think I've found out something big."

"What's going on?" I demanded. "What do you want?"

"I need you to check something out for me," he said.
"I'd do it myself, but I'm all the way up here in Bethesda
and I can't."

So much for his not telling me where he was.

"What do you need?" I asked.

"I think Boyd Jackson was treated at Memorial Hospital or maybe Duke before he transferred up to Bethesda
when the Senate convened. I need you to locate any
medical records on him that you can."

"Why?" I asked. "They should have the information
up there."

"They don't," he whispered. "Something's weird
about his file at Johns Hopkins. It begins when he
checked in nine months ago with a diagnosis of stomach
cancer. But I think he's been under treatment for a lot
longer than that. The history should be here. This is
supposed to be the best medical care in the world. It's
weird that it's missing."

"What makes you think he was treated down here?" I
asked.

"A handwritten note stuck in the file says to notify a
Dr. Robert Dahler if there are any changes in the
senator's treatment. The number listed for him has a 919
area code and a Chapel Hill exchange. And don't ask me
how I got my hands on the file."

I wasn't planning to. He'd tell me himself soon
enough. "Why don't you just call the doctor's number
and ask?" I said.

"They're not going to give me confidential patient
information over the phone," he hissed. "How amateur
do you think I am?" There was a long silence. "I tried,"
he finally admitted. "A woman answered and just said
'Doctor's office' and wouldn't tell me anything more.
She hung up on me. But this Dr. Dahler has got to be
affiliated with one of the hospitals down there."

"Unfortunately, there are many hospitals down here,"

I said patiently. "Besides Memorial and Duke, there are god knows how many smaller facilities in Durham. That's why it's called the City of Medicine, Einstein."

"Start with Memorial," he said. "His office was a Chapel Hill number and that makes the most sense."

"You seem to believe that I'm a magician," I said. I eyed my guest again, annoyed I could not get more specific without being overheard.

"I need your help, Casey," he pleaded. His voice took on a desperate, whining tone and the beginnings of an asthma attack lurked in every shortened breath. "What if I'm being followed? I'm risking my life."

"Are you sure this is important?" I asked. "I have a murder investigation on my hands."

"Of course it's important. Would I be risking my life if it wasn't?" He started breathing even more heavily. I knew if I didn't calm him, I'd lose him to a panic attack.

"Okay," I assured him. "I'll see what I can do. Call me tomorrow."

"I will," he promised. "From a secured line." Geeze, he'd been reading too much Tom Clancy.

After I hung up, Thornton Mitchell's daughter glared at me. "You're taking on another job?" she demanded. "When my father's killer is just roaming around free?"

"It may have something to do with his death," I assured her, though I didn't really believe it myself. What *could* it have to do with Mitchell's death? I intended to find out.

I was going to have to call in a marker to get a peek at Boyd Jackson's medical files. And I knew the perfect person to help. Someone who was smart and charming but without any scruples. My friend Jack.

It would have been easier to phone Jack—my human Labrador, loyal companion, and frequent paramour—but it was more effective to twist his arm in person. I ditched the black cardigan and told myself there were times when a tight dress came in handy. I was lucky with the traffic on I-40 and zoomed along toward the 15-501 exit, pitying the poor commuters stuck in the eastbound snarl created by Research Triangle workers heading home to Raleigh and its suburbs. I arrived at MacLaine's, a popular watering hole located between Durham and Chapel Hill, just as the after-work crowd was reaching a fever pitch. Jack was the king of the bar there and held court each weekday from four in the afternoon until some lucky lady dragged him home in the wee hours. I knew that Jack never went home alone and that he had a weakness for nurses. What man doesn't? But Jack was particularly susceptible to the white uniform. He went through more of them in a year than your local laundromat. He'd have plenty of contacts at Memorial Hospital.

"Casey, baby. Dangerous lady," he yelled over the raucous laughter, dropping his thumb to his forefinger as if shooting a gun. He began vigorously shaking a frosted silver container while the females at the bar admired his biceps and tight black jeans. "Grape shot?"

"No thanks," I said. "I'm trying to quit." Grape shots at seven o'clock at night? Ye gods.

"Little early for you to be dropping by," he said. "Hard day?"

"Yeah. Real hard. And I'm still on the job." I nodded toward the parking lot. "Got a minute?"

The look of alarm on his face made me laugh.

"Don't worry," I said, "I didn't hear from the health department. It's something else. I need your help."

He looked relieved. Jack is pretty good about keeping Trojan in business, but he's also well aware that he tempts the law of averages with each new close encounter he instigates. "Let me check with Hank," he said, expertly pouring a vile-looking purple concoction into a row of small shot glasses. A trio of well-tanned secretaries whooped with anticipation as he placed the drinks before

them. While Jack disappeared into the back office, the
women tossed the drinks down their throats. I listened to
their rebel yells with admiration. Believe me, secretaries
after work make truck drivers look like wimps.

"I got a minute or two," Jack said, steering me out the
door quickly. The secretaries watched in envy. Eat your
hearts out, ladies. You may be younger, you may be
thinner—but I got personality. Not to mention size
thirty-eights and an attitude.

I used it all when I got Jack in the car. "I need you to
do something for me," I told him and explained what I
wanted. "I know you must be fooling around with half
the day shift at Memorial," I said. "Do you think any of
them might pull the files for some serious money?"

Jack didn't waste any time protesting his playboy
status, which was what I liked about him. He was happy
being a handsome cad and I was happy being an
occasional cadet. I watched him think and thought how
criminal it was that such a lovely face and magnificent
body couldn't be replicated and packaged for women all
around America. Jack was just about the cutest thing this
side of the Rockies. He had thick glossy hair and delicate
features in a triangular face. His skin was an impossibly
healthy pink and his mouth was wide and talented. In a
few years he would start to get fat, thanks to too many late
nights and too many cocktails, but for now the man was
ready, willing and able. Oh, how the ladies of the
Triangle loved him.

"I've got it," he said after a moment of silence, having
taken my request seriously. He had searched an entire
mental catalog of women and settled on just the right one.
"She's got a problem, know what I mean?" He tapped
the side of his nose. "She's always on the prowl and
getting worse. I bet she needs the money. She works in
one of the offices there. I think the insurance section or
something."

"Good, she'll know the computer system," I said, trusting his judgment. After all, he adored me.

"But listen, Casey," he warned me. "It could cause me some trouble. This girl's a regular and comes in every night. I had a hard time getting rid of her the time we tumbled, you know what I mean?"

I knew. Women fell in love with Jack instantly and followed him around like puppy dogs. It was tough to be a sex symbol.

"I'll tell her we're engaged," I assured him. "I'll threaten to kick her ass if she messes with my man."

Jack nodded thoughtfully. "I like it," he said. "It'll work."

"How much should do it?" I asked. Everyone had their price. And drug users usually came cheap.

"Leave it to me," he said. "A couple hundred is plenty." He opened the car door. "I gotta get back. The natives are restless."

"Thanks, Jack," I said. "You're the best." And I meant it. "I owe you."

He leaned back in and planted a wet one on me for good luck. "Naw. Just call me in the morning."

What a guy.

I could have used a drink, but I was dog tired. And being dog tired reminded me that I had promised to check on Ramsey Lee's hounds. It was a long drive back to the other side of Raleigh, but I was cheered by the prospect of the mountain man's gratitude one day. Besides, if Ramsey really had seen a fisherman there the night that Thornton Mitchell was killed, there was a good chance the guy might return to his regular fishing spot. Unless he'd been permanently scared away. My theory was this: if a witness existed, he had no idea that he'd seen or heard something important. Otherwise, if he'd witnessed the actual murder, surely he would have contacted the police. Unless he were an illegal immigrant, of course.

And if that was the case, there was no way I'd get near
him, much less be able to talk to him. Which left me with
nowhere to turn but a shot in the dark. It was an
unfortunate metaphor to consider.

I pondered the possibilities as I neared the Neuse
River. The night had clouded over and the darkness was
absolute. U.S. 1 was deserted, the desolation broken only
by an occasional pair of headlights whizzing by. I had
trouble finding the turn-off to Ramsey's house and had to
double-back twice before I spotted it. I rolled down my
car window and cruised slowly down the rutted lane that
led to his cabin. A hint of rain in the air had stirred the
crickets and frogs. Their chirping softened the night.
Ramsey's dogs heard the car approaching and added their
own distinctive howls to the mix. Their high-pitched
baying split the darkness like the cries of banshees. A city
girl would have fled in terror but I was used to their
music. My grandpa once said that the singing of hounds
in a pack was the sweetest sound on earth. I wouldn't go
that far—I prefer the foamy pop that cold canned beer
makes on a hot day—but I wasn't frightened by it either,
not even when the howling escalated into a frenzy as I
approached the pen. I counted at least four assorted
coonhounds, a pair of Plott hounds, and two or three blue
ticks in the glow of my flashlight. They crowded around
me, tails wagging and bumping rear ends as they jockied
for pats on the head. This was no crowd of angry curs and
I suspected that tough old Ramsey Lee spent a lot of time
curled up with his pack by the fire.

I soon discovered the source of their eagerness: the
water pipe was fine but the automatic feeder had jammed
and several days' worth of dog food was backed up in the
hopper. I adjusted the chute and the dogs fell instantly
silent, crowding around the crescent-shaped feeder bowl
to chow down on their kibbles. I cleaned the water trough
and spent a few minutes scratching at the base of their

tails. Their scent reminded me of moonlit Florida nights and I kept expecting to hear the sound of my grandpa's familiar coughing in the silence. It was so real, I could almost hear it.

I *had* heard it.

I froze and separated the sounds of hounds slurping from the other night music. Ramsey had been right about the lay of the land. I could hear distant voices floating up from the banks of the Neuse. Gathering my courage, I crept through the trees and made my way down to the river.

The other side of the Neuse was hidden in blackness and I was afraid to use my flashlight. There was a chance that the SBI had posted a guard, though I doubted it. I was more concerned with scaring away a witness. My shoes made soft scrunching sounds in the bed of dead leaves covering the ground as I made my way further downstream. About fifty feet from the scene of the murder, I spotted an enclave of three small campfires. A hundred feet downstream, another small fire winked in the night, as if one of the fisherman had grown angry at his companions and was pouting by himself nearby. I heard laughter and the soft murmur of a foreign language. Great. The only foreign phrase I knew was "ein klein bier." It wasn't likely to help me much here.

I contemplated my options. I could swim for it, but the prospect of stroking copperheads out of the way as I swallowed the murky waters of the Neuse was decidedly unappealing. I could throw rocks across the muddy span until I got their attention, but sign language at fifty feet in the darkness was unlikely to prove useful. I finally hiked back to Ramsey's cabin and retrieved my car, returning to U.S. 1 until I could cut over a bridge to the other side of the Neuse. This time, the entrance was easy to spot: yellow crime scene tape blocked off a dirt road leading back into the shadows from a small gravel clearing that was otherwise distinguished only by a trio of large green dumpsters heaped high with trash. I left my car further down the road in a lane that went nowhere and walked back to the path, moving quickly alongside it, more concerned with speed than discretion. I slowed as I neared the river, taking care to remain outside the parameters of the road. I didn't want my footprints showing up as Exhibit B in court. The voices grew louder as I approached and I recognized the tongues: Spanish and another dialect that was harsher. Mayan, maybe. These night fishermen were clearly from the ranks of migrant workers who had settled permanently in the Raleigh area.

I was so pleased with my sleuthing that I grew careless and tripped over a tree root. I fell to the ground with a thud, skinning my knee and landing in a pile of dead branches that made more crackling noises than a vat of Rice Krispies in milk. There went my element of surprise.

And there went my witnesses. By the time I reached the clearing, they had disappeared. Three small campfires burned cheerfully along a deserted bank, sending golden-tongued reflections across the muddy surface of the Neuse. A lone fishing pole remained behind, leaning against a tree. Its red and white plastic bobber still swayed from when someone had brushed by. Curses. Foiled again.

I heard another cough and froze. It was phlegmy and full. The fourth campfire, the one further down the banks, wasn't part of this encampment after all. And whoever had built it didn't care if he was overheard. I made my way down the sandy shore, using the flames as a beacon. As I neared it, I heard a second cough followed by the splat of tobacco on sand.

At first, I thought I'd encountered another deserted campsite. The fisherman was so black that the night engulfed him. His face was shrouded in the darkness and his deep blue overalls invisible until I was no more than three feet from the old man.

"This your land now?" the fisherman asked calmly, his voice deep and gravelly, made rougher by the cough bubbling beneath the surface.

"No," I said. "Fish on. I'm just passing through." My eyes adjusted to the camp light: my companion was just about the oldest man I'd ever seen. Deep wrinkles creased his face, making it as puckered as an apple drying in the sun. His hair was white and buzzed close against a small, round skull. His eyes were large and calm.

"Funny time to be hiking," he said, waving me to one side so he could check his fishing lines. Two tall bamboo poles were firmly wedged into the sand, arcing gracefully toward the river.

"Catfish?" I asked.

"Whatever I can get," he answered.

"Mind if I sit down?"

"You want something," the man said. It was a statement, not a question.

"Just to talk," I promised.

"Talk about what?" he asked, not even looking my way.

I had the feeling this old man had dealt with thousands of white people in his day and had very little use for the lot of us.

"You live around here?" I asked.

"Close enough," he answered. "Got me a couple acres nearby."

He was probably the last of a dying breed in the South: a former tenant farmer left over from the old days, made obsolete by age and the disappearance of farmland, a lonely survivor in a sea of encroaching development. He was a man who would watch the demise of the green fields with the calm resignation that impending death provides.

"You come here to fish a lot?" I asked.

"Every night," he said, his eyes locked onto the bamboo fishing poles. "Why you asking? I got permission from the lady who used to own this land. Been fishing here for sixty years. Didn't think the new owner would care."

"She gave it to the city," I told him. "Raleigh's the new owner."

"Well, then Raleigh can come and make me leave."

He made Raleigh sound like the neighborhood bully out to cause him pain. And maybe to him, it was. "I'm not here to get you to move," I promised. "I just wanted to ask you a few questions."

"Why don't you ask them your questions instead," he said, nodding upstream toward the trio of deserted campfires. He spit out a wad of tobbacco and it splatted onto the sand, gleaming in the campfire for a second before it sank beneath the silt. His cough that followed rumbled in the silence.

"They're gone," I told him. "They heard me coming. I guess they're illegal immigrants or something."

"We've all got to come from somewhere," he said. His age and gravity made it sound like the wise pronouncement of a sage. "They're just trying to get themselves something to eat."

"Were you here three nights ago?" I asked.

"I done told you, I'm here every night." He looked at me briefly, as if wondering at my stupidity. Probably he was.

"Did you hear or see anything unusual?" I asked. "Do you know what happened further up the banks?"

He shook his head and shrugged. "I mind my own business. I expect others to do the same."

"Do you have a television?" I asked. Was it possible he didn't even know about the murder?

"Wouldn't do me no good," he confided. "I don't have electricity. Don't want it, neither. Those power folks can just go and charge somewhere else for their electricity. I can do without it.''

One of the bamboo poles bent slowly toward the river, its arc bowing until the tip nearly touched the water. The old man ambled up and pulled it from the sand, tugging toward the sky with a sharp motion to set the hook. Catfish don't fight like other fish. They just sort of lay there on your hook, letting their weight pull the line toward the bottom.

The old man ignored me while he went about his business. He pulled the line in and examined a dangling gray catfish that gleamed wetly in the campfire light, checking it for size. Satisfied, he grabbed it carefully around the middle with a work-worn hand, taking care to avoid the spiny horn at the top of its head. He laid it against a plank by the fire and bopped it smartly on the head with a thick branch. The fish lay still, its pewter body reflecting gold firelight. The old man pulled a long nail from his overall pocket and placed it just above one of the flat fish eyes, driving the nail through the head and into the board with his branch club. Once the fish was secured, he pulled a knife from a pocket and made several long incisions down the leathery skin. His seemingly bottomless pockets yielded a pair of pliers, which he used to strip the skin from the body, revealing a fat carcass of milky catfish meat. He quickly filleted it, then placed the strips of flesh tenderly on the top of some ice he had packed into a medium-size cooler. Grunting, he wiped his hands on his overalls and threw the catfish skin and guts deep into the woods for the raccoons. He then unscrewed a small jar and scooped out a dab of foul-smelling goo which he made into a small plug to wrap around the empty hook. He cast the line back into the water, jamming the pole deep into the sand to secure it. The whole operation took no more than three minutes. The man was old, but he was still mighty limber.

"Now what was you asking me?" he said when he rejoined me at the fire. The air had grown cold, reminding me that it was October. I huddled close to the flames, grateful for the warmth.

"I asked you if you had been fishing here three nights ago."

"Yep," he said. "I'm here every night. I got a lot of mouths to feed. My daughter ran away to Atlanta. Left us with three grandkids."

Personal details? Hey, he was warming up. Maybe as a reward for my not retching at the catfish display.

"Did you see anything unusual that night?" I asked. "Further upstream, maybe? Beyond those campfires there?" I nodded toward the trio of fires and saw that the fishermen had returned. They were being cautious and stood quietly by the bank, poles in hand. Every now and then, they would turn my way for a quick look.

"I didn't notice nothing along the banks," the old man said, punctuating this statement with a quick spit of tobacco and a juicy cough. "Just a pair of fools up on the road who got stuck. I had to help push one of them out."

"A pair of fools?" I asked, feeling a prickle of adrenaline.

"Yep. Some tall fellow who talked funny was driving a white car and some woman was trying to drive a big black car. She wasn't hardly big enough to see over the steering wheel. She was the one who was stuck. I had to push the car with the help of the young fellow until she could get it straightened out and down the road. It was pretty muddy. Darn stupid of her to be driving there in the middle of the night in the first place. I usually avoid that road. I walk in the other way."

"What did the man and woman look like?" I asked, wondering how any person could be so devoid of curiosity. He didn't care why they had been there or where they had gone.

"They were white," he answered, as if that said

everything. And for him, it probably did. "White and she was real snippy about it. Didn't bother with the pleases or thank yous, oh no, not that one. I walked me a ways to help them out. I had just gotten here and hardly got my fire set up when I heard the engine spinning and I was afraid they'd start scaring off the fish if they got any louder. When I got to the road, the tall fellow was pushing at the rear of the car and the lady was behind the wheel. I didn't say nothing, just started pushing alongside of the boy. The car was too heavy for that road. I had to use all of my strength to get it out of the mud. When the lady driving got a ways down the road, she stopped and came back to talk to the young fellow. Didn't say thank you, even. Just stood at the front of the car where I could hardly see her and looked at the boy and said 'Let's go' or something like that. The fellow thanked me, though. He shook my hand and got in the black car with the lady and I saw the two of them arguing, at least that's what it looked like to me. Then the fellow got out and went to his own car and the two of them drove away, one after the other, the lady leading the way. I was surprised the boy could drive, he was jerking around so much."

"You mean the car was jerking back and forth?" I asked.

The old man shook his head. "No, the fellow was. He was one of those nervous types, you know. He talked funny, like through his nose, and his hands were shaking like this." The old man held up a dark, gnarled hand and it trembled in the firelight. "City boy, probably scared of the dark. But not that lady. Oh, no." He shook his head. "She was cool as ice. Queen of the night. And I was her slave. Got no truck with people like that." He stared into the fire, remembering. "Not even a simple thank you."

"But what did they look like?" I asked again.

The old man shrugged. "The fellow was tall. Younger than me. Kind of skinny. He wasn't much help with the car. The lady was short. Didn't get a good look at her.

She stayed in the shadows. I just felt her, you know, and could hear her voice. She was used to ordering folks like me around, I could tell that, and I was sorry I had bothered to help her. A man deserves a thank you, at least. I was not put on this Earth to serve her, but I guess God forgot to tell her that.''

"What color was her hair?" I asked, frustrated. "Or his?"

He shrugged. "Couldn't tell you. The boy had on one of those baseball hats. It was white, I think, with black stripes on it. Not the Braves. Some other team. I don't know about the lady's hair. It was dark under the trees. I wasn't looking. I just wanted them out of there.''

I sighed.

"Sorry," he apologized. "I mind my own business. You the police?"

"No." I threw a few sticks into the fire and watched them blaze.

"What did those folks do?"

"Never mind," I told him. "Just keep on fishing." Thornton Mitchell's death had screwed up enough lives. And this old man had been through enough changes in his lifetime as it was.

"I plan to," he said, spitting a wad of juice into the fire. It sizzled and disappeared. "I plan to keep fishing here until the day I die.''

"Thanks for your help," I told him. "Thanks very much." I offered my hand. He took it gently, cradling it in a creased paw. "Good luck fishing.''

He nodded silently and turned his gaze back to his bamboo poles.

As I made my way down the banks, I heard the sound of leaves rustling. I passed by the other campsite and found nothing but three small fires burning brightly. The clearing was deserted and silent in the stillness of the Carolina night.

TWELVE

A tall man who talked funny? Who would the old man think talked funny? It could be Stoney, with his well-trained public speaking voice. Or Bradley Masters, for that matter, with his phony Boston boarding school accent. Maybe even Frank Waters with his asthma-laced television voice. I pondered the possibilities as I lay in bed that night. But not for long. I fell asleep for a well-deserved rest and didn't surface until Bobby D. woke me up with a phone call the next morning.

"Rise and shine, doll face!" His voice boomed through the answering machine, interrupting my dream of coonhounds chasing Mexican bandits along the banks of the Neuse. "We got a couple more days to solve this thing for that triple dinero bonus."

Only extra money could get Bobby so excited this early. I fumbled for the phone. "What's this 'we' crap?" I asked. "How are you helping any?"

"Hey," he protested in an injured tone of voice. "I'm calling with the goods. I've done my thing. It's time for you to do yours."

"What thing?" I asked sleepily. I found the clock wedged beneath the bed. It was nearly nine o'clock.

"Two shell companies invested in that failed Neuse Park project with Thornton Mitchell," he told me.

"One traces back to another company called Acorn Enterprises and that's owned by a local construction company. Probably hoping to build the houses along its edge."

"Legit?" I asked.

"Sure, babe. The owner is married to the mayor's sister. Can't get more legit than that. But the other company is giving me trouble. It traces back to yet another company and the trail ends there. I can't get any information beyond that. Either the files are lost or they never filed incorporation papers and it hasn't caught up with them yet."

"Lost?" I asked incredulously.

"Lost as in 'get lost,'" Bobby conceded. "What can I say? Maybe someone got there first with a bribe. I tried my best. The last company listed was called Sand Dollar Limited. I figure there must be some tie-in to beach properties."

"Sand Dollar?" I repeated. "How much were they on the hook for?"

"Fifty grand," Bobby said. "A fourth of the development partnership. I've checked out the other partners. They've all invested with Mitchell before. This one's the only one that ain't adding up."

"Thanks, Bobby," I said before I could stop myself. Thank him too much and he gets intolerable.

"Like I said, babe," he bragged. "Follow the money."

I hung up and lay in bed wondering if thirty minutes was too long a drive to take for fresh Krispy Kreme doughnuts. I needed a sugar infusion to jumpstart my brain. Instead, I dragged my sorry ass out of bed and rummaged through the kitchen in search of coffee. I finally found the can of Chock Full O' Nuts in the vegetable crisper—next to my missing pink bunny slipper. I didn't even want to know how it had gotten there. I made a pot of coffee, showered, and retrieved the morning paper from the stoop. For once, the paperboy had hit his mark. I pulled my sole chair up to the back window of my apartment and propped my feet up on the sill, jumbo mug of coffee in hand and the *N&O* at my feet. It was time for some serious thinking. Besides, Jack wouldn't be up for at least another two hours and there was no way he could come up with the medical records before mid-afternoon.

I tried to put it all together. What tall guy would hang out with what short woman? Stoney and his secret lady love? Thornton Mitchell's ex-wife or Stoney Maloney's mother and some young stud lover? None were likely scenarios. Shorty Shrimpboat from the SBI dressed in drag? An appealing but even more unlikely thought. Frank Waters and a contact from the Maloney campaign? I concentrated on what the old fisherman had said. The guy was tall. The guy talked funny. Stoney's father and his Eastern shore accent? Naw, he was old. But just about anyone could qualify as a young fellow to that old fisherman. Who knew?

I tried the other description. The woman was short. But how short? Maybe the old man had exaggerated. It was the middle of the night. Hard to see, but not hard to hear. And he had said that the woman talked nasty. That was Mary Lee Masters all right. Or Stoney's secret girlfriend. A campaign worker? I even tried casting Bradley Masters and a coed girlfriend in the starring roles, but failed when it came to a motive. I also wondered about the possible connection to Thornton Mitchell's Neuse River Park investor, Sand Dollar Limited. What did the name mean? Who had ties to the beach? I considered whether anyone of the gang was particularly suntanned and when I reached that point, I realized it was time to get a grip, preferably on something more concrete. I called Bobby back at the office.

"Can you get copies of the filing papers for Sand Dollar?" I asked.

"Sure. But I had my contact read them over the phone to me already. They aren't much help. The shareholders are two more companies: Sandman Properties and Dollar Inc. I hit a dead end on both of those."

"Get the filing anyway," I said. "Maybe there's a phone number or something. Have them fax copies over. I'll be in this afternoon."

"Have it your way," he said, hanging up to finish swallowing whatever it was he was chewing this time.

Maybe a run would help. I hated running. It was stupid. It was pointless. And a lot less fun than sex. But I had to kill some time and clear my head. Reluctantly, I pulled out my running shoes for a trip to the Duke campus where I could sneak onto their athletic track and at least be distracted by sweaty young bodies while I jogged. The run proved so invigorating that I was forced to stop and eat a huge late breakfast afterward. A pound of grits and butter later—never mind the fried eggs, sausage, and biscuits—I returned home and showered again, killing time until it was safe to call Jack.

At noon, I broke down and phoned him. He was groggy but at least he was home. Jack's sleeping habits—and habitats—tended toward the erratic.

"Don't tell me you stumbled home alone last night?" I asked. "Will wonders never cease?"

"A man's got to save his strength when he hangs out with you," he replied.

I wanted to drive over and test his theory, but duty called. "Did you get the stuff?" I asked, feeling like I was back in the land of drug deals.

"She went for it," he said. "I thought I'd have to do her to seal the deal, but some drunken schmuck snaked me, thank god, and she wanted to make me jealous so she took him home instead. He probably offered her more in the way of incentive, if you know what I mean. I never touch the stuff.''

"I hope to god she made it to work today," I said, alarmed. "I need those records this afternoon."

"She's there," Jack promised. "She's the type who thinks that if she can drag her ass into work, it proves she doesn't have a problem. She said she'd have the files sometime after lunch."

"Great. I'm picking you up in thirty minutes." I hung up before he could protest.

Jack hunched miserably in my front seat to let me know the sacrifice he was making to be up and conscious so close to noon. He pouted until I stopped at a Wendy's and refueled him with two double cheese-burgers, fries, and a large Coke. It never took him long to recover from a bad mood, especially when you bribed him with food.

Jack's best trait is his good nature—which is one of the biggest reasons why we remain friends. He is like a perpetual four-year-old, hiding his true intelligence, running around a giant playpen pulling all the pigtails he can grab and charming his way into being totally spoiled. But he is quick to repent when he crosses a boundary he should never have approached, and he is careful about his real friends' feelings. In the five years I have known him, Jack has never let me down. Which isn't to say he is perfect. I caught him sneaking looks at his hair in the sideview mirror and was once again reminded of his carefully concealed vanity.

"Looking good," I told him as we arrived at Memorial Hospital. I licked the mustard off one corner of his mouth and fixed his hair with my fingers. "Just use your charm. And cold hard cash."

"Got it," he said, patting a pocket.

He was back within half an hour, holding a manila

envelope. "Bingo," he announced. "But that bitch held me up for an extra hundred. Said one of the files was hard to locate."

"Should have gone home with her last night," I suggested. I reimbursed him three hundred dollars and he handed over the envelope. We like to keep our business relationship formal.

The package was fat and felt promising. I held it in my hands, reluctant to open it and burst the bubble of optimism rising within me.

"Who are these people anyway?" Jack asked, popping the last of his french fries into his mouth. "Their names sound familiar."

"No one important," I assured him. Hey, if Jack didn't think that the names of his current senator and one of the top candidates to replace him were important enough to remember, who was I to set him straight? I dropped Jack off at his apartment then drove to Duke Gardens to review the material. I was getting more than a little paranoid and wanted to be sure I was alone. It was too late in the year for the roses to be in bloom and the walkways were deserted. I found a bench in the middle of a cluster of silver oaks where I felt safe from prying eyes. Slowly, I unclasped the fastener and slid a stack of Xeroxed papers onto my lap. A hastily scrawled note on the top of the pile read: "You don't know what you're missing. Call me sometime. Love, Sylvia." She dotted her *i*'s with little hearts. Barf. I spared Jack the trouble of replying by tossing the note into a nearby trash can.

The first few pages were short and to the point: the patient had been admitted briefly in 1974 while a student at the University of North Carolina at Chapel Hill. When you cut through the medical jargon, the reason why was pretty clear: Mary Lee Masters had suffered complications following a routine first-trimester abortion, legally performed by doctors at a Memorial Hospital outpatient clinic. She had been referred by a resident physician affiliated with Student Health Services. The complications had not been severe. Basically she had been scraped, stabilized, and released.

Yuk. And no wonder she had freaked out at the thought of my snooping through medical files. If she had only kept her mouth shut and showed some restraint, I would never have asked Jack's contact to search for a file under her name as well. But now I understood Mary Lee's panic and her sudden interest in my progress. An abortion was not an extraordinary event in the 1970's for a college girl. But in the political climate of the 1990's, it was a most definite liability. She could hardly claim not to have inhaled. The voters would not be forgiving. Especially since she had failed to redeem herself by offloading a few kids as penance. So this was what she had been hiding. And this was why she stayed married to Bradley Masters. He was probably the father and knew her secret. If she cut him off or complained about his spending or his affairs, he could leak the news to the public. It was just what the Maloney campaign needed to seal their victory.

Aren't people grand? A man responsible for half a deed turns around and blackmails his partner for that same deed, knowing the public will condemn her while never thinking to look twice at him.

I couldn't decide whether to tell Mary Lee that I knew or not. Or that I might have a way out of the dilemma for her, thanks to Bill Butler and his investigative buddies. For now, I kept it to myself and began to thumb through the rest of the copied files. I was in for an even bigger surprise.

I was a little rusty on technical terms, but I could damn sure read a schematic when I ran across one. And a carefully marked map of the human body that traced the path of cancer through Senator Boyd Jackson's innards told me something I had never suspected: he was dying from lung cancer.

Now, you may be asking: lung cancer, stomach cancer—what's the difference? He'll still be dead in the end.

The difference is that Senator Boyd Jackson spent about fifty percent of his political life defending the interests of North Carolina's twenty thousand tobacco farmers and a handful of contribution-rich tobacco companies. If the world found out that the most visible champion of tobacco rights was dying from lung cancer, the war against cigarettes would never be the same. But I wondered if his motives for hiding the truth weren't even more personal: Boyd Jackson had devoted much of his life to defending tobacco interests. Would condemning tobacco now—or conceding its dangers— be too much like admitting he had sacrificed his life to an unworthy cause? I didn't know the man, so I didn't know the answer. But I knew that this was a secret that was possibly worth killing for. There was no way that Boyd Jackson or his overly proud family would have let his true illness be made public knowledge. I checked the rest of his records and had to give nervous old Frank Waters some credit—the television reporter had been right about Dr. Robert Dahler. He was the key to the trail that led to this file. He was listed as the treating physician and appeared on all forms, prescriptions, and assessments—in itself unusual, given the team treatment approach preferred in medical circles these days. But I knew why: he was probably a family friend and sworn to secrecy.

I tucked the papers back in the envelope and hurried home, anxious to confirm a few crucial facts that might help me connect the senator's medical condition with the murder. Just as I was walking in my apartment door, Detective First Class Bill Butler called and sounded so forlorn that I actually picked up the telephone. I could afford to be generous. I had a lead. All he had was his good looks.

"Having any luck?" I asked him.

"Nothing," he conceded. "The SBI is about to release Ramsey Lee and they don't like it. But there's no physical evidence to link him."

"That's because he didn't do it," I said.

"So you've been saying all along. But what else is there?"

"Did they question people along the river?" I asked, feeling sorry for him, but not wanting to give the old fisherman away. Besides, Bill played his cards pretty close to his chest. I wanted to return the favor.

"What people?" Bill asked. "Except for Lee, no one lives there."

I was silent, weighing my conscience against my desire to upstage the SBI. "Okay," I finally conceded, "if I tell you something, you must swear, absolutely swear, that it is never to be traced back to me and that you won't try to contact my witness."

"A witness?!" he screamed, nearly puncturing my eardrum.

"Down, boy," I cautioned him. "Not a witness to the murder. A witness to two people at the murder scene on that night. I found an old man who says he saw two people, cars stuck in the mud, on the road leading up to the murder scene at about the right time."

"How do you know about the murder scene?" he asked.

I ignored the question. "He said it was a man and a woman." I described them both. Bill remained silent, his innate northern skepticism creeping through the wires.

"Not much of a description," he said when I finished. "Tall? Talks funny? That's the whole population down here."

"Speak for yourself," I told him. "I'd say most people down here think you talk funny with your Long Island drawl."

Then it hit me. *Of course.*

"Hey, are you a baseball fan?" I asked him.

"I've been to a few Durham Bulls games," he said cautiously.

"Relax. I'm not asking you out on a date. I just want to know if you know your baseball teams."

"Most of them," he admitted. "Why?"

"What team has a white uniform with black stripes?"

He thought for a moment. "None of them," he said. "The New York Yankees are white with dark blue stripes. That's as close as you get."

I didn't say anything more. I hadn't told him about the baseball hat the tall man had been wearing, but it gave me the answer I needed.

"I need to talk to your witness," he said firmly.

"The old man was just visiting his daughter," I lied. "He left today for Atlanta. You'll never find him. But maybe the information will help put you on the right track."

"Or maybe you're going to help me track him down." His voice softened. "Listen, thanks for the tip anyway." He was silent for a moment. "I can be a jerk. You've been a big help. I wish there was some way . . ." His voice trailed off. I didn't prompt him to finish. Best to leave that avenue open.

I hung up more wired than I had been since this whole case began. Because now I knew the identity of the tall guy who talked funny. I just needed to nail his lady friend. And I would do it by taking the most direct route possible. If I knew my people, he wouldn't stay silent for long. He didn't have the nerve. First, I would stop by my office to pick up my gun. Then I would do a little fishing of my own.

Bobby D. was napping when I arrived and unimpressed with my burst of energy. "Jesus," he said when I pushed his feet off his desk. "Can't a guy get a little well-deserved rest?"

"I'll let you know when you deserve it. Where's today's paper?"

"On your desk," he said irritably, checking the trashcan to see if his new six pack was sufficiently iced yet. "Next to a faxed copy of those incorporation papers. Closing in?" He did not look hopeful.

"I might be," I said. "I just need to check today's campaign schedule."

"We're going to make the triple fee deadline?" he asked, his face transformed into a seedy Santa-like beaming. "Jesus, you like to cut it close. We've only got until tomorrow night."

"We'll make it," I said, anxious to track down my quarry. According to the *N&O,* Stoney was in Raleigh for the afternoon but scheduled to speak at a dinner in Winston-Salem that night. I checked the time. His entourage would just now be mobilizing for the two-hour drive out of town.

I wanted to dash out the door, but checked the faxed incorporation papers first. I was rewarded for my diligence. The company that had invested in Thornton Mitchell's failed Neuse River Park project was not Sand Dollar Limited like Bobby had said. It was "Sand-Dahler" and that made a big difference. A very big difference indeed. In fact, it was just what the doctor had ordered.

I checked the clip of my .380 and pulled the slide back to eject the first bullet. Then I made sure the safety was on. No sense shooting my toe off until I had to. I was wearing jeans and a tee shirt, which made it tough to conceal a gun. So I did what any self-

respecting lady dick would do: I stashed it in my
pocketbook. I grabbed a beer from the trash can on my
way out the door and tucked it in next to my gun. I
would celebrate later, I was sure. If my hunch proved
correct.

The receptionist at Maloney headquarters was not
pleased to see me again. I suppose I should have been
flattered that she remembered me at all. The frown that
crossed her pretty little face stayed in place until she
had returned with the object of my interest.

Adam Stoltz didn't look much friendlier. He glanced
at my jeans, then at his watch, and then at a clock on the
wall.

"I get the point," I said. "This will only take a
minute. A routine couple of questions is all."

He frowned. "I'm leaving in half an hour and I have to
go over some items with Stoney first."

"Don't worry," I assured him. "I just want to show
you a photo in the car." I looked around me, feigning
nervousness. "It's highly confidential. Can you come
out?" I cocked my head toward the exit.

He sighed in annoyance, but followed me out. I had
parked at the far end of the lot, forcing him to walk a
good hundred yards before we reached my Valiant.

"Jesus," he muttered as I unlocked the doors. "I
should have worn my hiking boots."

I motioned for him to get in. For the first time, I saw
alarm flicker in his eyes. "Look," I said, acting impa-
tient. "You said to let you know first if I came up with
anything so Stoney could prepare a statement. This is it.
I'm keeping my promise."

He climbed in without another word. He really should
have greased those wheels in his head. I could hear them
turning.

I joined him in the front seat, locked both doors, put
my pocketbook on my lap, reached inside, and aimed the

gun at his chest so that the outline of it against the fabric was obvious. I didn't have one in the hole, but he didn't know that.

"I have a gun pointed at your heart," I told him calmly.

"What?!" His head hit the ceiling and he reached for the door knob.

"Don't move," I warned him. "Just sit back and shut up."

He obeyed, his Adam's apple bobbing up and down as he gulped for air.

"I know you were there the night that Thornton Mitchell was killed," I explained quietly. "I have a witness who helped you push a car out of the mud. You were wearing a Yankees baseball cap. You were afraid."

"The old man," he said sourly, looking out the window. "She said we ought to get rid of him, too. I should have listened to her."

"You should never have listened to her in the first place." He had given me an opening I hadn't expected. I didn't know who she was, but he thought I did. Maybe I could trick him into telling me.

"She's pretty bossy, isn't she?" I said. "Must get under your skin."

Something in my voice gave me away.

"You don't know who she is, do you?" he said, sitting up straight. I moved the gun and he sat back against the seat cushion. "You have no idea who I was with. She stayed in the shadows. God, she's smarter than us all."

I could try to bluff or I could go ahead and scare the shit out of him. I opted for the most reliable route. I removed the .380 from my pocketbook and placed it on my lap with the barrel pointed at his crotch.

"I'm not really in the mood to fuck around," I

explained. "So let me put it this way: you can try to protect her or you can tell me who she is. First let me tell you why it's in your best interests to spill your guts. Okay? One, you need to spill your guts before I do. Understand?" I jiggled the gun.

His eyes were trained on me, silent and wide. He nodded nervously.

"Number two, the state of North Carolina is all too happy to impose the death penalty in capital murder cases. If this woman is smart enough to keep her identity hidden, she's smart enough to pin the murder on you. I don't think you did it. I don't think you have the nerve. I don't think you have the temperament. I don't think you're that kind of guy. If you tell me who she is and if you cooperate with the police by testifying in court, there's a good chance you can live. In fact, who knows what kind of deal a good lawyer could cut for you under those circumstances. But you aren't going to get anywhere except pointed down a long hallway toward the death chamber if you don't tell me right here and right now who you were with the night that Thornton Mitchell was murdered. That's it. That's all. Tell me and save your life, maybe even your career, if you have a good enough story for the jury."

He went for it without a moment's hesitation. Call it the ultimate in spin control. "But it *wasn't* my fault," he said. "I had no idea she would shoot him. She said it was only to talk, to work things out, that he was trying to blackmail her. When she opened the trunk of her car, I thought she was getting out a flashlight. I didn't know she had a shotgun. I'd never even seen one before that night." His voice squeaked like a boy in puberty.

"Who is she?" I interrupted. I had my money on the mystery girlfriend.

He told me. His version was precise and well thought

out. Either he was telling the truth or he had anticipated this moment. The only time he showed any surprise was when I asked about Dr. Robert Dahler.

"You know about that?" he asked.

"I know," I said.

He talked some more and I listened some more. Then I tucked the gun away in my purse and started the car.

"Where are we going?" he asked in alarm.

"Relax," I said. "We're going to see a friend of mine."

"I have to go with Stoney," he protested. "We have a dinner in Winston-Salem tonight."

"That part of your life is over," I told him. "Get used to it now."

He gave me no trouble during the drive. I parked illegally and we took the stairs instead of the elevator. I didn't even have to use my gun as an incentive. Adam Stoltz marched stiffly up the steps, head back, as if he were already a dead man walking.

I found Bill Butler in front of an automatic coffee machine staring morosely into his cup. His eyes locked with mine when he saw me.

"Brought you a present," I said. "We need some place private."

He looked at Adam Stoltz and then at the gleam in my eye. "In here," he said, pushing open a conference room door with a foot. "Right this way."

We sat at a table and Adam told his story. I drank my victory beer and listened to it again. Bill Butler didn't say a word. When it was over, he looked at me in astonishment.

"The *mother?*" he asked incredulously. "Stoney's mother?"

"The mother of all mothers," I said.

THIRTEEN

It turned into a late night, though, compared to Adam Stoltz, I had little to complain about. When I left him around ten, at the conclusion of the initial interview, he was huddled with the two lawyers he had called as soon as he realized that he should never have opened his mouth in the first place. Bill Butler had dangled the word "deal" in front of that northern boy like a hungry man dangling rotten meat in front of a crab. Adam was ready to bite—he just wanted to make sure he cut the very best deal he could. In the meantime, he was in custody and under orders to speak to no one in the Maloney campaign. He'd had no problem sounding sick as a dog when he phoned campaign headquarters and informed them he had taken ill. Just to be safe, Bill hovered over him during the call, his hand above the disconnect button. The two lawyers sat mute, their minds silently calculating exactly what they might demand for their client.

After the call, Bill and I retired to the hall while Adam and his lawyers figured out their poker hand. For someone who had just been bested, Bill was quite the gentleman.

"I apologize, Casey," he told me and I had to give the man credit—he looked me right in the eye when he said it. "I misjudged you. You didn't have to bring this to me and I want to thank you."

"No problem," I told him. "Better you than the SBI."

He held my gaze and I felt those butterflies nibbling at my stomach again. Never had hard work and exhaustion looked so good on one man. I wanted to run my fingers through his gray-flecked hair but managed some restraint. One day, I promised myself, one day.

"How about a drink?" he said. "A real one? After we wrap the deal?"

"Deal," I said. "On the drink, I mean. But what's the deal on the deal?"

He told me what he wanted to do. He couldn't do it without me. That was the part I liked the best. I thought it over and agreed on two conditions: no SBI and I had to remain anonymous.

"I'll risk moving ahead without the SBI," he agreed. "They haven't returned my phone calls in two days anyway. I can come up with a cover, say we were just going out there to talk to her. But keeping you anonymous is going to be hard if this works out. The press will be all over it."

"Tell them I work undercover for you and you can't blow my identity. What's a little lie between friends?"

He agreed and returned to the conference room to outline his conditions to Adam's lawyers. I waited for him downstairs in my car, happy for the fresh air and time alone. I was starting to feel anxious and miserable, no doubt having caught it from Adam Stoltz. That always happens to me. I can't be around lowlifes without feeling like a lowlife. I can't tolerate unhappiness without taking it on. It's a good thing I didn't grow up to be a shrink.

An hour later, Bill and I were sitting in the darkest corner of a transvestite bar on Morgan Street. It was the only place downtown that we could find open without going where we would be recognized.

"You're not going to pull off a wig and announce

you're a woman, are you?" I asked him. "Because that would kill a lot of my fantasies."

He smiled. The wrinkles around his mouth crinkled slowly as if he were unused to wearing a grin. "Your fantasies are safe with me," he said, touching my hand. Just then the willowy black waitress arrived with our drinks. I wanted to rip off her falsies and stuff them down her throat for interrupting at such a delicate moment, but I admired her sequined getup too much to mar her illusion.

He didn't touch my hand again, but he did relax. I could have stayed in that dark corner with Bill Butler all night long but we had too much to go over—and too much at stake—to begin the next day slowed down by hangovers. Instead, we reviewed the game plan several times for flaws and discussed the best place to hide a wire.

"Between my breasts," I insisted. "Where else? That woman is not going fishing between these babies, believe me."

Bill stared at my chest. "It might muffle the sound," he said dubiously.

"I'll let you personally place the mike and check it out. Okay?"

He nodded. "I'm something of an expert."

"I'll bet."

We agreed I would avoid the office the next day and wait at home until he called. It would be a long day, I knew, but I was too superstitious to hurry the process. It wouldn't work if Sandy Jackson suspected anything—or if Adam Stoltz got cold feet. He was trouble enough as it was.

"Do I have to bring him along?" I asked.

"Yes, you do," Bill replied. "You'll need him to convince her you're on the level. Don't worry. If she's the kind of person you say she is, she'll have no trouble believing your motives and she'll just think he's nervous because he's scared."

"What about me?" I asked. "How do I explain away my own knocking knees?"

"You have knees?" He peeked under the table at them. "Why do I have a feeling that you're going to be the least nervous one of us all?"

He smiled. I smiled. My thoughts turned from business. I brought them back and bid him adieu.

By morning, I was ready and rested. I called Bobby D. and let him know where I was, cautioning him to stave off everyone but a few select callers. But I didn't tell him what was going on. Bobby likes to trade information as much as he likes to buy it and this was too important to risk.

The morning passed as if it were a week. I knew Bill was meeting with the department's attorneys to deal with the legalities and hand-picking a backup team he could trust. When the phone rang around noon, I was sure he was calling with a repeat of his explicit instructions about what I could and could not say without endangering the case. I picked up the telephone without screening the call first.

"Casey," a breathless voice announced. "What's going on? I called you at the office and that fat guy said to try you here. Why are you home?" A faint wheeze lurked beneath the voice. I could hear traffic whizzing by in the background. Frank Waters—calling from the interstate.

"I can't tell you everything right now," I said. "But get back here by tonight and I'll give you the story of your life plus the footage you need to start a whole new career."

"You're kidding? What's it about?"

I told him enough to extract a promise that he would be waiting by his phone at his station office all evening for my instructions. "I'm in Virginia near Petersburg," he said. "I'll be back by four."

"Stay low," I warned him. "And remember—just you and a cameraman. You have to stay hidden until we come out the front door. You'll know when to approach because backup will start swarming all over the lawn. Don't let the cops see you until then. And when you're filming, I don't want any zooming in on me. I have a lot of personal reasons for staying out of the limelight."

"Got it," he said quickly, as well he should. For the career boost I was about to give him, he owed me at least his firstborn child.

"Make a big deal about the arresting officer," I told him. I explained who Bill Butler was, gave him some background, and said he had been a maverick during the investigation, always questioning the official lines of inquiry and refusing to be swayed by false evidence. It was a big fat lie but it sounded good and it would make Bill look good. I'd have a friend for life. One right in the middle of the Raleigh Police Department. And Shrimpboat Shorty could just kiss my refrigerator butt when all was said and done.

The rest of the afternoon passed by more quickly. I took my .380 out of my pocketbook and practiced drawing it from the back of my waistband. Reach around, quick tug, half turn, extend, and squeeze. I felt like Emma Peel by the time Bill Butler called.

"It's on," he said. "Adam's going to make the call in an hour. She's on her way back from some fundraiser in New Bern. He says she has a dinner in Raleigh tonight and he'll try for after that."

"I want to be there when he calls her," I told him. "The more I can find out about her and what she's thinking, the better."

"Better hurry," he said, hanging up.

I made it to Raleigh in twenty minutes, fast enough that Bill checked his watch twice. "I guess the highway patrol was at lunch."

"No sense taking chances," I said.

Adam Stoltz was dressed in a bright orange jumpsuit

that hung from his body like loose skin. His face was a parchment white, as if a vampire had sucked out all his blood overnight. And he looked about twenty years less confident.

"I guess you got your deal," I said to him. His lawyers stared at me like I just flashed the guy. Adam said nothing.

The table had been cleared of old coffee cups and was now dominated by a Star Trek–like circular phone system and recording device. Bill and a technician fiddled with the controls so long I wanted to scream, but at last Adam made the call.

"Maloney Headquarters," a perky voice chirped. "Vote for a better Carolina."

"Molly?" Adam said, his voice quavering. "It's Adam."

"Adam? How are you feeling? I heard you had the flu or something. Do you want me to get you anything from the store?" Her genuine concern permeated the cold steel atmosphere of the tense conference room. Ah, for simpler times.

"It's pretty bad," he said. "But I'm okay. Don't worry." He sounded like a bullfrog about to collapse from the heat. The boy may have had nerves of steel about politics, but he sure didn't have the temperament for crime. "Is Sandy there? I need to talk to her."

The girl's voice dropped. "Sure you're feeling well enough? She's in some kind of a temper. She had a fight with Stoney and she's mad enough to spit. She threw a stack of bumper stickers at Roger."

"Yeah, put me through," he said hoarsely. "It's important."

"It's your funeral," she replied and transferred him.

"I told you I didn't want to be disturbed." Sandy Jackson's tightly controlled twang snaked out of the telephone wire and coiled on the table.

"Sandy," Adam said. "It's me."

"Where the hell are you?" she demanded. "We don't pay you six figures to get the flu. There will be no sick days until this election is over, do you understand? Do you think I can do this all myself?"

"She knows," Adam interrupted. He shut his eyes and waited.

There was a short silence. "Who knows?" Her voice was steady. Sandy Jackson was either mighty cool or mighty heartless. Possibly both.

"The detective. The one Mary Lee Masters hired."

"What?" she demanded. "The trashy one?"

I winced but no one else seemed to notice.

"Well . . ." Adam said, his voice trailing off as he nervously eyed me.

"How did she find out anything?" she demanded. "What did you tell her?"

"Nothing!" he protested, real fear in his voice. "I didn't say anything at all. You have to believe me. She found out somehow, though, and she wants to cut a deal." His voice cracked and he choked on what sounded like a sob. That was when I realized that Adam Stoltz wasn't afraid of the police or of what his family might think. He was afraid of Sandy Jackson.

"She *would* try to cut a deal," Stoney's mother said nastily. "She's the type. First chance she gets to make a buck, she'd throw all her scruples out the window. I'm not surprised. I pegged her for a cheap tramp the minute I set eyes on her."

Well, how do you like that? The bitch had blown away an old friend in cold blood and she was calling me names?

"But she wants a lot of money," Adam added, glancing at me with contempt as if he were telling the truth.

"I'll just see about that," the woman replied. Her

laugh was even nastier than her voice. "How does she want to do it?"

"She wants to meet and settle on the price. She says she's left behind a letter in case something happens to her so we better not touch her."

"Touch her?" Sandy Jackson laughed. "I wouldn't touch a hair on her trashy head. And I'm giving in to her only because the easiest and smartest thing to do is to buy her off. Especially since she can be bought off cheap. She'll come down easy, believe you me. I know her type."

Oh boy, was that old biddy digging her grave. Any hesitation I felt, any nagging doubts of moral entrapment, any sympathy for her age and lost opportunities went right out the window with that crack. I was bringing that woman down.

I was so lost in my plans for revenge that I hardly noticed while Adam made the final arrangements and hung up the phone.

"Done," he said, looking at Bill Butler for approval.

Uneasily, I noticed that the lawyers were all staring at me as if trying to decide whether I was cheap or not.

"It's on," Bill said. Then he stared at me, too. I tried to think of something trashy to do, but failed.

"You're still in, right?" he asked me. "Ten o'clock tonight?"

"Ten o'clock," I confirmed. "Aloha. Be there."

I had to wear a bulky sweater to conceal the gun and I was suffocating in it. The night was cool enough, all right, but I was sweating like a pig. My armpits were soaked and rivulets trickled down my neck, making the hidden microphone itch. Any other time I would have been pleased to have Bill Butler's face buried between my breasts, but right now it was embarrassing.

"Try to relax," he told me. "We'll be nearby. I'm not going to let anything happen to you."

"It's not fear," I lied. "It's this synthetic sweater. I hate rayon."

He smiled and adjusted the tiny microphone so that it pointed up above the band of my bra. "How's it sound, Mark? It looks good from here." He looked up at me and winked and, against all odds, I managed a smile. He cupped his hand to his ear receiver and nodded. "She'll be okay. Maybe we should spray?" He nodded again and excused himself for a moment, returning with a small can of Arrid Extra Dry. "Hold still," he commanded, prying the microphone free and spraying my chest with the anti-perspirant. "Hope you don't take this too personally."

I groaned. My ego would never recover.

The police van pulled over to the side of a darkened cul-de-sac a few minutes before ten o'clock. We were parked at the top of a small, heavily wooded hill overlooking the backyard of Sandy Jackson's house.

"Can't risk covering the front," Bill had explained on the way over. "She's tight with the neighbors. The yards are too close. And she's too smart. We'll come in from the back and I'll send people around the sides and front of the yard as soon as you're inside. If some do-gooder doesn't call the police to report prowlers, we'll be okay."

"*You'll* be okay no matter what," I reminded him.

"You're going to be okay, too," he said. "I guaran-damn-tee it."

My gun felt heavy and clammy against the small of my back, but its weight was reassuring. I checked to make sure the safety was off and the clip fully loaded, shrugging away Bill's warnings. I'd rather risk shooting off a few inches of cellulite from my butt than lose time when I needed it the most.

"Let's go," I told Adam when I was ready. An officer had followed the van in my Plymouth Valiant and we climbed silently inside. Adam had turned a greenish white and sweat shone above his upper lip. "Stop it," I told him as we pulled up in front of Sandy Jackson's home. "You're making me nervous."

"I can't help it," he whined. "I'm scared."

"I'm armed," I replied. "And if you don't calm down, I may be forced to shoot." I don't think the poor kid knew I was kidding.

When Sandy Jackson answered the door with a shotgun in her hand, I knew we were off to a bad start. "Hurry up and get inside," she demanded. "I don't want the neighbors to see me associating with someone like you."

"At least I'm not a murderer," I said evenly, stepping across a doormat that was decorated with magnolia blossoms, dogwoods, and a banner that read A HEARTY SOUTHERN WELCOME. Yeah, right.

"A blackmailer's the lowest form of life on earth," she spit at me, waving the barrel of the shotgun toward her living room.

"Is that why you killed Thornton Mitchell?" I asked.

"Shut up and get away from the front windows," she commanded.

No problem. I wanted the whole scene to go down as close to the back windows as possible where I had someone to watch over me.

The plush carpet was thick beneath my feet and dyed a creamy white. It shone in the glow from several expensive standing lamps. The furniture was top of the line and the paintings that decorated the walls were originals. Sandy Jackson liked her status symbols.

"Pat her down," she commanded Adam.

"What?" he asked stupidly. The dim lighting helped conceal the sweat on his forehead but I was afraid he might pass out.

"Check her for a gun, you idiot," Stoney's mother commanded, swinging the long stock of the shotgun toward Adam. He scurried over and began to pat his hands up and down my body like he was plumping up a limp scarecrow.

"Hey, watch it!" I complained when he reached my breasts. This distracted the old biddy enough to take her mind off the lousy job Adam was doing. The last thing I needed was for her to take over. But even Adam had enough sense to block the search from her view with his body and my gun remained safely concealed in my waistband.

"She's okay," Adam croaked. "Can I sit down now?"

"For god's sakes," Sandy said in disgust. "Just don't put your feet on the furniture."

Adam sank gratefully onto the white brocade couch and loosened his collar with a finger. I remained standing, staring at my opponent, wondering what in the world made that woman think that the rules didn't apply to her.

"Let's get started," she said nastily. "I'm not paying your price and you better be prepared to deal. You saw what happened to the last person who tried to blackmail me."

"So that was it," I said, memorizing the layout of the living room while I blathered. An entrance off the rear led to the kitchen and beyond that was a garage door. Straight ahead was the archway to the front foyer. Two ways out. "Thornton Mitchell was trying to blackmail you. About what? About your brother dying from lung cancer?"

"Shut up," she squawked, the shotgun jumping an inch.

Yikes. I'd better take it easier than that. "I'm sorry your brother is dying from lung cancer," I said, "but people are going to find out eventually. You didn't have to kill Thornton Mitchell for knowing." I was verbally tap dancing, trying to get her to talk about the murder without putting words in her mouth.

"He wasn't going to quit," she told me, her narrowed eyes glinting in the reflected glare of a nearby lamp. "He'd come to me once before to say that if I didn't give him money for some damn fool project of his, he would let the world know that he had paid for Stoney's tuition at Duke, which was his idea in the first place. But I knew people would twist it into something wrong, so I gave in and invested in his Neuse Park scheme. But then he came back and wanted more. You ought to keep that in mind when you leave tonight. Because this is the only deal I'm going to make with you. I want you out of my house and my life but quick. You don't belong here. You're nothing but white trash.''

"We've all got to come from somewhere," I said, remembering the words of the old black fisherman who Sandy Jackson had insulted. If only she had been a shade more polite, I believed, I wouldn't be standing where I was.

"Let's talk about where you're going," she replied. "Name your price and name it now so you can get your cheap ass out of my home."

"My ass is not so cheap," I improvised. "Concealing a murder should have a bigger price tag than concealing lung cancer, wouldn't you say?"

"How much bigger?" she demanded.

"She wants half a million," Adam croaked from the sofa.

I could have strangled him. He was stepping on my lines. What was he trying to pull? I glanced at his stricken face and decided he only wanted to look good when sentencing time came. He was kissing ass as best he could.

"Half a million dollars?" Sandy Jackson repeated. She threw back her head and laughed. "For half a million dollars, I could buy air time every day between now and the election. What would a girl like you do with half a million dollars?" She lowered the shotgun in disgust and shook her head. "I'll give you $25,000. That's it. Take it or leave it."

"Twenty-five thousand dollars?" I repeated incredulously. "For keeping my mouth shut about a murder?"
Come on lady, I silently willed her. You're arrogant. Take
the bait.

"You can't prove I killed him," she said tightly.
"Adam here isn't going to talk, are you?" She turned the
shotgun on him and I thought he might faint. His mouth
opened and closed like a fish gasping for air, but no sound
came out. The old bitch laughed. "See what I mean? If
he makes so much as a peep, his career is ruined and that
boy is a political whore. He doesn't know how to do
anything else. Do you, Adam?" She smiled at him and
her teeth seemed small and sharp, like the teeth of a cat
stripping a mouse of its flesh. Adam looked down at the
floor and gulped for air.

"You're gonna have to do better than $25,000," I
said. "I have a witness I have to pay off."

She froze. "That old colored man." Her face was a
blank. "I told you we should have gotten rid of him," she
said to Adam.

Bingo. She had just confirmed that Adam was telling
the truth. It would hurt her if it went to court.

"The old man'll keep quiet," I assured her. "But I
need cash for him, too. Make it $200,000 in all."

She lost her temper. "I'm not going to stand here and
haggle with some white trash, two-bit tramp," she said.
"You can take the money I offer or you can take your
chances with me. I killed one time and you listen to me
good sister, because I won't have any trouble doing it
again. You can take the money and walk out of here
tonight and I never see your trashy face again or you can
spend the rest of your life wondering when I am going to
come and find you. I've been shooting since I could walk
and you won't ever know what hit you. And no one will
ever know. If not for my son trying to be such a do-
gooder, you would never have found out about that fat old
blackmailer. My son's a good man and you're not

bringing him down. I'll kill you and dump your body on the capitol lawn if I have a mind to.''

I had her. She had just dug a big enough grave for an entire jury to roll over in once the case went to court.

"How long did you say you'd been shooting?" I asked suddenly. It threw her off guard.

"Since I was three years old," she said. "Growing up on a farm. I could shoot the eyes out of a squirrel from twenty yards. And, honey, you're a much bigger target than that."

"Three years old, huh? Well, I hate to tell you, but I've been shooting the ticks off a hound since I was two." I pulled the .380 out from behind my back in one smooth motion and rushed her, pushing the barrel of her shotgun down toward the floor and clamping her hand tightly shut around it. I had my gun in her face before she could blink. And it felt real good.

"Now you listen to me," I told her through clenched teeth. "I don't appreciate having a shotgun pointed at my face. How do you like having a pistol pointed at yours?" Bill Butler was probably pissing in his pants.

God almighty if that woman hardly blinked. "You aren't going to get your money that way," she hissed. "And I'm not scared of the likes of you."

"Drop the shotgun," I told her, squeezing her wrist even tighter until I could tell the nerves had deadened.

I released her hand and the shotgun fell to the carpet. I motioned for her to step away from it and to sit on the couch beside Adam. She sat there sullenly, glaring at her companion. "I told you to search her," she spat at him. "You can't do a goddamn thing right, can you?" She stared at me, her face ugly with fury. "You won't get your precious money that way."

"I don't care about your money," I started to say but the change in her expression stopped me cold. Her eyes had slid beyond me. She was staring toward the kitchen, her face transformed by a grotesque smile.

"Stonewall!" she cried. "Just look at this. This woman has burst into my home with all sorts of accusations. She's working for that awful woman, Mary Lee Masters. She's trying to ruin the campaign."

Stoney Maloney stepped out of the kitchen doorway, his car keys in hand. He looked at his mother's weird smile and then at the gun in my hand. "What's going on?" he said warily.

"What are *you* doing here?" I asked him, eyeing the distance between the shotgun and the kitchen door. What if he tried to go for it?

"I think you know why I'm here," he said. His voice was calm. "I'm surprised you'd be a part of this, Casey. My mother deserves representation."

"Who told you we were here?" I asked. Was he in on it, too? Had his mother told him everything? Did Adam know Stoney was involved and had he been trying to save his candidacy by saying nothing? I felt outnumbered and out of control.

"I have friends in the department," he said, shrugging as if it were no big deal. "One of them called me and said the police were planning to question my mother tonight. What are you doing here? Where are the cops? Why didn't you let her know she could have a lawyer present?"

Maybe he didn't know, I thought. Oh, please god, don't let him be a part of it. I glanced at his face for a clue and that was my mistake.

As soon as I took my eyes off her, she went for the gun. That old biddy flew off the couch and snatched the shotgun off the floor faster than I have ever seen a human being move in my life. She had it pointed at my head before I could swallow.

"Throw the gun over there by the fireplace!" she screeched. "Or I'll blow your head into pumpkin pulp."

I believed her. I tossed my pistol across the carpet and prayed it wouldn't go off. Or that it would shoot anyone but me if it did. It fell harmlessly into the thick nap of the carpet.

"What are you doing?" Stoney asked, appalled. He stared at the shotgun, then turned his eyes to his mother. His voice quavered but he did not flinch. "What the fuck are you doing, Momma? Put the gun down."

"I'm not putting it down!" his mother screamed. "This cheap little bitch is a liar. She's trying to make it seem like I'm the one who shot Thornton. They're trying to make me take the blame. She works for that Masters woman. She did it. They probably both did it together."

"Mary Lee did not kill Thornton Mitchell," Stoney said. He moved closer, hand outstretched. His voice softened. "Put the gun down, Momma."

"She did it," his mother insisted. "I'm telling you she did. She's the type. They just want to make me look bad. They want to make you look bad. They're trying to take us down. I'm not going to let them."

Stoney stepped between me and his mother. "Give me the shotgun," he repeated slowly, a hand outstretched. "This woman did not kill Thornton Mitchell," he told her. "And Mary Lee could not have killed him, either. She's not that type of person, Momma. She couldn't take another life. Think of what you're saying. She's not the kind of person to take another life."

"Not take another life?" the old woman shouted. "She's trying to take yours. Can't you see that? She'd do anything to win. She'd kill and cheat and steal and she'd use this cheap tramp here to help her. Why can't you see what kind of person you're up against? We could lose this election, Stonewall. We could lose it all. She'll stop at nothing to defeat you."

"Momma!" Stoney's voice grew louder until it filled the room. "Give me the gun. They had nothing to do with Mr. Mitchell's murder. Let the police find out who did."

"I won't," she shouted back. "Why won't you ever listen to me! I've tried to tell you from the start what that Masters woman was like, but you won't listen to me."

Stoney pushed the barrel to one side and grabbed his mother's arm, forcing the shotgun toward the roof. "Mother," he said evenly—and every word that followed was slowly and clearly pronounced, as if it pained him to say them out loud: "Stop saying such things right this minute. Mary Lee Masters could not have shot Thornton Mitchell. She was with me when he was killed."

FOURTEEN

I almost felt sorry for the old bird after that. She melted to the floor with a godawful sobbing and curled up on the carpet like a baby, gulping for air and moaning nonsense. For sixty-five years she had maintained that steely southern woman control and now that she was losing her shit, she was losing it big time.

I don't even think she noticed when the backup unit finally arrived, bursting through the front door about ten minutes too late to do anyone any good. They'd been too busy standing around outside arguing about what to do ever since Stoney had driven up and gone inside the house. What if he was in on it? They didn't want to blow their chance to get him on tape. No one had been too worried about blowing my chances, it seemed.

Stoney didn't have a clue as to what was going on. I was the lucky one who got to break it to him. "She killed him," I said when he tried to interfere with the female officer who was snapping handcuffs on his mother.

He stared at me blankly.

"Your mother shot Thornton Mitchell," I explained. "Ask *him*."

I nodded toward the sofa. Adam Stoltz was leaning over the arm of the couch, throwing up on the white carpet. He nodded miserably and wiped his mouth with his sleeve. "Something's the matter with that woman," he said.

Stoney stared after his mother. She looked shrunken and frail, hunched up between two officers as they practically carried her outside. He didn't say a word to me. He just turned around and went after her.

Frank Waters and his cameraman were waiting at the edge of the lawn. They were up and shooting before Bill Butler or anyone else could stop them, at least not without being captured on film attempting to squelch Frank's First Amendment rights.

The story led all the morning news shows, including the national ones. Footage showed Stoney Maloney comforting his mother as she was led to a waiting police car while arresting officer Bill Butler held court on the front steps, explaining how he had tracked down the killer of Thornton Mitchell. Frank Waters did an admirable job of filling in available background information and viewers could detect nary a wheeze as he rumbled on about Mitchell's connection to Senator Boyd Jackson who, by the way, he told an astonished nation, was dying from lung cancer.

His followup story aired a week later and it ended up saving the district attorney about $20,000 in investigative fees. Frank had done all the legwork for him. Thornton Mitchell, he reported, had long been contributing cash to Boyd Jackson's campaigns and, though it had been hidden from Stoney Maloney's knowledge by his own family, Thornton had also secretly bankrolled Stoney's tuition and expenses through his undergraduate and law school years at Duke as a way to compensate the Senator for favors rendered—without the public knowing. When Mitchell's business went sour once Boyd Jackson was too ill to protect him, he had approached Sandy Jackson for help. It was time to repay past favors and to help an old friend. She had responded by investing in his new project: the failed Neuse River Park. In typically efficient fashion, she had killed two birds with one stone, paying back her old family medical advisor, Dr. Robert Dahler, for his silence on Boyd Jackson's true medical condition by making him a partner in the venture.

When the proposal failed, it left her angry, Dahler without payment, and Thornton Mitchell still in the hole. Worse, Mitchell discovered that a local reporter was planning a story on his dealings. Frustrated, he had called the reporter numerous times, as Frank could personally attest, perhaps to trade information on Boyd Jackson in return for Frank's silence. But he had hung up without speaking and continued running scared.

Desperate, Mitchell had returned to Sandy Jackson with another ace card up his sleeve: he knew that Boyd Jackson was dying from lung cancer. He had spotted the senator at Memorial Hospital while attending a heart clinic there and uncovered the information he needed once he realized the family was trying to keep their visits quiet. He had agreed to meet Sandy Jackson in the most secluded spot they knew: the banks of the failed Neuse River Park plot. Both felt betrayed. One had a shotgun. The murder had been a surprise. Thornton had been killed in front of a terrified Adam Stoltz and dumped in Mary Lee's driveway in an attempt to discredit her campaign. Mitchell's car had been dumped on Ramsey Lee's land because of his past record and in hopes of promoting a conspiracy theory between the two cousins. Sandy Jackson herself had called the police, posing as a teenage girl who'd been out parking with her boyfriend.

It was, I thought, pure Sandra Douglas Jackson. That woman always tried to do a little too much at once.

By the time the show was over, Frank Waters had left the local stations of North Carolina far behind. He has his own national news show now. It airs right after ''Firing Line.'' The fame didn't stop him from losing his hair.

Stoney Maloney came through the ordeal looking like an Eagle scout. He had never known of Thornton Mitchell's involvement in his life and his statements were convincing. So was the volunteer lie detector test he took to prove his innocence. He released the tape of the proceedings in their entirety and clips were played on the evening news. I recognized Stoney's father by his side. Without Sandy Jackson blocking the way, Albert Maloney had turned into a father at last. He looked like he was there to stay. Stoney had lost a mother, but gained a father. It could have been a far worse deal. Most of all, Stoney's unwavering support of his mother and his behavior following her indictment showed him to be a man who believed in doing the right thing, no matter how difficult or personally embarrassing. He was even discovered by the press visiting the daughter of Thornton Mitchell to offer his condolences on her loss and his apologies for the role his family had played in it.

This grace in the face of constant press coverage won him the election four weeks later—and I was one of the people who voted for him. I stood before the ballot machine finding myself the first family member in history to ever cast a vote in favor of a Republican. But I think my grandpa would have approved. He hated fat cats, but he hated phonies even more. Stoney Maloney was no phony. I think I finally knew who he really was.

Mary Lee remained a mystery. She never did get back into politics after she lost the race to Stoney. At least, not as a candidate.

I met with her the day after the arrest of Sandra Douglas Jackson. It was the only honest conversation I believe we ever had.

"So," I said to her. "You're Stoney Maloney's mystery woman."

"I don't want to talk about it, Casey," she said. "I really love him. If this gets out, he'll be ruined."

"I don't plan to talk about it," I told her, marveling that she was actually thinking about someone else for a change. "I wish you both the best of luck. You'll need it."

"Here." She slid a blank check across the desk toward me. "Fill in whatever you want. You've earned it. I know you don't like me, but you did a good job for me anyway. I'm willing to pay the price."

"All right," I agreed, filling out the check so she could see the amount. I billed her exactly what we had agreed on: triple my usual rate plus expenses. And I threw in another thousand for a new Anne Klein pantsuit as I was unlikely to discover another thrift shop bargain in this century.

Then I saved her about ten thousand dollars in divorce costs.

"I have a present for you," I told her. "It's on the house."

Her eyes narrowed. She was one of the few people in the world even more suspicious than me. "What kind of present?" she asked.

"You know those obscene phone calls you've been getting?" I asked.

"Yes," she said. "Is there a connection?"

"In a way." I smiled. "Bradley's been making them. And I have the phone records to prove it."

"Bradley?" she said, astonished. "Who makes obscene phone calls to their own wife?"

"Bradley. I guess he really does feel threatened by your success." I shrugged. "You started moving up in the polls, his business started going south. He cracked. That's why the caller knew so much about you. But I think he was really getting off on it, Mary Lee. He even called you all the way from Nassau just to scare the shit out of you. That's how I caught him. And that was *after* he knew Mitchell's body had been found in your car. It turns out that Channel Five is the CBS affiliate down in the Bahamas. He saw the report on it and didn't even bother to come home. He stayed there boffing his coed and dialing your private number so he could talk to you about tying you up in your panties during your darkest hour. He's a true prince among men.''

"What a creep.'' She stared out the office door, her mind calculating when he had called and just what he had said. And how she could get rid of him. And that was where I could help her out.

"Bradley's not embarrassed by his screwing around, is he?'' I asked.

She shook her head. "I suspect he thinks it makes him look better.''

"But he would be embarrassed if the whole world knew he was a weasely pervert who got off whispering into the phone about high heels and lingerie?''

"Oh, yeah.'' Mary Lee nodded emphatically. "Bradley likes his country clubs and well-connected friends. He'd die if anyone knew. And his father would kill him. Bradley's already run through his share of his grandmother's money. His only hope is to inherit more when his father kicks off.''

"Well, then, Mary Lee,'' I explained slowly. "Let's just say, for argument's sakes, that you and Bradley shared a past secret and that you were staying married to him because of that secret.''

She stared at me but did not open her mouth. It was a once-in-a-lifetime experience.

"Only now that you have something on him,'' I explained, "you can dump the bastard without fear, if you want.''

She wanted. Within a year, she had gotten her divorce and moved to Washington, D.C. She arrived in the capitol the very same week that the former Senator Boyd

Jackson died of lung cancer, his devoted nephew by his side. Mary Lee married Stoney Maloney the following autumn and every political reporter from here to California cracked the same dumb joke about politics making for strange bedfellows. I wondered if Mary Lee accompanied Stoney on his monthly visits to see Momma at the Women's Correctional Center in Raleigh. Somehow I doubted it.

Yes, Sandra Douglas Jackson was convicted. She was found perfectly sane, perfectly crafty, and perfectly guilty of first-degree murder. Mostly because Adam Stoltz crowed like a rooster on Easter Sunday once he took that witness stand. What a performance. But in a way, Sandy Jackson escaped punishment. They didn't give her the death penalty. They only gave her life. And that had already been taken from her.

Adam Stoltz survived with a better deal than anyone of us could ever have imagined. He wrote a best-selling book while in jail serving his time. It was supposed to be about politics. That way, Thornton Mitchell's family couldn't claim the profits. But it sold like hotcakes because everyone knew that the author had been there that cool October night when a genteel southern woman of the highest social order had pumped a round of shells into the chest of her oldest and most secret friend.

Thornton Mitchell had bought a lifetime of secret favors from Boyd Jackson, exchanging badly needed cash for forty years of closed-door deals. It had been an arrangement made as both men were just starting out, with Sandy Jackson serving as broker. But Mitchell had ultimately paid for the association with his life. Four decades of mutual corruption had ended with the jerk of a trigger finger and a pool of blood in the sand. Being a witness to this conclusion made Adam Stoltz a very rich convict.

The rest of us didn't do too bad, either. Ramsey Lee

could have sued for false arrest but the SBI had been embarrassed enough, and he had better things to do with his money. He's still blocking development along the Neuse today.

Bobby D. got his cut of the fee but lost it betting on the Braves in the final game of the World Series a few days later. It upset him so much he couldn't eat for an hour and almost lost half a pound.

As for me, I waited over a week for Bill Butler to show up at my front door to say thanks and to ask if I'd care to share the rest of my life with him.

The call finally came early one Friday night as I was dressing to meet a new friend for dinner. "Casey?" Bill's voice filled my apartment, stopping my eyeliner wand a quarter inch from my left eye. "I know you're there. Pick up. I need to see you."

"How about you need to thank me?" I told him, cradling the phone in one hand as I untangled a pair of black fishnet stockings with the other.

"That, too," Bill said. "But it's something I feel I should do in person. Besides, there's something important I want to share with you. Can I come over? Just for a few minutes?"

"You're going to drive thirty minutes from Raleigh to tell me thanks?" I asked skeptically.

There was a silence. "Trust me, Casey," he finally said. "I know what I'm doing. And I want to come over."

I stared at the phone for a moment. A lot of thoughts went through my head. I thought of my ex-husband and how often a handsome face hid a spoiled heart. I thought of Bill Butler's dark eyes and his long hands, the way he moved like a big cat stalking the night. And I thought of his smile, so seldom seen, yet so spectacular when it finally appeared. It was the memory of his smile that did me in. I am a sucker for a great smile.

"All right," I said at last. "I'll be here until seven-thirty."

My doorbell rang barely thirty minutes later. I opened it cautiously and peered out. Bill had both hands hidden behind his back. "I brought you a present," he said. "It's my way of saying thanks." He flashed his smile and the door came open. I decided to let him into my life.

What entered my life, however, was the most astonishing excuse for a dog I have ever seen in my life. It was a large hound, completely covered in multicolored specks that made it look as if an ink bomb had exploded in the air above him. He had black spots sprinkled over his sway back, red freckles peppering all four tall legs, velvety russet ears as long as a basset hound's, and a gray-speckled snoot shaped like a beagle's. A large black dot marked the base of his long tail, which was turning in lazy circles as it curved inward like a plume without feathers.

"What the hell is that?" I asked as the hound staggered past me, bumped into my armchair, careened off the base of the bed, and flopped down in the center of my rug. The beast gave an enormous sigh and began to snore loudly, all four of his legs splayed out to the side as if he were 100 percent skin and no bones.

"That's Beauford," Bill explained. "He's all yours."

"Mine." I stared at Bill. My voice grew grim. "No way in hell."

"Casey, you have to take him," Bill begged, his voice rising in pitch until he sounded like a kid. "If you don't, they're going to put him to sleep. I can't take him home with me. I already have a dog and he hates other dogs."

"*Who* is going to put this animal to sleep?" I asked slowly. "And wouldn't it be redundant?"

We stared down at the huge mound of hound flesh, rising and falling as the dog snored lustily, his body a mass of multicolored ticking against the pale blue rug. I watched in horror as a trickle of urine spread from the center of the mound and leaked across the rug like a tiny tributary seeking the sea.

"That dog just pissed on my carpet," I pointed out. "No one pisses on my carpet, man or beast."

Bill looked momentarily ashamed. "He flunked out of DEA school."

"What?" Drug Enforcement Agency dogs sniffed out the presence of drugs in luggage and cargo holds, they did not go around pissing on people's carpets.

"He got kicked out of training school today."

"For what? Peeing on the instructor's leg?"

Bill looked uncomfortable. "He ate an ounce of evidence."

I started to laugh. "You mean *that* dog"—I pointed to the slumbering hound—"ate an ounce of marijuana today? Is that what you're telling me?"

Bill nodded solemnly. "Including the plastic bag."

I couldn't stop laughing.

"Does that mean Beauford gets to stay?" Bill asked hopefully. "He's really a good-natured dog."

"I'm sure he is," I said, trying to catch my breath, "but I'm not sure I can afford to keep him that way."

As if on cue, Beauford raised his head and stared sleepily at me, brown eyes large and glassy in his stupor. He had enormous wattles that hung from each side of his jaw and a magnificent brisket of red-speckled fur. My grandfather would have adored him.

"Can he stay?" Bill pleaded. "Please, Casey. He's not the kind of dog people pick from the pound. They'll put him to sleep."

"Yeah, he can stay," I said. "I know a good home for him. But you have a mighty peculiar way of thanking your friends for services rendered."

Bill let out a long, relieved whistle. "Actually, I consider Beauford another reason why I owe you one. But this is partial payment on the debt." He brought a big bouquet of flowers out from behind his back. A bribe in reserve to convince me to take in the dog? Or truly a gesture of thanks?

"I thought maybe I could take you out to dinner tonight while I'm at it?" His eyes met mine and those long lashes of his were in fine form, framing a pair of innocent brown peepers.

Oh, mamma. This look was what I had thought about for many a night as I drifted off to sleep, my mind wandering from my work. Here was my chance to explore the long motif, my chance to check for silver chest hair, heck—here was my chance to date a man out of grade school for a change.

And, yet, thoughts of my ex-husband kept popping into my mind. I had waited for Bill Butler to call me just as surely as I had waited for that fatal call from the ex so many years ago. And Bill would keep me waiting again, I knew. He was a cop. He was the type. Was I going to keep doing this for the rest of my life? I had made promises to myself. How much did those promises mean?

More to the point, I needed Bill Butler in my debt more than I needed him in my bed.

"I don't think so," I said, surprising myself more than him.

"What?" he asked, the flowers rustling in his agitation.

"We're going to be working together," I said. "I don't think it's such a good idea."

"Casey." He stared at me. I stared at the dog. "The only women I meet are the women I work with. Or the ones I arrest."

"Well," I said brightly. "Think of the advantages. If you stick to the ones you arrest, you can preview them with a full body search."

"Very funny." He was silent for a moment. "This is because I didn't help you out very much, isn't it?"

"No," I promised him, taking the flowers and turning

him toward the door. I gave him a gentle push. "Believe it or not, this has very little to do with you."

After he left, I put the flowers in water and stared down at my new canine friend. I nudged him with my foot and he shifted slightly. There was a slim chance he could still walk. "Come on, Beauford," I shouted down at him. He didn't move. I lifted one of his long silky ears and hollered into the canal: "Supper time!" This time he opened an eye and blinked it at me. "Time to move out," I told him firmly, grabbing his collar and hoisting the hound to his feet. He wobbled obediently after me and, after falling over while trying to urinate on the landlady's boxwoods, he made it to my car in one piece.

Halfway across Wake County, I had to roll down the window or I'd have arrived for my dinner smelling like the pet of a Mexican drug lord. I was making good time and would even arrive early. My host was in for more than one surprise.

The driveway was easy to find in the dark. I'd been there at night before. A strange truck was parked by the side of the cabin, though the license plate seemed familiar. I dragged Beauford from the back seat of the Valiant and managed to pull and push him toward the front porch. The outdoor lights blazed on as we reached the steps.

"What the hell happened to that dog?" Ramsey Lee asked, his voice breaking into laughter. "If I didn't know better, I'd say he was stoned to the gills."

"It's a long story," I admitted. "Sorry I'm early. This is Beauford. Can he stay here with your dogs? I'm at my wit's end with him. He sits around stoned all day, absolutely refuses to get a job, does nothing but watch television and won't even pick up his own dirty clothes. Just smell him."

He laughed even harder. "Sure. He can stay. The old fellow looks like a good hunting dog. Let me get a better look at him. Slim—come on out and take a look at what the cat dragged in."

Slim Jim Jones—keeper of the canoe and obedient son to crusty old Momma—stepped out onto the front porch of Ramsey Lee's cabin. Our eyes locked across the crouched form of our host. "I didn't realize you knew Ramsey," I said evenly. "Small world, isn't it?"

Slim Jim shrugged. "Shoot, Casey. That's what I always say." He spat a wad of tobacco juice over the side of the porch and, unless the lights were playing a trick on me, I could have sworn he threw a wink my way.

God, mountain men. Even without a mountain behind them, you could recognize them at a glance. They were stubborn. Self-assured. Scrawny. Hard-working. And just about the last damn men on earth who cared about something other than money.

"How long have you known Ramsey?" I asked him.

"Long enough," Slim Jim answered, giving Beauford a pat on the head. "I best be getting home to Momma," he said as he headed into the yard. "That dog's got good bones there, Ramsey. Soon as he sobers up, you might have a good working dog." Beauford chose that moment to plop down for another serious snooze, his body stretching upward over four steps, the skin all sliding to the lower rear end where it collected in accordion folds around his tail. Slim Jim began to laugh and I listened as his merriment gave way to the sound of his truck motor fading down the lane.

"You're a good man, Ramsey Lee," I told him. "You take in wayward dogs. And, you never did give the cops the names of the men who helped you out that time you dynamited that construction site, now did you?"

Ramsey scratched behind Beauford's ears. "I'm not the sort of man who likes to kiss and tell," he said. "Let's go inside and eat."

He'd made us homemade Brunswick stew, the right

way, complete with shredded beef, chicken, pork, and squirrel meat. "Been cooking all day," he promised. "So I expect you to eat all night."

We ate in happy silence—as we have done many times since. Ramsey doesn't like to talk and I'm perfectly happy not to. Talk only exposes people's weaknesses. That's why I prefer the strong and silent type.

That night was the start of a very good winter, all things considered. Over the months that followed, I spent a lot of time out at Ramsey's cabin, walking in the snow along the banks of the Neuse by day and sharing his bed at night. Like me, he mostly, but not always, prefers to be alone. Best of all, I spent many a lazy hour curled up in front of his fireplace with a pack of very spoiled hounds.

They say that if you lay down with dogs, you'll get up with fleas. But do you know what I think? I think there's worse things in life than fleas.